Subway
AND THE PLACES WE MEET **STOPS**

MINDY MICHELE

Edited by Samatha Eaton-Roberts

ALSO BY MINDY MICHELE

Pratt Family Stories

Paper Planes and Other Things We Lost

Subway Stops and the Places We Meet

Chasing Cars and the Lessons We Learned

The Backroads Duet

Love in C Minor, Vol one

Loss in A Major, Vol two

Nothing Compares To You, a 90s novella

Also by Michele G. Miller

Last Call

The Prophecy of Tyalbrook

Never Let You Fall

Never Let You Go

Never Without You

From The Wreckage Series

From The Wreckage

Out of Ruins

All That Remains

Standalone FTW spinoffs

West: A male POV Novel

Into the Fire - Dani's story

After The Fall - Austin's story (17+)

Until We Crash - Jess and Carter's story (17+)

Havenwood Falls Series

Awaken the Soul, Havenwood Falls High

Avenge the Heart, Havenwood Falls High

Co-written with R.K. Ryals:

Dark Seduction, Havenwood Falls Sin & Silk

Sign up for Michele's newsletter for exclusive first peeks and other perks.

http://bit.ly/MGMNews

Also by Mindy Hayes

The Faylinn Series - YA Fantasy

Kaleidoscope

Ember

Luminary

Glimmer

The Willowhaven Series - Adult Romance

Me After You

Me Without You

Me To You

Individual titles

The Day That Saved Us – Coming of Age Romance

Stain - Romantic Psychological Suspense

Sign up for Mindy's newsletter

http://bit.ly/mindyhayesnews

For Ryan and Jonathan

———

He said to her
don't fall in love with me...
She thought to herself
silly boy we are best friends
we've been madly in love since the
day we met

N.R. HART

FOUND OUT ABOUT YOU

FLIGHT 397 MEMORIAL—JUNE 17, 1993

ONE YEAR AGO, metal and debris washed upon this shore, littering the sand with bits and pieces. Lingering smoke marred the peaceful blue of the early summer sky where a plane fell in a ball of fire.

One year ago, phone calls were made. Loved ones were lost. Lives were changed. Families were shattered. And new ones built.

I search out Brett and Amber. I barely knew them a year ago. Today they're my family. My brother and sister. Brett's standing near the water, pensive as he gazes out at the horizon. He's the opposite of Amber, who's heading my way in a hurry. She appears tense and angry, even from this far away.

The briny tang of the ocean rides past on a warm breeze. I close my eyes, imagining the scene from a year ago as I say goodbye to the nightmare of the crash. I open my eyes again when screams of high-pitched, childish laughter reach me. Children chasing the rolling tide superimpose my vision of loss. My lips twitch. Joy is preferable to grief.

Sand clings stubbornly to the soles of my dress shoes as I leave the beach. I stomp on the boardwalk as I shake my pant legs. Pants at the beach in June. I'm dying here.

. . .

A BLUR OF BLACK APPEARS IN MY PERIPHERAL VISION. Amber. Her blonde head tilts toward the ground as she makes her way across the sand and steps onto the boardwalk.

"Hey." My voice is barely audible. A funeral voice.

She ignores me.

"Amber?"

Her head shakes hastily. Her hand lifts, waving me off as she hurries by, the floral scent of her mother's perfume mixing with that of the beach.

"Wait, what's wrong?" My shoes tap noisily on the wooden boardwalk as I pursue her.

"I'm fine. I need a minute." Her words come out broken. Strained.

"Amber? Talk to me about it."

She runs headlong into a couple, her hand covering her mouth as she shakes her head once again.

"Amber?" Curious glances turn my way from the lingering memorial attendees and a few beachgoers who didn't know today's memorial would take over their vacation spot.

What happened? Where's Brett? What am I supposed to do with her? She ducks into the women's restroom. What is she doing? Now what? Sweat beads across my forehead. Do I leave her alone? Stay here? What's the protocol for handling over-emotional teenage girls? Why didn't we cover this in med school?

"Is she okay? Can I help you in some way?" I turn toward the voice and find a gorgeous brunette standing behind me.

"Can you tell me how to lure a teenage girl out of the restroom?" The brunette's eyes go wide, the greenish-gray bolts of shock threatening to strike me down. What the ...

"Oh, no! No, no, no." My head won't shake fast enough. "She's my sister, I swear. We're—" I shove my fingers through my hair, barely controlling the urge to tear the strands out. "Her

2

parents died in the crash. Flight 397." I point toward the memorial in case she has no clue what I'm talking about. That's dumb, everyone here knows about 397. "She's upset. I don't know—" Where is Brett when I need him?

"Okay, okay." Her fingertips carefully graze my arm. "Let me go in there and check on her for you." She vanishes through the doorway, leaving me gaping.

She doesn't believe me. That was a patented 'okay, creeper' response if I ever heard one. She's probably preparing herself to grab Amber and run.

I search for Brett once again, my eyes scanning past the dunes to the shore beyond. He's finally heading my way.

"Brett." I wave him over. "Something upset Amber and she hightailed it into the girls' room and won't come out."

"She what?" He picks up his pace, panic morphing his facial expression.

I catch his elbow as he tries plowing by. "Hey, you can't go in there. I got help. Hang on." Should that have been my response? There's no mistaking his worry for his—no, *our* sister. I still suck at this sibling concept.

"What happened?"

I shrug his question off with a shake of my head. I haven't a clue what's going on.

"Here she is." The brunette appears in the doorway with Amber beside her. She wasn't preparing for a grab and run after all. Thank goodness for small miracles.

Brett moves forward, immediately wrapping an arm over Amber's shoulders. "Am?"

Take notes, Cole.

Amber's swollen eyes flick my way. "I'm okay. I'm fine," she sniffles as she leans into Brett's side.

Brett nods, steering her away. Just like that? He made it seem so easy. My eyes follow them for a few steps. Amber's back straightens as she swipes at her face. Brett lowers his head, whispering something as they walk away. At work I can console strangers when they lose a loved one, but I can't handle my own sister? I shove my hands into my pockets. Today has been a day.

"Thank you for helping my sister," I sigh heavily, turning my head for a better look at my bathroom hero's profile. Not a bad sight at all.

"It was no problem. I'm really glad you weren't lying." The corner of her mouth pulls up slightly.

Those curiously colored eyes look back at me, and for a moment, time stands silently still. Remember, Cole, joy is preferable to grief. I turn and face her fully. "Yeah? What would you have done if I were?"

"I probably would've sought the help of all the other ladies in the restroom to gang up on you while we made a run for it."

I draw a deep breath, standing taller and flexing my chest muscles. Schwarzenegger I am not. "I'm unsure whether I should be offended that you think I look like the type of guy who preys on teenage girls or grateful you felt the need to enlist the help of others to get past me."

"Definitely the latter," she laughs. It comes in waves, muffled behind her hand, then loud and throaty as she throws her head back.

Her laughter is contagious, and I easily join in. "Thanks for attempting to make me feel better. I had a moment of helplessness there. I'm not good at handling teenage girls." Foot in mouth, dude. "I mean, I'm normally not so bad with my bedside manner."

Her laughter softens to small chuckles beneath her breath. "Bedside manner, huh?"

"Doctor. I'm a doctor. I'm not bragging about my *bedside* bedside manner. I should shut up now." Holy cow, I'm unnerved. The urge to slap my hand over my mouth is strong. If only it wouldn't make me look like a bigger idiot.

She chews on her bottom lip, curbing a smile. "In my

experience with teenage girls, it's best to stay quiet and let them ride out their emotional roller coaster."

"Stay quiet? I think I can do that. Any other advice?"

"She's always right."

"She is, is she? Now, is that advice pertaining to Amber specifically? Or all women in general?"

"All women." Her raspy laughter sets my pulse racing.

"I'll file that away for later use." I push the sleeves of my dress shirt up my forearms, deliberately flexing my muscles with each movement. Her eyes follow me, and I sneak a peek at the time to hide the obviousness of my little show. It's getting late. Afternoon shadows from the rapidly setting sun cover the bathhouse. "I should probably go check on them." My gaze drifts back to this woman. A chunk of her dark hair rests in the V of her dress at her chest. I struggle to pry my eyes away.

"Oh, yeah. Of course." Her hand spreads over where my gaze rested, her fingers nervously playing with the neckline of her dress. She sweeps her long hair over one shoulder, covering herself. She absolutely caught me staring. "Your family needs you."

"Thank you again, honestly." I lower my head, confiding with a wink. "I don't know if you noticed, but I was panicking before you came along."

"I now see that's what it was." Her smile wavers as her eyes flit around the memorial before she looks at me again. "I'm glad I was the one to stumble onto you, *doctor*."

"Me, too." I tap two fingers to my temple, lifting my brows. "I'll lock your advice away for safekeeping until I need it."

I step backward. I don't see beautiful women like her often, and I don't want to walk away too quickly. I should get her name. See if she's local. My lips part, but I swallow the words. We're at a memorial site. She probably lost someone. She is dressed in black. It wouldn't be appropriate. Shoving my hands into my pants pockets, I turn away with a nod and a smile, forcing the little voice telling me to 'do something' back into its box.

Get her name, Cole. I roll my eyes; the voice won't stay locked away. He's—I'm—completely nuts. Halfway down the boardwalk, I give in and turn around.

She's gone.

A heaviness settles in my chest as my gaze scans over the area. There's no one around. The

pavilion is vacant. The beach and boardwalk are nearly empty, too. Dwelling on it won't help. Amber and Brett are making their way up the beach toward me as their Gram heads my way from the memorial site. I drop my search for my mystery hero.

What kind of guy picks up a girl at a memorial service anyway? I grin. If I could rewind the moment, the answer would be me.

My lips twitch. I'm just that kind of guy.

HARD WORKIN' MAN
SMITH'S GYRO CART—JULY 26, 1993

TEN MINUTES. I have ten minutes to grab a breath of fresh air, find a bite to eat, and haul tail back to the hospital, or Dr. Evil will stick me on bedpan duty for the remainder of my shift. Such is the life of a first-year resident. The eclectic aromas of Manhattan in the summer assault me as I cross over 1st Avenue. The scent of trash, urine, and gasoline is marginally better than the stench of the blood and antiseptic I've been inhaling for the last six hours. Admiring the scents of New York streets and hospitals, that's not sad at all. I've got to get out more often.

I verify the time—nine minutes left. The tapping of my feet on the pavement gets a little quicker as I pick up my pace. Why can I find a hot dog vendor on every corner when I don't want one, but they're nowhere to be found when my butt is on the line? Ahh, food truck umbrellas! Thank God it's only one block away. Seven and a half minutes left; I can't be picky today.

The aroma of meat and peppers sizzling on a grill replaces the less appetizing scents of the city as I reach 1st and Mt. Carmel. Smith's Gyros. Not my favorite, but it'll have to do because I'm starving and out of time.

I join the short line of suits waiting to order. Two third-year residents ahead of me nod a greeting as they wait for their food. Does my face have the same sallow, exhausted expression as theirs? I bounce in place, rubbing my palms over my eyes and shoving my fingers through my hair in an effort to liven myself up a bit. I'm third in line, mentally finalizing my order, soaking in the sunshine, and checking out the park and playground on my left when my eyes land on the brunette in line behind me.

Wait...

My head snaps back for a second look. Is that? I skim over the lean frame dressed in workout clothing behind me. There's something so familiar about her. Something about the way she stands. She slips her black sunglasses on top of her head and I see her face. Holy crap, it *is* her!

She's run through my mind more than once in the last month. The girl in the black dress with the smoky voice who made my pulse race. What are the chances I'd see her again?

Her hands lift, adjusting the dark ponytail at the top of her head; and her eyes, those amazingly colored greenish-gray eyes, meet mine. There's a glint of uncertainty, a spark of 'Do I know you?' mixed with 'Why are you staring at me, you freak?'

I'm probably creeping her out with the way I'm ogling and smiling.

"Hey," I say once I can muster the words. "You're ... I mean, we met on Long Island last month."

Her hands drop from her hair as recognition dawns. "Oh, right. Doctor—"

"Cole." I turn, facing her fully.

"Dr. Cole. It's nice to see you again." She extends her hand. No rings, but she's in workout clothing, so that might mean nothing.

I chuckle, "No, it's Dr. Rossner. You can call me Cole, though." My hand closes around hers as my eyes rove back over her body. My wandering eyes can't be helped; she's dressed in tight spandex, after all.

She tugs her hand from mine and tucks a stray hair behind her ear with a polite smile. "I'm Samantha. You can call me Sam."

"Sam," I repeat under my breath. "I have to tell you, I kicked myself for not getting your name that day at the beach. You were a life-saver."

Her lip twitches, not quite a full smile, but more of a knowing smirk. Like she thinks she has me figured out. "How *is* your sister?"

"She's—" She's Amber. In the two weeks since she was in the city with Brett and me, I've barely slept, let alone had time to check in on my teenage sister. Brett says she's okay, and I'm working on trusting his judgment of his twin. He knows her better than I do. "She's dealing with a lot, but she's coping."

Sam nods slowly. She understands the pain the crash left behind. She was at the memorial, too.

A suit nods behind her, pointing out the moving line, so I turn back to the cart.

"Here," I step aside, extending my arm and waving Sam up. "Go before me."

"You really don't have to do that. It's okay. You were here first."

"I insist."

Sam hesitates before ducking her head as she brushes past me. "Thanks."

"No problem. Do you live around here?" I ask, checking out her backside in her workout gear.

"Umm..." She hesitates long enough for the vender to cut her off.

Beep, beep, beep.

My beeper goes off now? Figures. My hand moves to my waist, and a sigh falls from my lips as I read the numbers. *911.* Crap.

"Well, Sam, duty calls," I say to the back of her head as I check my watch again. I had three minutes left. Dang it.

9

I'm already backing away when she looks down at my beeper. "Oh, no! You didn't get to eat lunch. If you wait a second, you can have mine."

"I'm a first-year resident; not eating goes with the title." I shrug, my stomach growling in protest as I take off toward Bellevue. Something tugs at me and I turn, calling over my shoulder, "It was really good seeing you again."

"You, too." Her voice is all but lost on the wind as I jog away.

I curse all the way back to the hospital and right up until I'm running through the ER doors and elbows deep in blood. I have her first name, but I'm no closer to knowing who she is than I was the first time we met. What are the odds I'll bump into her a third time?

3

ARE YOU GONNA GO MY WAY
N TRAIN—OCTOBER 14, 1993

The subway whirls through the tunnel, coming to a screeching halt in front of the platform. It's late enough that the subway car is mostly empty. Wrapping my scarf tighter around my neck, I move toward a row of vacant seats and get comfortable for the long ride to Queens. My foot taps to the trumpets in my ska music as I flip through my *People* magazine. The squealing breaks alert me we've arrived at our next stop before the doors open.

With my head down, I feel someone sit next to me. Ignoring them, I continue leafing through the pages, bobbing my head to Stretch Armstrong. I nonchalantly cross my legs, shifting away from the stranger. Of course there's an entire empty car and this person decides to sit right next to me. A manly freshly showered scent wafts over, masking the musty subway. Well, at least he smells pleasant.

The subway rolls forward, picking up speed. Fingers graze my earlobe, pulling my headphone away from my ear. On reflex, my arm shoots up and forcibly smacks the hand away, the other hand quickly following as I bring my fist up to punch him ... when I see his face.

Dr. Long Island mouths something with his arms raised defensively. My music is still blaring in my other ear, so I awkwardly yank off my headphones.

"Oh my gosh, you scared me," I breathe.

With his hands raised, he says, "Sorry. So, so sorry. I didn't mean to scare you." He offers an apologetic smile as he lowers his hands.

My adrenaline pounds in my ears. "This is New York, at night, on a subway. You can't go around touching women. I nearly punched you in the face."

His rich laughter fills the car. "Then I thank you for sparing my face. I don't think I would have liked that very much. I'm betting you have quite the punch."

I slowly relax, unclenching my fist as I take a deep breath. "Well, when a woman travels alone in the city, self-defense is a necessary skill."

"I'm gonna go out on a limb and say I think you're safe." He nods, shaking out his left arm where I hit him as if it hurt. "All joking aside, I'm sorry for scaring you. I wasn't thinking. I was shocked to see you again and merely wanted to say hi." He settles back into the seat beside me. "Maybe you can offer me some advice on how to approach a woman alone on a train who is wearing a headset, since you were so good with the whole luring a girl out of the bathroom scenario."

Did he seriously wink at me? Uncomfortable laughter escapes from my lips. He's trying to be charming. Okay, he *is* charming. Admit it, Samantha.

He lowers his head, shaking it. "I haven't exactly made the best impression on you, have I?" The corner of his mouth turns up.

It's not his fault handsome men make me uncomfortable. I offer him a forgiving smile. He is ridiculously handsome, but that doesn't mean he'll get anywhere with me. "No, there probably is no good way to approach a woman on the subway who's wearing headphones. I would've punched you no matter what. I'm sorry, by the way."

"No, I get it. If my sister repeated this tale to me, I would tell her to run as fast and as far as she could." His hands scrub over his exhausted face. "I swear I'm not as creepy as I seem. You keep catching me on bad days." His hands drop and he peers over at me with bright blue eyes. *Dang*, his eyes are so blue. "So, really, it's your fault."

"Oh, my bad." I laugh softly. "I'll try looking less approachable."

His eyes roam around my face, and my stomach starts feeling funny. "I'm not sure that's possible."

My face flushes. I try focusing back on the magazine in my lap. Maybe if I don't encourage him with conversation, he'll get the hint. Right? It's been a long day, and the last thing I want is to deal with is an attractive man hitting on me on my way to Monica's for a girls' night.

"Hey, think you could give me some advice on Amber again?"

I clear my throat and force myself to meet his eyes. "Sure."

"She started Penn this fall. How often can I check in with her and not come off looking like an overprotective big brother?"

"I don't think you can ever get away from the overprotective big brother stigma no matter how little you call," I chuckle.

His face clouds over as he inhales. "Yeah. Just … she lost her parents, you know? She's delicate, but thinks she isn't."

My heart stops, restricting my breathing. Offering up the information is so easy for him. I can't remember the last time I freely talked with someone about Flight 397.

"Sorry, I kinda dumped that on you. I didn't mean to bring up the crash."

"No, I'm sorry." I look down at my lap, releasing a quiet cynical laugh. 'I'm sorry' is always an automated response when someone hears about a loss from 397, but it doesn't do much.

"You were at the memorial that day. I assume you lost someone, too?"

I nod, not willing to give a stranger more than that.

"I'm sorry." His hand hesitates over my thigh, as though he wants to offer me comfort, before he pulls it back. He leans forward, resting his elbows on his knees, and stares straight ahead at the blur of the scenery flying past the subway windows. "I bet I use those words a hundred times a month at the hospital, but I hate them. They don't make you feel better, do they?"

I shake my head, but he isn't looking. "So ... *Doctor*, what kind of doctor are you?"

His head swivels my way, a small smile playing on his lips. "You can call me Cole." His brow rises as though he's expecting a reply, so I nod, bringing a crooked grin to his face. A player's grin. His brain is formulating how to ask me out. I swear, his intentions couldn't be clearer if they were written across his forehead.

"I think I mentioned I'm doing my residency that day we ran into each other at the food cart. I work in the ER. Ultimately, my goal is specializing in pediatric surgery, but I'm exploring all of my options."

"You better with kids than you are with women?" My amusement bubbles under the surface, threatening to be released.

"I sure hope so." He sits back again and shoots me a confident side-smile, clearly pleased with himself.

Nervous laughter flows from my lips. Gosh, that grin makes me flustered. "Being an ER doctor must be stressful. You probably see a lot."

"Are you kidding? I've got a wealth of crazy stories up in here I could share." He taps his temple. "I'll spare you all of the gore and craziness, though. I *can* tell you that the number of people who visit the ER because they tripped over their assassin pets is staggering. I hope you don't have one. They're a health hazard."

I bite back yet another smile. "No, I'm safe. One health hazard dodged."

"That's a relief."

We lapse into silence. The constant clack, clack, clacking of the subway on the tracks fills the space between us as our gaze drifts apart.

"You know, even with the strange cases, I love my job. It's all I ever wanted to be," Cole says out of the blue after a few minutes. I lift my eyes from my lap. He pinches the bridge of his nose. "It's stressful and exhausting, but sometimes I have cases like the ones I had today where I help a panicked parent with a choking toddler, or I help deliver an overly eager newborn. Those moments make everything worth it."

Everyone has highs and lows in their job fields, but going from those kinds of extremes in one day, it takes a special kind of person. And that's definitely not me.

"It must be very rewarding, making an actual difference in the lives of others the way you do."

"Sure. I mean, it's what I do, you know? It's my job." His foot slides across the scuff-marked subway floor. His well-worn black Converse nudges mine. Bonus points for the amazing shoe choice. "What about you? You must be a superhero with those killer fighting skills."

I smirk and stare at his foot next to mine, coolly scooting it away. "Working girl by day, vigilante by night. Someone has to save this city."

He regards me thoughtfully, a hint of a smile playing on his lips. And nice lips they are. I shake the unbidden thought away as we reach Broadway station.

I grab my purse and stand. "Well, this is my stop. It was nice bumping into you again." I move quickly toward the doors, waiting anxiously for them to open.

"Hey, Supergirl," he calls after me, and I turn. "I had a long shift and was planning on grabbing something at McGuinty's Pub, if you're up for it."

I hesitate. What kind of a day must this man have had? In between saving people and bringing life into this world. Did he lose any patients? Give devastating news to unsuspecting family members? He could probably use some company.

"I'm sorry. I'm headed to my best friend's house." The doors slide open and I don't want to miss my window, so I toss him a wave. "Have a drink for me."

Standing on the platform, I watch Cole lean back as the doors close and the subway departs. There are only three stops left. That means Dr. Cole Rossner lives within a few blocks of my best friend. This may not be the only time we meet on the subway. Does that make me excited or anxious? It's possible it's a little bit of both.

4

ROUND HERE

MARKET ON BROADWAY—DECEMBER 23, 1993

"You know you don't have to cook anything special for us," Brett reminds me for the third time as we wander up and down the overflowing aisles of the market. "You finally have a night off. I feel like I should be cooking for you."

I pull two cans of green beans from the shelf. "Nope. I never see you guys. I want to cook. I mean, it's not like you're getting a gourmet meal here."

We survey the contents of our cart. I'm roasting a chicken, making a green bean casserole, and baking potatoes. Simple, but it's a family meal with Brett, Amber, and Ruby. And it's the holidays.

"Jingle Bells" plays over the store speaker system and my brain subconsciously sings the words as we round an aisle. I scan the colorful packaging on the endcap stacked with holiday cookies and treats.

"Whoa," Brett warns, his hand gripping the side of the cart and stopping me a moment shy of bowling over another shopper.

"So sorry," I apologize, pulling my cart back a step. I look up from the fudge-covered graham crackers I'm craving to the girl dressed in red standing before us. "Hey," I utter as the air vanishes from my lungs.

"Cole, hi," she breathes. Her eyes shift to Brett and back to me.

"We keep running into each other. It's getting a little weird, don't you think?"

Does she get more beautiful each time I see her? My hands grip the cart as I look her over. I'm done asking what are the chances I'll see her again. Evidently, the chances are very good.

"Ha. This is—what—the third time in six months? Are you stalking me?"

She's counting the encounters. That's something. "Stalk, Supergirl? I'd have to have a death wish to do that." I shoot her an exaggerated look of fear. "Besides, I live in this neighborhood, so if anyone is stalking, it's you."

It's an opening for her to clue me in on where she lives. She doesn't take the hint. She merely shakes her head slightly, her red lips tugging up at the edges.

Brett clears his throat and I spare him a glance. He's inspecting Sam thoroughly, his brows nearly touching as though he's working out how he knows her, the same way I did that day at the gyro cart.

"Oh, so, Brett, this is Samantha. She's the one who helped Amber that day at the memorial."

Recognition lights up Brett's face as I focus on Sam again. "This is my brother, Brett. I guess you didn't officially meet that day."

Sam surveys us before she extends her hand to Brett. "I see the resemblance. It's the eyes."

Brett and I exchange looks. Blue eyes. It's one of the only traits I share with my half-siblings. Our dad's eyes.

"I thought you looked familiar," Brett nods as he takes Sam's hand in his. My insides heat up. He's touching her. My hand twitches for the same. "Thanks for whatever you said to her that day."

"It was nothing." She waves off his thanks. "Just some woman-to-woman stuff."

"Nah, it was definitely something," I disagree.

Our eyes hold, mine silently confirming how helpful she was that day.

"Hey, I'll go grab the drinks. It was nice meeting you," Brett blurts out, excusing himself without a backward glance.

I'm left with Sam, the cookies, and Bing Crosby serenading over the speaker system.

"You look nice. Going to a party?" Keeping my eyes from scanning over her body more than once is an effort.

"Oh," she pauses like she's never received a compliment before and peers down at herself. "Thanks. Yeah. My best friend is having a Christmas party, so I'm just picking up some last-minute things for her."

Ahhh, so the best friend lives nearby. Good to know.

"Oh, nice. I'm cooking for my brother, his girlfriend, and Amber. A little party of four." Why did I share that? Why do I sound like an idiot around her? I shove my hand through my hair. "I should catch up with Brett."

An array of emotions flicker in those hazel eyes of hers before she blinks them away.

"Right. Of course."

She inches her cart to the side so I can pass.

"It was good to see you." I tip my head in her direction. "Have a Merry Christmas, Sam."

"Yeah. Merry Christmas, Cole. Maybe we'll bump into each other again sometime."

"I'd like that." I pause when we're side by side and give her a smile. "It's a big city, but you know where I work," I hint.

I'm walking away reluctantly. I want to get to know her, but I don't have time for relationships. I don't have time for the chase she is intent on sending me on. I don't even know her last name. Clarity returns the further I retreat from her side. She deflected when I asked about her job, she turned me down when I asked her out on the train. She hasn't offered me even half a bone in our three meetings. Maybe she'll pick up on the hint this time and come see me, or maybe she isn't interested.

My mother's nagging voice echoes in the back of my mind. Her constant complaints on how I need to bring home a good girl from the hospital for her to meet drives me insane. If it were only that easy, Mom. Her love of *General Hospital* gives her a warped sense of my day-to-day life. Too bad things never play out in life as they do on television.

5

CRAZY

MONICA STANDS behind the counter and lifts her head when I walk into the studio, her blonde ponytail swishing to the side. "What are you doing here so early? Your first class doesn't start for another hour."

I push my sunglasses back. "I know. I'm still getting used to traveling all the way from Queens. It was so much faster coming from the East Village."

"But living with me is so much more fun," she croons.

"Yeah, yeah." I hike up my gym bag and peek around her shoulder to see how many people have signed up for my class. "Fifteen. That's not bad."

"It could be better, but it's a great start."

I nod. "Considering my other two classes are always overflowing, it's nice to have a lighter load."

"Shawn signed up again for your class tonight," she gripes. "If he doesn't stop hitting on every female member, I'm going to have to cut him off. He's becoming a liability."

I laugh. "I could always *accidentally* elbow him in the stomach while walking around the class helping others work on form. He might get the message then."

21

"Doubtful."

"The man can't help himself, Mon. I think he does it to get a rise out of you. Ever since you turned him down, he's had to find a way to get your attention."

"Negative attention. He gets negative attention from me."

"But it's attention nonetheless."

"SHAWN JUST WALKED IN WITH AN INCREDIBLY SEXY specimen, but if he's anything like Shawn, I will kick them both out on the spot."

My eyes wander to the front of the studio. A man with sinewy arms in a fitted white T-shirt and basketball shorts bends over, setting down a duffle bag against the wall. When he stands, he turns and we make eye-contact. Holy crap. My stomach flips. His features twitch with surprise before he smiles.

I figured since it's been almost a year, I'd never see Cole again, but now he's standing in my kickboxing studio with Shawn, the epitome of a womanizer. All the times we've bumped into each other and he's hit on me become crystal clear.

Even though we've only met a few times, a strange pang of longing runs through me when he smiles, like I've been missing a good friend and we're finally reconnecting.

Cole leisurely saunters across the wood floors as I return his smile. "Well, if it isn't Dr. Long Island."

"This is where you perfect that killer punch of yours, huh?" he asks, arching his brow.

I peer around the studio Monica and I established over a year ago. "Secret's out of the bag. This is my studio. Or rather, it's both mine and Monica's." Monica clears her throat at my side. "Oh, sorry. Cole, this is Monica, my best friend and business partner. Monica, this is Cole."

"Hi." He nods at Monica. "I've actually heard quite a bit about you from Shawn. It's nice to finally meet you."

Monica appraises him. She is going to grill me as soon as he's out of earshot. "I bet you have," she says dryly. Cole smirks like he knows exactly what she means. "How do you know Sam?" Or she's going to cut straight to the chase.

"Umm..." I pause.

"Supergirl, here?" He gives me a wink. Why do I like it when he winks? Winking is so skeezy.

Well, not when Cole does it. Ugh.

"She came to my sister's rescue about ... what? A year ago?"

I nod. "Sounds about right." It's actually been a year and two months, but I won't correct him. He'll think I'm keeping a tally because of him, not the anniversary of the crash.

"Thankfully, she's more adept at dealing with teenage girls than I am." His toned arms cross over his chest, accentuating his biceps. Don't ogle his biceps, Samantha. "I had no idea you would be here." His eyes appraise me from my ponytail to my Nikes. I shift from one foot to the other, unsettled by his blatant disregard for subtlety.

Monica gives me the side-eye, her elbow digging into my waist. Yeah, she's definitely going to want more information.

"I'm surprised you haven't heard more from Shawn," I say.

"Oh, I have, but it's all about Monica." The corner of his mouth turns up, giving her a hard time.

"Well, on that note." Monica clears her throat. "It was nice to meet you, Cole."

Girly laughter peels through the studio and I spot Shawn in the center of several women who haven't learned their lesson. They playfully slap his shoulder or nudge him with their elbows.

Cole looks over to the commotion, rolling his eyes. "I should probably go keep him in check. He tends to hit on every woman in the room. Something tells me I don't have to warn you two about that."

"Ha! Definitely not," Monica grumbles.

As though he knows we're talking about him, Shawn strolls over to us before Cole has even taken two steps.

"Ladies." Shawn's arm flings around Monica's shoulders. "I see you've met my lovely neighbors." He looks at Cole with a confident grin.

Monica shrugs out from under his arm and squares her shoulders. "And I already wish *he* was our neighbor."

No. No, we don't. Stop it, Monica. Do not encourage him.

"What? And miss seeing me every day?" Shawn clutches his heart. "That hurts."

"One could only hope."

"Wait, you two are roommates?" Cole's eyes narrow as he looks at Shawn.

"It's a new thing," I say. "I moved in with Monica about two weeks ago."

Cole's mouth curves into a smile. "Now I wish I were your neighbor, too."

Heat rises to my cheeks. Thankfully, Monica saves me from answering. "Please take Shawn's apartment."

Or not. She's not supposed to encourage the man. He'll get the wrong impression.

"Okay." I begin backing away. "I think it's time for me to get this class started."

6

I BURN

PURE KICKBOXING—AUGUST 22, 1994

OF ALL THE COINCIDENCES. How in the world is it that Shawn lives in the same building as Sam? I share a walkup with a young family and a widow, and he gets Sam and Monica?

I check them out as Sam calls the class together and we move into lines in the center of the room. I haven't seen her in over six months. Since that night Brett and I ran into her at the market. I even ate at Smith's gyro cart a couple of times this spring hoping I might run into her again, not that I would admit that out loud. I don't even particularly like gyros. Looking at her reminds me why I was interested. She's gorgeous, but more than that, she came off like a genuine person that day in Long Island with Amber. I wanted to get to know her better, but dang, if she wasn't putting up some heavy shields when I hit on her. And now here we are.

"You know, secretly she loves me," Shawn whispers, leaning in, his gaze following mine.

"Who, Sam?" The woman in front of me peers over her shoulder. Did my voice go up two octaves?

Shawn winks at her, mouthing a greeting, and she returns her focus to the front.

"No, Monica." He pulls an arm across his chest, stretching out. "But now that you mention it—"

"Don't go there," I warn.

He regards me with amusement, but music cuts off his reply as Sam steps in front of the class. "Alright, who's ready to break a sweat?" she asks, her husky voice amplified by the headset she's wearing.

FORTY MINUTES LATER, SWEAT DRIPS FROM MY BROW. WHEN Shawn cornered me at the hospital and asked me to come with him to this class, I figured it would be a cream puff workout. An easy way to blow off a little steam, but dang, Sam and Monica are brutal. His selling point was the 'two hot chicks' who run the place. He's talked about Monica over the last year often enough, but he's never mentioned Sam. She isn't on his radar. That's a good thing, I'd hate to have to take him down.

I sigh with relief when we lower our bodies to the floor for an ab workout. I catch my breath as Sam demonstrates the proper way to do sitting punches for the newer attendees in the room.

"You're going to contract your ab muscles as you sit up, then cross. Right shoulder to your left hip. And punch," she calls out, her well-toned arms throwing perfect punches across her thigh before she lowers back to the floor and sits up again. She's not even breathing hard!

The class joins in. Sit ups, punching, side-to-side leg raises—we do it all until my abs are screaming. I've been working too hard lately. My body hates me right now.

"Give me one more. Good job. Sit up and hold, then cross punch. There you go. If you want to make it harder, lift your feet."

At some point, I'm doing half the work and watching Sam the rest of the time. Her tank top has bunched up around her ribs, giving me a nice view of her flat stomach. This is why Shawn comes here on a weekly basis; between Monica, Sam, and all the other ladies working out, a guy could get used to this.

"Okay. Cool down time. You made it. Take it easy. Loosen up those arms. Open up that chest." She smiles as her eyes scan the room, never meeting mine. "Doesn't that feel good?"

No, Sam, it feels like torture. New goal, join a gym and find time to get some workouts in.

She ends with ten deep, cleansing breaths, then the class claps before breaking up, gathering bags and water bottles, chatting happily. Why did they do that? Clap as though they're *applauding* Sam and Monica? I want to curse them, not applaud.

I swipe the sweat from my face and grab my water bottle, purposefully taking my time so the class can clear out before I approach Sam again.

"It's your first time here."

I look up to find the blonde who worked out to my right stands before me. "Yeah."

"I'm Natalie." She offers her hand.

"Cole." I nod, lifting my full hands as an apology for not accepting hers.

"You picked the right place. Sam and Monica are two of the best instructors in Manhattan." Natalie dabs at the sweat peppering her forehead and neck. "Sam went a bit harder than usual today, but you kept up nicely."

She went a bit harder today, huh? I wonder...

"It was a great workout," I agree, glancing in the mirror lining the back wall of the studio in search of Sam. She's chatting with two girls near the front.

Natalie interrupts my staring. "Some of us like to grab drinks after class. You have plans?"

My eyes skim over the woman before me. Her sports bra and spandex shorts leave little to the imagination. This is the appeal of this place for Shawn. If my attention wasn't distracted by Sam, I'd walk out the door with Natalie right now.

I check Sam's position once more. She looks like she's finishing up her conversation.

"If you'll excuse me, I need to speak with Sam." Halfway across the floor, my step slows. I didn't reply or thank Natalie for her invitation. I shrug it off with a rueful shake of my head. I highly doubt she cares.

One of the girls talking with Sam, notices me walking their way. She flashes a knowing smile. Are my intentions so clear?

"Okay, we'll let you go, Sam. Great class. See you Wednesday."

"See ya." Sam waves as she turns from the door.

"Hey."

Sam jumps as she nearly runs into my chest when I step in front of her, and her hand flies to her heart. "As if that class didn't get my heart pumping enough."

"Did it? I swear you looked like this was another day at the office for you. I mean—" I lean closer, and she draws back as my eyes study her flushed face. "I think that might be one drop of sweat right there on your temple."

She grins and straightens as I pull back.

"I'm bathed in sweat here. I'm impressed, Sam. That was a really good class."

"I guess teaching several classes a day helps build my stamina."

Oh, I do love a girl with stamina.

"I have to admit when Shawn asked me to come, I seriously thought it was for women. Case in point," I jerk my head toward the back corner of the studio where my friend has Monica cornered. He's turning himself inside out for her attention. "I think for him it is all about the women."

Sam's eyebrow raises. "How did you and Shawn become friends?"

"We work at Bellevue together."

"Shawn's a doctor?" Her jaw drops. She's seriously concerned by this thought.

"No way." A bark of laughter escapes my lips at the picture of Shawn practicing medicine. I should feel bad, but I don't. "He's a patient care advocate."

"Really. So, he's the guy that speaks for the patient and helps them understand all the medical jargon?"

She knows what his title entails. Amazing. "Surprising, isn't it?"

Sam peers over at Shawn with her head tilted, studying him as he annoys Monica. She appears to be looking at him with different eyes, seeing him in a different light. It puts a smile on my face.

"Don't hold his sleazy womanizing against him. I promise he has a really big heart."

She suppresses a laugh. "If he showed that side to Monica, he might make things a little easier on himself." We check them out, watching as Monica rolls her eyes and shoves at Shawn's chest. Shawn merely laughs and catches her wrist.

"I seem to recall you telling me that women are always right," I remind her, returning my attention to her profile. "I'll pass your advice to him."

"Wise decision." Sam bends down, picking up her water bottle and weights.

I step back as she pushes a kick bag toward the wall with her foot. I move to help, then check myself. It might not go over so well. She comes off as an independent woman. "Are you done for the night?"

"Yeah. This was the last class."

Except for the four of us, the studio is empty now. "Are you heading back to Queens, then?" I ask with hesitation. Should I suggest grabbing drinks or dinner? My sweaty clothing and wake-up call for tomorrow's shift make that decision for me and I push the idea out of my mind.

She considers me like she isn't sure how she wants to answer. "Yeah. As soon as Monica balances out."

I nod like an idiot. "Do you want me to grab Shawn and get out of your hair? Or would you mind if we stuck around and caught the train with you? We're going to the same place, after all."

"Oh, um ... yeah. Sure. I mean, Monica might feel differently," she laughs and spares Monica a glance. "But, maybe Shawn will use his time wisely."

Maybe I'm reading the situation wrong, but Sam might be mistaken about Monica. She looks as though she enjoys Shawn's attention.

"I'll grab him so you two can finish up whatever you need to. Can we help with anything while we wait?"

"No, we've got it. Thanks, though."

I wrangle Shawn away from a grateful Monica, who disappears into a small office in the corner of the studio near the front door.

"Did you see the way she was looking at me?" Shawn nudges my side as we grab our duffels. "She totally wants me."

"You're delusional, man. Want my advice?"

"Your advice? The guy who hasn't gone out with anyone more than once since he moved to New York."

I punch his arm. "I work eighty hour weeks. Dating is a foreign concept to me right now."

"You guys ready?" Sam asks before I can finish. She's standing near the front door with Monica at her side. Judging by Monica's scowl, she's super excited for our company.

"Sure, let's go." Sam flips off the studio lights as we cross the floor toward the exit. Bumping into Shawn's side, I offer him a little advice. "Tone down your obnoxious flirting before you make us both look like jerks."

"Whoa, wait." He stops walking. "Sam? She's the girl you told me about, isn't she?"

How did he guess that? Did my face give me away? Did he note the way I can't keep my eyes off her? I turn my head.

"Holy crap! What are the odds?"

I cover his whisper-shout by coughing loudly. "Shut up or she'll hear you. Yes, she's the girl."

"That's crazy."

It is crazy, but I dismiss it. "It doesn't matter. I need to keep my focus on work and get through my residency."

Shawn looks at me as though I have two heads. If I were him I'd look at myself the same way.

FREAK LIKE ME

N TRAIN --AUGUST 22, 1994

"I CAN'T BELIEVE you told them they could ride home with us," Monica hisses into my ear as we walk down the stairwell to the N Train with Shawn and Cole close behind us. Deep murmurs drift our way. I can't make out what they're saying to each other, but if I can hear them whispering, they can probably hear us.

I shush Monica as I shoulder past someone coming up the stairs. "We're going to the same place."

"I don't care."

I'm not fighting with her in front of them. "We'll talk at home."

"You bet we will," she mutters.

Once we're home she's going to want to do more than chew me out, and I don't want to get into how I know Cole and all the times we've run into each other over the last year. Knowing Monica, she'll go all hopeless romantic on me and read the situation completely wrong.

"Just keep your cool for twenty minutes."

"My cool is always present," she huffs.

On the platform, Cole stands on my other side as the Q

Train passes. I smell fabulous all covered in sweat. Good thing the mingling smells of the subway tunnel overpower me.

"I told him to chill out," Cole confides, moving close to my ear and speaking over the roar of the train. His breath tickles my earlobe and I refrain from rubbing it on my shoulder. I'd look revolted, when really, I don't know how to handle men in my personal space anymore.

"Honestly, that works for your and my benefit more than anything," I chuckle.

He looks back at Shawn and Monica and laughs lightly, nodding his agreement. "So, you moved in with Monica a few weeks ago? Where did you move from?"

"The East Village."

His eyes go wide, his mouth opening and closing like he's wondering why in the world someone would move from the East Village to Queens, but he's too polite to ask. He nods. "When did you two open the studio?"

"It was—" I count back, tapping the months on my fingers. "May of last year? Yeah. May. She'd been wanting to open a kickboxing studio for a while, but she couldn't do it alone. When she asked me, it felt right, so we went for it."

"That's amazing. Owning your own business at your age." Cole leisurely looks me up and down. A shiver runs up my spine at the heat reflecting in his eyes. "I mean, how old are you?"

Did he seriously ask me my age?

"Oh, wait! I shouldn't ask you that, should I?" He cups the bill of his *Yankees* cap.

I laugh to put him at ease. He doesn't have to know how it was possible for us to afford it. "I know we look too young to own a business. I'm twenty-four. Monica's twenty-five."

"Really? I was still in school at your age." He shakes his head. "I'll say it again, I'm impressed."

"You were also going to school to become a *doctor. That's*

34

impressive. All we did was open up a place for people to work out."

It's not like Monica and I would've been able to start up Pure Kickboxing without the money I had access to. It's not like it was money I saved, or earned, or borrowed from a bank. It's money I don't want anything to do with.

The N Train whistles to a halt in front of us. Monica practically shoves Cole out of the way as she boards behind me, away from Shawn. I pick the last two seats in a row, hoping Cole and Shawn will sit across the aisle from us. Instead, Cole takes the seat adjacent, putting himself right next to me. When the subway jerks forward, Cole's knee knocks into mine. Even after the subway gains momentum, he doesn't move away. Do I want his knee to keep touching mine? Yes, and that is exactly why I shift away in my seat and tuck my foot under my other knee, trying to look like I'm only getting comfortable for the long haul. With as much as I dodge him, I'm probably giving him a complex.

"So, Cole, what do you do for a living?" Monica asks a few minutes into the ride.

"I work with Shawn at Bellevue."

I shoot him a look. Why is he holding back his profession?

"So, you kind of work with the patients?"

"Kinda." He catches me looking accusingly at him from the corner of his eye before he offers, "Actually, I'm an ER doctor." He's almost reluctant. I've never known a guy with a job like that —doctor, lawyer, dentist—where he hasn't willingly bragged about his title.

Monica's eyes burn a hole through me. "That's why you called him Dr.—what was it—Long Island?"

Shawn laughs. "Dr. Long Island? That's cute."

"So, why Long Island?" Monica asks as she leans forward, too intrigued for my taste. "Are you from Long Island?"

I guess we're having this conversation now. As soon as she finds out that's where we met, she'll know.

"No, I'm from Pennsylvania. Sam calls me that because we met there. You know how I told you Sam helped me out with my sister?" Monica nods and Cole continues, "We were at a memorial service for Flight 397. I assume you know of it?"

Monica's eyes dart to me, and I discreetly grab her hand resting between us and squeeze, hoping she catches my lack of desire to talk about it. "Yeah. I'm familiar with it. I don't think there's a person in New York that isn't."

Cole nods. "My sister had a bit of a breakdown during the memorial, and Sam was kind enough to help me get Amber out of the restroom. She was a big help. Plus, she gave me a few pointers for dealing with overly emotional teenagers."

"Teenagers are overly emotional? I don't know about you, but I was an angel."

I give Monica a grateful smile for steering the conversation away from 397.

Cole chuckles. "Amber is definitely not an angel. I love my sister, but I'm still trying to figure out how to handle her."

"I don't think any brother knows how to handle his sister," I say. "My big brother, Jamie, sure doesn't." Being an older brother for twenty-four years hasn't taught him anything.

"So ... *Doctor*, what do I have to do to get an appointment with you?"

"Oh, c'mon!" Shawn blurts. "You want him just because he's a doctor?"

I bite back my laughter. Monica shrugs one shoulder like he isn't wrong. "Maybe you should've been a doctor."

With an eye roll, Shawn slouches in his seat and shakes his head.

"First, you can call me Cole, not Doctor. As for getting an appointment with me, I wouldn't recommend any of the typical injuries I see, I mean, unless you're partial to being shot or stabbed."

"Dang it. It was worth a shot."

I snort. "Oh my gosh, Monica."

She laughs and winks at Cole. "No pun intended. So, you're from Pennsylvania. You're a doctor. You have a little sister. You're handsome and have good taste in workout methods, but for some reason you associate with this guy." Monica points her thumb at Shawn. "That seems to be the only flaw I can find."

What is she getting at?

"You're searching for my flaws other than my friendship with this loser?" Shawn shoots daggers at Cole who seems immune as he continues, "Trust me, I have plenty of flaws, and Shawn's the least of them."

"Somehow I doubt that." Monica bats her eyelashes. What a shameless flirt. Poor Shawn.

"Whoa," Shawn interjects. "I am an asset to any relationship."

"Asset. Liability. Same difference," Cole laughs lightly. "Alright, Monica, you don't think I have any flaws? I don't typically offer this type of information up to people I just met, but I'll share a secret with you." He leans forward in his seat and Monica does the same in anticipation. "I drink milk straight from the carton," he stage whispers, his jaw dropping with mock severity.

I laugh as Monica sits back with a smirk. "Touché, Doctor. Touché."

"What about you?" Cole turns to me. "You have any horrible flaws I should know about?"

Me? Ask Monica. She's the one initiating the conversation. He doesn't *need* to know *anything* about me.

"She can't carry a tune," Shawn interjects.

My eyes flit to him. "How do you know that?"

"I've heard you outside my door. What do you listen to in

that Discman of yours, because you're always screeching some tune when you're coming up the stairs? You're gorgeous, but, man, you can't sing."

Cole gives Shawn a look I can't decipher. A mixture of shock and irritation, I think.

"Well, God had to give her at least one imperfection." Monica knocks into my shoulder, her lips pursed.

"Oh, shut up." I roll my eyes. "There's plenty more where my tone-deafness comes from."

"Name one." Cole's eyes twinkle with the challenge.

I laugh, accepting and raising the stakes. "I'll give you five." I tick them off on my fingers. "I have the hardest time returning phone calls. I ... Oh, I never remember to close my cereal boxes. Don't bother talking to me if I'm hungry or tired. There will be no rational conversation had. Umm, I'm a neat freak. And ... I become enraged when I'm lost."

"Define enraged," Shawn quips.

"Shut up." Cole's foot kicks at Shawn's.

"No, really," Monica says. "There's a level of anger you've never experienced until Sam is lost. And she's not lying about being a neat freak. She vacuums and mops every morning."

Cole rests his hand on my thigh. It's a light touch to get my attention, but I have to keep my eyes from shooting in that direction. Breathe normally, Samantha. "If it makes you feel any better, I leave my wet towels on the floor."

"I have to eat my Skittles in a certain color order."

"I dip my French fries in mayonnaise. I've been told that's disgusting."

"I have serious road rage."

"In New York City? Surely you can't be any worse than anyone else out there on the streets."

"Why do you think I take the subway?"

Monica sighs. "This is getting ridiculous. How do you two have so many flaws?"

"Seriously," Shawn chimes in. "Monica and I are obviously perfect. You two are lucky you have us in your lives."

Cole and I exchange looks. His brow quirks up. "They're right," he sighs. "Two people as messed up as we are should probably stick together. Especially in a city like New York. I mean, who else could help you overcome this serious issue with road rage, if not me? Did I mention I'm especially patient? It's one of my few good points."

"He tells the truth." Shawn nods.

Their friendship is evidence of that patience, but what is Cole trying to get from me? Is he just being flirty? Or does he want more from me?

I'm saved from answering by the slowing of the train as we arrive at Broadway station.

"Are you sure you ladies feel comfortable with this clown walking you home?" Cole stands as we do, his brows arch in question

"We'll be fine," I say.

"If anything," Monica chuckles as she hikes her duffle onto her shoulder, "he'll get jumped and we'll be safe."

"Oh, right. What was I thinking? I should be asking you two to protect *him*."

"Ha ha. You guys are so funny," Shawn groans as he and Cole do a little handshake.

"Okay, Sam." Cole turns to me. "I think it's safe to say we're going to keep bumping into each other. I mean, the last time we met I told you how to find me at work and you didn't take the hint. This time you're in trouble because now I know where you live."

He's definitely hitting on me. And I like it a whole lot more than I should. The question now is, how am I going to evade him?

"I think you're right." The smugly please smirk on his face doesn't go unnoticed as I continue, "Have a good night, Cole,"

We make our way to the doors as they're about to open.

"You, too. Be safe."

Something in the way he says those last two words causes me to peer over my shoulder as the doors close behind us. When our eyes meet, I know Cole is genuinely concerned about us making it home safely, and my heart warms. Without a man in the city, it's a nice feeling knowing there's someone like Cole worrying about me.

8

BE MY BABY TONIGHT
THE ROOF—SEPTEMBER 2, 1994

WHAT AM I DOING HERE? I survey the crowd. The bar is predictably crowded for a Friday night in Manhattan. Most of these people are likely my age, but I feel so old. Carefree smiles, tight dresses, and cocky-looking businessmen are all around me. I'm walking dead, I'm so tired. The bar is cool, though. Open and airy, completely different from McGuinty's, thanks to the large panels of windows flanking the back wall and the two wide open doors that lead out onto a rooftop patio. Hence the name The Roof. Original. The patio is the appeal of this place. The late-night Manhattan skyline is breathtaking, the view made more spectacular by the gorgeous brunette sitting in an oversized chair.

Sam. Right, *that's* why I'm here.

Zigzagging my way through the crowd in the indoor portion of the bar, I try watching where my hands go. I do a little dance with a blonde in a slinky black number, squeezing between her and a table full of suits, as she turns around.

"Well, well, well, Dr. Long Island, I didn't know if you were going to show up." Monica smiles. "You're late."

Wow, for best friends, Monica and Sam are so different.

Monica exudes flirtation and mischief, her crystal blue eyes always shimmering as though she's keeping a secret.

"Another one of my flaws." I nod my greeting. "And an occupational hazard. Happy birthday, by the way." My gaze floats over Monica's head, verifying Sam hasn't vacated her solitary spot.

"She's outside." Monica sees right through me, though I won't admit I already located her.

"Hey, is Shawn lurking around here somewhere?" How is he not lingering by Monica's side? He has a thing for marking his territory when he's into a girl, and he's more than into the stunning blonde in front of me.

"He's probably trapped some unsuspecting woman in a dark corner." She waves her hand with an air of annoyance.

"Naturally," I smirk. "I'm gonna go speak with Sam. I owe you a birthday drink later, though, okay?"

"I won't say no." She raises the half-full glass in her hand and smiles.

SAM IS IN A TRANCE, STARING OVER THE CITY SKYSCAPE AS I approach. Her profile is stoic, odd for someone at her best friend's birthday party.

"Is this seat taken?"

Her head whips up. "Cole," she spits out, startled by my appearance.

"Hey." I sink down beside her on the loveseat, not waiting for an invitation.

"What are you doing here?" she breathes, her long lashes fluttering rapidly.

I chuckle, resisting the urge to shake my head. "I'm good, and how are you?" I ask pointedly. Why does she always seem so uncomfortable around me?

A moment ticks by as we stare at each other before her mouth turns up. The smile instantly softens her features. "Sorry. I just didn't know you were going to be here. Monica didn't mention it."

"So I gathered by your reception. She invited me through Shawn, I guess. I mean, I think I was invited. Shawn told me about it yesterday afternoon, but I worked an eighteen, so I wasn't sure if I'd be able to make it."

I'm a dead man walking, but I wasn't passing up the chance to see her again. I've tried coming up with good reasons to stop by their place since the other night, and this party saved me the embarrassment of showing up with a lame excuse.

"I'm sure Monica is happy you're here. She loves the spotlight." The words don't come out in a resentful way, in fact they are more endearing than anything else. How long have they known each other?

"Is Monica the only one who is happy I'm here?" I knock my knee against hers. Sam's mouth twists. "I mean, I left some mighty big hints our last two meetings, hoping I'd hear from you."

"Well, I don't—Cole, I'm—" Her teeth catch her bottom lip as her eyes look everywhere but at mine.

"Tell me about you and Monica," I try, throwing her a bone. I'm not ready to be turned down by this woman yet. Maybe after some conversation she'll relax and I can win her over. "How did you two meet?"

Sam pauses before answering me. She does this a lot. Is she holding something back?

"Um, when I moved to New York a few years ago, a mutual friend introduced us."

A waitress balancing a tray of test tube shots stops at my side. "Can I get you two something?"

"I'm good, thanks." I glance at Sam who lifts her untouched wine glass. The waitress leaves us her name as she saunters off.

I pick up our conversation. "You were introduced by a friend?

You two seem very different. What is it about her that makes you two such great friends?"

"Are you saying two people have to be alike to be friends? Is that your way of saying you're a player like your buddy Shawn?"

Sam's got a little sass of her own. Touché. "Shawn forced me to go out with him and a bunch of friends the first week I moved here. We work together. He cares about my patients and his job. That gave us something to bond over. Plus, we're both huge sports fans. That's all guys really need to maintain a friendship."

She cocks her head. "So, you're not a player?"

"Are you especially worried about that?"

"What?" She pops up, sitting straighter and shaking her head. "It doesn't matter to me."

Her nervous energy and the way her words rush from her lips speaks differently.

"Hey, Sam," I incline my head. "You want to mingle with the others?"

She takes in a deep breath, the lines around her mouth relaxing. "Sure. Why not?"

We make our rounds through the crowded bar with Sam introducing me to her and Monica's friends. I'm able to place a few faces from the kickboxing class I took the other night.

"Are you planning on joining us again sometime soon?" asks the blonde who hit on me last Monday after class. What was her name? Natalie?

"I wish I could, but I work a crazy schedule, so I don't have a whole lot of free time to get workouts in."

Her predatory eyes peruse my body. So this is how Shawn's conquests feel.

"You don't look like you suffer for it," she insinuates. Sam groans under her breath.

Looping Sam's arm under mine, I give Natalie a nod. "Excuse us, we need to talk with the birthday girl," I offer politely.

We're barely five feet away when Sam's shoulders shake with

suppressed laughter. I peer down at her flushed face, holding back laughter of my own. She was so pale when I spotted her on the patio earlier. I like this Sam better.

"What can I say? Women love me," I tease out the side of my mouth.

"Oh, my gosh. She was undressing you with her eyes in the most uncomfortable way possible. *I* was uncomfortable for you." Her gaze slides up to mine.

Several retorts spring to mind, but the way her eyes glisten in the overhead lights distracts me from speaking them. I compliment her instead. "You have beautiful eyes."

Sam eyes me warily, conflicting emotions battling in the sea of colors.

I pause, tucking her arm closer. "I mean, they're chameleon, changing colors each time I see you."

Her lips part. What is she going to say? What is she thinking?

"There you two are." Shawn bellows as he arrives with Monica at his side. He slaps my back, his attitude as carefree as the other twenty-somethings around the bar. He raises a beer mug. "Dr. Evil let you get out of there? I'm shocked."

"Not talking work." I give him a side-eye as Monica and Sam whisper to each other. "Sam and I were talking about her amazing eyes."

Sam's head pops up. "What are you doing?" she asks me, hushed, almost accusing.

"Oh really?" Monica and Shawn ask simultaneously.

Sam's arm untangles from mine and cross over her chest. "He says I'm like a chameleon," she deadpans.

I bite the inside of my cheek as Monica grimaces and Shawn silently questions my player skills. Chameleon? What was I thinking?

"I thought they were greenish-gray when we first met. Tonight they're more blue," my explanation is lame.

Shawn sends me an all too knowing look. "Let me have a

look," he says smoothly, taking Sam's face in his hands and drawing her close.

"They're hazel, you idiot," Monica gripes, slapping at his arm.

Sam effortlessly pulls away from his hands. "What she said. Without the 'idiot' part."

Shawn throws his hands up. "Sorry, I didn't mean to mess with your girl." I punch his bicep. His face takes on an innocent look of shock. "What? The tension between you two is so thick I could cut it with a knife."

Monica nods, laughing, "You think?"

"What is happening right now?" Sam sputters, her face flushing. "We're standing right here."

"Hold up," I jump in. How did this conversation go from Sam's eye color to this? "The two of you," I wag my finger between Monica and Shawn, "are not seriously going to give us crap about tension?"

Sam snorts. "Hey, pot. Meet the kettle."

"Do not confuse you two with Shawn and me. This," Monica exaggeratedly waves her hand between them, "is *never* going to happen."

"And neither is this," Sam retorts. That shuts Monica up and stuns me. Is this argument helping or hurting my case?

"Wait, do I not get a say in this?" asks Shawn.

Exactly. Do *I* not get a say in this?

"No," Monica says tersely.

"You know you want me."

Monica's blue eyes roll. "Gag me."

My hand shoots up. "How about we get some drinks?" I suggest, flagging down the nearest waitress.

Shawn hounds Monica about her comment until we're each handed a drink and Sam clears her throat to gain their attention. Lifting her wine glass, she grins. "One more year closer to thirty!"

"Only one year ahead of you," Monica sasses back.

"To Monica." I raise my glass. "May you finally rid yourself of this guy."

"I'll drink to that," Monica giggles.

Shawn elbows my ribs. "Really, wingman?" he grumbles for my ears only.

"You dug your own grave, man," I whisper as the girls laugh and knock back their drinks.

Monica's laughter fades when she spots Shawn's frown. She kisses his cheek, murmuring something in his ear that's good enough to return a smile to his face again.

I lean closer to Sam. "You know, I don't think those two are so unlikely."

She eyes our friends. "No?"

"No." I take a drink. "I don't think we are either." I lift my glass smoothly throwing a wink her way.

THE BARS PULSATING MUSIC FINALLY SLOWS TO A SOULFUL groove, calling couples to the dance floor. Soon the dark floor is teeming with bodies. I'm nursing a beer as Sam sips on wine, and Shawn and Monica order another round. A merry-go-round of friends stop by our bar side table giving Monica their best wishes.

"Wanna dance?" I ask Sam when the four of us are alone.

"Umm..." Sam looks across the table at Monica, like she's asking for permission, or maybe she's asking her to come to her rescue. Monica doesn't spare her a glance. Sam takes a deep breath and looks at me with a hesitant smile. "Yeah, okay."

Not the most promising acceptance, but it'll do. As Sam's hand takes mine, I overhear Shawn behind us.

"Good idea. How about it, birthday girl? Want to grind up on this?"

"That couldn't sound more unappealing than if you called me 'hot stuff' and smacked my butt."

The smack of palm to butt rings clear and Monica yelps as we're swallowed up by the crowd.

"She might murder him tonight," Sam shouts over the music. "It's her birthday. She'll take it as a free pass."

"He'll deserve it." I swing her around into my arms.

"You should know, if that happens," Sam's hands land on my chest, her face inches from mine, "I'll be an accomplice to the murder. I'll have to help her bury the body."

"A girl who's got her friend's back. I like it." I tip my head, giving credit where credit is due.

She smirks, her distance from the beginning of the night wearing off. The wine, maybe? "My loyalty runs deep."

Monica's giggles reach me over the music and I glance up, finding her and Shawn swaying to the beat a few couples over. Shawn's mouth hovers over Monica's ear, his lips curved into a smile as he speaks.

"Do you think he'll win her over?" I ask Sam without removing my gaze from our best friends.

"It'll take a lot more than a few shots and a spin on the dance floor, that's for sure."

The words are a challenge issued.

"Yeah? Like what?" My hand applies pressure to her back. "What would it take to win you over?" I ask, lowering my voice, teasing her.

She pulls her attention away from Shawn and Monica, eyes wide.

"What if someone drew you onto the dance floor and wrapped his arm around your waist like this—" My hand slides down along the curve of her spine, coming to rest at the small of her back. My palm touches the heat of her skin flashing between the hem of her shirt and waist of her skirt each time she moves. She sucks in a breath. "And what if he took your other hand like this," I ask, tucking our clasped hands close to our chests between our bodies.

"It'll take more than some suave words and dance moves for me." Her voice is husky, uncertain. A quiver mars her breathing.

My pulse accelerates and I grin, more than willing to continue this game. "Suave words, huh?"

Inching my face closer, our foreheads nearly touch as I gaze into her eyes. "I wasn't kidding earlier. You do have the most exquisite eyes I've ever seen."

She clears her throat and murmurs, "Thank you."

"But do you know what I never noticed until I pulled you into my arms?"

Sam waits, expectantly. The beat of her heart pounds beneath our clasped hands.

My fingers, intertwined with hers between our chests, loosen as I aim my pointer finger up, dragging her hand with mine as the tip of my finger skims along her exposed collarbone and up the slim column of her neck.

"You ... have ... an ... amazing ... neck," I whisper, dragging the words out as I drop my face closer to hers.

She draws air into her lungs as though she hasn't taken a breath since we entered the dance floor.

My nose nudges her hair. I inhale. "And you smell like honey."

"It's my lotion," she utters, remaining still.

I long to kiss her neck. Does it taste as good as it smells? My mouth brushes against her cheek as I move toward her ear. "I love dancing with you, Samantha," I murmur, creeping closer to the pulse of her neck.

She swallows. "I'm not much of a dancer." Her words say one thing, but her moves prove otherwise.

This challenge takes on a life of its own. Releasing her hand, I curl my fingers around the back of her neck and into her hair. My thumb lingers along the edge of her jaw, rubbing back and forth, back and forth. One of her hands grips my shoulder while the other clutches the back of my neck.

"Not true." I kiss behind her ear, no longer able to keep my lips from touching her skin. "You dance perfectly. Everything about you is perfect."

I'd pull her closer, but there's no room left between us. Is there something going on around us? I've forgotten where I am. I'm lost.

"Hey, Sam?"

She hums a reply, saying nothing more as we sway.

"I'm going to kiss you now." My hand skates up her spine to rest between her shoulder blades. The bridge of my nose makes the return trip, following along her jawline until my forehead is pressed against hers. Our noses touch as I inhale deeply and curse softly. "I have to kiss you." I growl, the need to feel her mouth against mine primal. This isn't a game anymore.

This isn't a sweet, simple kiss. Our lips collide, both of us giving and taking. I drop my hand from her neck, no longer worried she'll pull away, and wrap it around her back. I want to hold her as close as possible. I want to wrap her up and fall through the floor to where no one can see us. To where we can be alone.

She pushes up onto her toes, her hands taking control of the back of my head. Her fingers threading through the hair at the nape of my neck, tugging, wanting.

Sam sighs, or maybe it was me? Around us, the music builds to a crescendo, providing the perfect backdrop to the pacing of this kiss.

I can't. I ... I tear myself away from her mouth. The dance floor remains dark, but the music is different. Faster. The bodies around us liven up. The tone of the room changes.

But I'm not done. I want more of Sam. And by the way her hands remain in my hair and her eyes are sleepily closed, she wants more, too.

"C'mere," I order softly, grabbing her hand and dragging her through the dancing crowd, outside onto the rooftop, and into an empty corner. I press her backside into the brick wall behind her and brace my arms on either side of her head.

Sam doesn't waste a second. She takes my jaw in her hands, drawing me down, and seals our lips together. The music is a distant sound compared to the sensual whimpers coming from her mouth. This woman might kill me. My body takes control, molding itself against her figure. I remove one hand from the wall and curl it behind her neck, gripping her hair, controlling the movements of her head.

Her fingers crawl down the side of my neck and dig in my shoulders, forcing me closer still. With one hand, she trails down my back, playing my muscles like a musical instrument.

Without pause, Sam loudly inhales through her nose and gently pushes against my chest. "I can't do this."

I grin. "We're already doing this," I remind her, placing little kisses on her chin and jaw when she turns her head.

"No, Cole. I'm sorry." She shakes her head, her eyes not meeting mine. "This was a mistake. I shouldn't have done that."

"There is no way something like that was a mistake." I shake my head, barely able to catch my breath.

I lean down and tilt her chin up to look at me. What is stopping her? "Sam," I whisper. She shows no resistance as her eyes rise to meet mine. Our lips a breath apart. Her mouth hesitantly brushes mine, teasing. Her eyes flutter closed. She *does* want this. I can't resist her. And I don't have to; she closes the gap.

It doesn't last. As quickly as she kisses me, a cry rips from her lungs, "What am I doing?" She tears herself away from the brick wall, from me. "Cole, I can't do this. *We* can't do this."

"You kissed me." I jump back, shocked at the pleading tone in her voice.

"I know. It was a lapse in judgment. The wine, the dim lighting, the music, your cologne. I lost my head."

"A lapse in judgment?" I'm so worked up I can't see straight, and she wants to blame the atmosphere for what happened between us? "You must know I like you, Sam. I've asked you out several times. I'm not hiding my interest. Seriously, even Shawn and Monica know. If you weren't ... if you didn't want to—"

"I did want to. I do," she stutters. Her eyes dart around the patio, searching. Is she searching for the moment she just killed? "I ... it's not right. We're not right."

Ouch.

"I'm tired, Sam. I've worked all day and I've got to be back in the morning. I don't know ... I don't know what you want from me. I've never—" My fingers dig into her hips. I force myself to push her away when all I want is to pull her back in. "I can't play this game." I lift my hands in surrender.

I step back, staring her down before I turn and walk away. I almost told her I've never felt an array of emotions like the ones those two kisses brought out in me. We'd made progress. Hadn't we? I rub the back of my neck, shaking my head at my stupidity as I walk away.

9

FEEL THE PAIN
PURE KICKBOXING—OCTOBER 25, 1994

FINALLY, the shipment of new weights arrives. I carry the box to the counter up front while Monica finishes up her last class. We didn't expect so many people to sign up for classes. It sucks only having enough for half of the people. With the recent turnout, these weights couldn't have gotten here fast enough.

I can't wait to use them for my next class. Snagging the box cutter from the desk drawer, I press it to the tape on top. With one swipe, I lose my grip and the blade slices right across my palm.

"Ouch, ouch, ouch, ouch, ouch." I suck in a pained breath and press my other hand over the cut.

"And that's it for today," Monica says from the floor. "Great job, guys!"

Shawn shows up at my side. "What did you do?"

Did he hear my gasp all the way at the back of the class? "I cut myself with the box cutter. I'm too afraid to look and see how bad it is." Red seeps out from between my clenched hands.

"Let me see it." I lift my hand as blood drips down my wrist, pouring out of the gaping slit. His mouth twists in shared pain.

"It's not going to stop bleeding. You'll need to keep pressure on it. Where are your towels?"

"In the back office."

Monica appears next to us. "What's going on?"

"Sam cut herself opening that box."

"Well, what are you standing around for? Shawn, go grab her a towel."

He sighs, but doesn't argue as he jogs to the back of the studio.

"Maybe you should let me open the shipments from now on?"

"I'm not incapable of using a box cutter. I lost my grip."

"Clearly, you don't know where to put your hands so you don't cut yourself if you slip up."

"Is this really the time, Monica?"

Shawn returns, towel in hand. "Maybe you should go to the emergency room."

"No, it's fine." Adamantly, I shake my head. "I don't think it's deep enough."

I lift my hand off the cut so Shawn can cover it with the towel. The wound gushes more blood, pooling in the center of my palm.

"I think you should go. It looks pretty deep. Cole is there tonight. He'll take care of you." He wraps the towel around my hand tightly.

My head tingles. "We haven't seen each other in like two months. I don't think he wants to see me. I think I hurt his feelings."

"Stop being such a girl," Monica snaps.

Shawn's eyes narrow, picking up on my slip-up. "How would you have hurt his feelings? What's going on with you two?"

"Nothing, I ... he ..." I ramble. Cole didn't tell him? If Cole didn't tell him, I definitely don't want Shawn to know.

He pushes for more. "Last time we were all together was at

Monica's birthday, and you two looked mighty cozy. Did something happen? He won't tell me a thing."

I glance at Monica who knows most of the story.

"You need to stop bleeding all over our floor," she jumps in, pulling Shawn's focus from Cole and back to my injured hand.

"Okay, ER it is. Let's go."

"I'm fine, really—" I protest as Shawn's hand goes around my back, propelling me from my spot.

"Do I have to pick you up and carry you there?" he asks firmly. "Because I will."

I breathe a heavy sigh, defeated. "I have a class in fifteen minutes."

"Wow. It's a good thing you have a partner who can cover for you," Monica says. "Go to the hospital."

BELLEVUE HOSPITAL

ADRENALINE KICKS IN AS SOON AS WE ENTER THE BUSTLING emergency room. Somewhere, Cole is beyond those walls and I'm gonna see him. I sign in, take a clipboard of forms to fill out, and follow Shawn as he helps me find a seat. Every other seat in the waiting room is occupied.

"We're gonna be here for hours, aren't we?"

Shawn frowns and looks toward the front desk. "I know Trisha. She loves me. Let me see what I can do," he offers, getting to his feet.

Shawn leans over the desk, a debonair smile on his handsome face. He chats for a few minutes while I fill out my paperwork. Will Trisha tell him I have to wait with everybody else? She might be immune to his charm. Hopefully, he hasn't screwed her over in the past.

Cole saunters through a set of double doors to the left of the nurses' station wearing green scrubs. A stethoscope wraps around his neck and he carries a clipboard in his hand, like a real doctor. Duh, he *is* a real doctor. My mouth hangs open. I immediately snap it shut.

Yes, Samantha. He is extremely attractive, but it can't go anywhere. Calm yourself.

His face brightens as he spots Shawn with Trisha and approaches them.

Shawn's head bobs as he points me out in the sea of ailing people. I want to shrink and blend into the rest of the waiting room. Cole's expression dims when he finds me. He doesn't look happy to see me.

He mouths, "I'll get her." Cole calls my name, jerking his head back in a signal for me to follow him. I keep my towel pressed to the meat of my palm as I walk toward him with my paperwork tucked under my arm.

"But what about all of these other people?" I hiss.

"They aren't life-threatening. None of them are losing blood and need stitches. And there are plenty of other doctors on staff tonight."

There are at least ten other people holding bloody bandages to one appendage or another, but I drop it.

"Don't you have protocols? Doesn't a nurse need to check my vitals or blood pressure and weight and all that stuff?" I whisper as we walk toward the double doors. He's going to know how much I weigh. Why does that matter?

"Sam, I went to medical school, you know. I can do those things."

"I know. This feels illegal or something."

"Okay. Well, Miss Cooper, you are welcome to take a seat here in the waiting room and someone will be with you in, say," he pauses as he glances around at the patients before continuing, "three hours."

I swallow hard. "Now is good."

"Somehow I figured that's what you'd say. Don't worry. If I'm needed, they'll page me. No one is going to get subpar treatment because I'm helping you." His reassurance helps me relax.

"C'mon, I've got an open bay over here. Take a seat in the chair," he instructs as he pulls the curtain closed. "What happened?"

He pulls on latex gloves and takes a seat in front of me, rolling over on his stool, close enough that his legs scissor mine.

I pause, staring at his legs' proximity, which clearly doesn't bother him, before answering when he takes my hand, "I was opening a new shipment." Cole unwraps the towel, and I continue, "And the box cutter slipped, slicing my palm."

Cole gently holds the back of my hand, shifting it back and forth under the lighting as he examines the cut.

"Any allergies I should know about?"

'Not that I know of, unless you're worried about my cat allergy."

The corner of his mouth twitches. "I think you're safe here." His eyes hold mine for a moment. What is he thinking? He goes back to probing my hand. "When was the last time you had a tetanus shot? Do you know?"

"No idea. Does anyone ever know?"

This time the twitch holds, curving into a soft smile—the first he's offered tonight—as he rolls away on the stool. "Most people don't. Looks like you're going to need about five stitches. I'll send in a nurse to give you a booster while I grab the tray."

Cole pushes back the curtain and instructs a nearby nurse what to do with me. My eyes drift down his nice backside. Lucky nurses get to spend every day watching him in those scrubs. I shake away the absurd thought. An older nurse comes in and asks me more questions as she gives me the shot. After she leaves, I wait for a good ten to fifteen minutes before Cole comes back. He's spewing out doctorly orders as he steps back behind the curtain.

"Sorry for the wait. I had to check on a patient."

"That's fine." I avoid looking at him as he sits down on the stool and scoots over, wedging his leg in between mine again. He's not acting like the Cole he was that night at the bar. He's standoffish and formal. I knew coming was a bad idea. I *did* hurt his feelings, or completely bruised his ego. He must hate me.

Cole rolls over a tray containing the instruments he needs and holds out his hand, waiting for me to give him mine. Resting my hand on the tray, he cleans the wound. His hand works with gentle precision as he swipes the gauze across my palm. It stings more than I anticipated, but his soft touch helps.

"I'm going to numb you up a little." He waves a needle before my eyes. "You're going to feel a slight pinch." The needle pierces my skin before I can brace myself, causing me to suck in a breath.

"And another." The anesthetic tingles as it enters my bloodstream, numbing my palm and working its way to the base of my fingers. By the time he sets the needle down, my hand is heavy and numb.

"Anything?" His face watches mine as he pokes around the laceration.

"Not a thing."

Cole nods, picking up the thread and fishhook-shaped needle and hovering over my palm. He gives me one last look—somehow it comes as pained—before he pulls the edges of my skin together and sews. He's silent as he works.

I want to get out of here. Stupid Shawn convincing me to come. I could've put some liquid Band-Aid on the cut, secured it with a bandage, and gone on my way. Or gone to a different hospital, at least. Instead, I have to endure distant Cole. I don't like distant Cole. Treating me is probably the last thing he wants to be doing. I would have done us both a favor by not coming here.

He clears his throat. "Shawn tells me your studio has taken off in the past couple months. I think his exact words were, 'There are twice as many hot chicks to hit on.'"

"Ha. Sounds about right. Yeah. Business is steady. Nothing crazy."

"Steady is good."

The awkward silence continues. Suddenly, I miss what little friendship we'd created before. His earnest smiles and easy conversation. I miss Cole, and I don't understand how that's possible.

If only I could keep my mouth shut. "I'm sorry about that night at Monica's birthday thing."

Cole's brows pinch together and his lips pucker, but he remains professional, concentrating on my hand. "Hey, it was two months ago. We don't have to talk about it." He pauses, tugging a stitch through my skin and pulling the thread taut. "We can forget it even happened."

"Right. Okay." I nod, shutting up. Should've kept my mouth shut.

I shouldn't have ended things the way I did, or rather, I shouldn't have let things happen in the first place. Things never should've gotten so far. It wasn't my intention to let things go anywhere with Cole. Things can never go anywhere with anyone.

"I do owe you an apology, though. I shouldn't have left the way I did."

"No, no. It's fine. You don't owe me anything. I get it."

We lapse into silence again.

"Speaking of birthdays," I nearly jump at the abrupt comment. "According to your forms, you had one last week." His eyes flicker to my face. He pauses mid-stitch again, then returns to work. "Happy late birthday. Did you do anything special?"

He sounds so much like a doctor, trying to come up with safe topics of conversation with a stranger. So, I give him an answer a patient would give. "Thanks. I went home to spend it with my brother and mom."

"Oh? Where's home?"

"Vermont. Newport area."

"Small world, my brother has his heart set on moving to Burlington after he graduates from NYU."

"That's such a beautiful area. Why does he want to move there?"

"He's an outdoors enthusiast. His dream job is working for Burton Snowboards there in Burlington. He's interested in doing design and marketing for their products. He met one of their engineers two years ago, and he's had stars in his eyes ever since."

"Well, that sounds really cool."

Any easy conversation we tried establishing is gone the moment Cole focuses back on my hand. Why am I so bothered by that? I'm the one who wanted to set boundaries for him. I can't be mad about it now.

He finishes stitching in silence.

"Alright, you're good to go. Keep the bandages dry, but you can wash your hands or shower like normal. Just be sure to dry the area completely and use an antibiotic ointment before you cover it." Cole covers the area with gauze, his touch light as he uses medical tape to secure it. "You need to keep an eye out for infection. Any red puffiness, streaking around the wound, or if you start running a fever. You can check in with your primary doctor." He rubs his palms against his thighs as he rolls back on his chair. "Or feel free to call me," he says on an exhale, like he had to force himself to make the offer.

"Thank you, *Dr. Rossner*." I don't feel like I can call him Cole anymore. There wasn't a flirtatious glint in his eyes once.

"Do you have insurance?"

"I don't," I admit, but I'm not concerned about it.

"You'll need to have the stitches removed in two weeks, so if you want, I could stop by the studio and do it for you. It's quick and painless." He smirks. "I mean, there's no need for you to incur another huge bill for something that simple. It's up to you."

"Yeah, I'll let you know." I grab my purse with my unstitched hand and stand.

"I'd walk you out, but I've got patients to see. Take care." He knocks his chin in the air as his farewell.

I don't want to leave with this awkwardness between us, but I only have myself to blame.

"Bye." I barely have a chance to toss a wave before Cole is walking down the hall.

10

THERE GOES MY HEART
BELLEVUE SOUTH PARK—NOVEMBER 1, 1994

THE LAUGHTER on the small playground is a welcome distraction today. I'm two blocks from Bellevue, but it seems like worlds away. The shouts of toddlers begging for pushes on swings drown out the voices in my head. The sun warming my face pushes the memory of a cold hand from my fingertips. I hate my job on days like these.

Loss. I've seen it enough now. Suffered through it myself. It never gets easier.

"Cole?"

I shield my eyes as I look up. Sam stares down at me, her face twisted with worry.

"Hey." I shake myself to the present and slide forward on the bench.

"Hey, you don't have to get up." Her hand motions for me to remain seated. "I said your name a few times. Are you okay?"

"What? Oh, yeah, I'm sorry. I was deep in thought." I check out her workout gear. "You on a lunch break?"

"Yeah. I just finished with a class. How about you?" Her brows furrow with concern.

I nod. Does she think it's strange that I'm sitting here midday in my scrubs?

Her feet shift. "Did you eat already? I was just passing through the park to grab a gyro. If you feel like talking, you can join me."

As if on cue, I spot Trisha making her way toward us, bag in hand, and I stand and wave her way. "Actually, I think my lunch has arrived."

Trisha breaks into a wide smile as she nears. "There you are. I thought you were going to wait in the break room, but Shawn said you needed to get out." Her hand settles on my bicep as she steps into my side. She rubs it once, twice.

Sam steps back, eyeing Trisha with surprise.

"Sam, this is Trisha. Trisha, Sam."

Sam's posture changes instantly. Her shoulders lift, tensing around her neck. She turns away from me and addresses Trisha with a polite smile. "You were in the ER on Tuesday night when I came in."

"Oh, yeah. You're Shawn's girl."

Shawn's girl? Did I miss something?

"Oh, no, no," Sam laughs, shaking her head so wildly her ponytail smacks her face. "No. He's just a friend who was with me when I cut my hand."

Oh, right. Shawn was the one who brought her in the other night. How could I forget that?

"How's your hand, by the way? You been fighting any more box cutters since I last saw you?" I reach for her, intending to examine her palm out of habit. Trisha's hand around my arm applies the barest amount of pressure, stopping me.

Sam holds her hands at her waist, rubbing her thumb over the stitches. "Monica's been needing to pull her weight around the studio, and I've had to modify some of my techniques in class, but it's fine. Healing great. Thank you."

"Studio?" Recognition sweeps over Trisha's face and she

finally releases my arm. "Oh, Pure Kickboxing. Now I see your shirt. You work there? I have several friends that rave about that place."

"She's the owner," I point out, crossing my arms over my chest. "Don't let her innocent face fool you, she packs a mean punch. I should know, I found out the hard way." I give Sam a meaningful look.

I really need to let that kiss go. Sam's smile falls, and I frown. Low blow, Cole.

"Anyway," Trisha coughs, and I plaster a smile on my face. "Lunch is getting cold. We should eat."

"Yeah, I'll leave you two to your date. I'm sure you don't have much time left."

"It was nice to meet you," Trisha's says quickly, her hand tugging on my sleeve.

"Tell Monica I said hey, and don't forget to come see me to get those stitches out. Okay?" I hold Sam's gaze, willing her to agree. There's no reason for her to make an appointment to get them cut out. She has a crazy work schedule like me. I mean, it's the least I can do.

"Sure." She offers a forced smile of her own. "I won't forget. I'm counting down the days until I can get back to a normal routine."

"I bet."

Trisha tugs on me once again, and I relent, waving to Sam as we turn and head deeper into the park.

11

CONFIDE IN ME

MONICA & SAM'S—NOVEMBER 6, 1994

SITTING on the edge of my bed, I hold the black picture frame in my hands. Every day I look at this picture and function perfectly fine, but today I'm a basket case. Tears fall onto the frame and I brush them aside, smearing the glass. Tugging my long sleeve over my palm, I mop away the smudges to see our smiling faces. Why do I torture myself with this picture? I hiccup a sob.

Putting the frame face down on my nightstand, I get to my feet. I have to get out of this apartment. The pain is too much today.

Wiping my cheeks, I snag my coat and purse from the hook by the door. Over my shoulder, I shout out to Monica, "I'm heading out."

She emerges from her bedroom. "Where are you going?"

I refuse to meet her eyes as I shrug into my coat and wrap my scarf around my neck. "I'm just going out. I'll be back in a couple hours." She knows what today is.

Any second, she's going to walk toward me and try to hug me or ask if she can come. She searches my face in silence, debating.

Finally, she says, "Okay. Call if you need anything. I'm not leaving the apartment today."

I nod. "I'll be back." Waving and forcing a smile, I hurriedly close the door behind me. I lock it and turn to the hallway with my eyes shut, heaving a sigh.

"Fancy meeting you here."

Startled, my hand flies to my chest and I look down the old hallway. "Cole." I blink rapidly, trying to clear away any remaining tears. Too bad I probably have red eyes and puffy eyelids. Perfect timing. I brace myself for the onslaught of questions.

"Hey, how are—" His smile fades with each leisurely step he takes. "Are you crying? Is everything okay?"

Using my fingertips, I wipe under my eyes, trying to remove any streaking mascara. Why didn't I think of waterproof today? "Oh, everything is fine."

"Sam?" Cole steps into my space, taking me by the shoulders. I'm surprised he's willingly touching me.

He tilts his face, drawing my eyes to his. "What's wrong?"

How can I blatantly lie to him when he's looking right at my tear-stained face and seeming so attentive and concerned? "Today is just a rough day for me. I needed to get out of my apartment."

His hands give my shoulders a squeeze. The doctor in him radiates through his gentle touch and tone. "I'm sorry you're having a bad day. Sometimes we need a break, don't we?"

You have no idea. But he does, only on a different level. "Yeah," I agree for lack of anything better to say.

"Want some company?"

Do I tell him no? Do I want his company? Today wouldn't really be appropriate for him to tag along. But then I hear Monica. *It's okay to let people in. You don't have to mourn alone.* Having his presence wouldn't be so bad. It would be comforting, actually. Maybe we can patch things up, start new. And maybe it's time Cole learns the truth.

"Yeah, okay. That would be nice."

"Really?" He steps back. "I didn't expect you to say yes."

Was he asking to be polite? Or have I shot him down so much that he doesn't feel like I want him around at all? "Well, don't feel like you have to."

"No, I want to." He glances over his shoulder at Shawn's apartment. "I'd love to, actually. Let me tell Shawn I have a change of plans."

I nod and wait by my door as Cole walks to Shawn's door and knocks. After a minute of chatting with him, Shawn pops his head out into the hallway. "Hey, Sammy."

Despite myself, I offer a small smile. "Hi, Shawn."

Cole shoves Shawn out of sight, and after another moment, he heads my way. "Alright, so where are we going?"

"Well, I was gonna go to one of my favorite Italian bakeries. Jio and Marie's. Have you heard of it?"

"No, but I like dessert. Lead the way, Supergirl."

I wish I felt more like Supergirl today.

JIO AND MARIE'S ITALIAN BAKERY

WE WALK TO THE BAKERY IN SILENCE. IT'S COMPANIONABLE, but slightly awkward. Once we walk inside and Jiovanni appears from the back while dusting his hands off on his white apron, my mood picks up almost immediately.

"Samantha, bella! It's so good to see you." His warm smile brightens his jovial, tanned face.

"Hi, Jio. It's good to see you, too."

"Samantha?" Ann Marie's voice lights up as she comes through the same doorway behind the counter. "We've missed you!"

"I've missed you, too. Business has kept me pretty busy, so I haven't had much time to come."

Jiovanni reads between the lines and nods. "You here for Paul's favorite?"

"Yes, sir."

"We'll bring it right out to you, sweetheart," Ann Marie says.

"Thank you." I smile.

Jiovanni turns to Cole. "Something for you?"

"That cappuccino machine looks killer. I'll take one, and a pistachio cannoli, please."

Jiovanni hands Cole a small plate with his dessert sitting atop a paper lace doily. "Have a seat and I'll bring your drink out to you once it's finished."

Cole and I find a two-seater table against the wall and sit opposite each other.

"They know your name and your order? You eat here often?"

I nod. "I used to. Now I drop by when I get the chance. Every few months, I guess. I haven't been here in a while."

"It's always nice to find hidden gems in the city." He looks around the quiet bakery. "I hope it's as good as it smells. Although, it'll be dangerous to my health if it is."

"Get ready to gain twenty pounds."

Ann Marie sets down a giant pile of little dough balls covered with rainbow candies on the center of the table. Cole's eyes grow wide. "Enjoy, you two." She kisses the top of my head and walks away.

"Whoa. I guess you *are* having a rough day," Cole chuckles. "I assumed you were getting a little slice of tiramisu or something. What is this monstrosity?"

"Struffoli. They're deep-fried dough balls coated in honey. They're delicious." And exactly what Paul would've wanted today. "I'm definitely going to need your help eating them."

"Lucky for you, I'm a human trash compactor."

Jiovanni arrives with Cole's drink in hand. He throws me another sad smile and rubs my back before he leaves the two of us alone with our treats. Cole follows the exchange as he inhales the scent of his cappuccino, testing it with a small sip.

"That's perfect," he sighs. "Wanna tell me what has you so upset today?"

I pop a dough ball into my mouth. Am I ready to tell him?

"You know, I'm a doctor, which makes me a good listener. Plus, I'm bound by the doctor-patient confidentiality rule. Sooo—"

I quirk my eyebrow. "I'm not really your patient."

He reaches across the bistro table, his hand taking mine and flipping my palm over. "Not my patient, huh?" He eyes the large bandage covering my mostly-healed cut.

My lips curve upward against my will. "And what makes you think there's something wrong?"

Cole shakes his head and eyes me pointedly. "It's not polite of me to mention the red-rimmed eyes and running nose you had back at your apartment. And I'd hate to point out the dark circles you're wearing under those normally bright eyes of yours because that's not exactly gentlemanly of me, either."

I purse my lips at his unflattering, if not accurate, description of my current state.

"Sam, I know the look you were wearing when I saw you outside your door. I'm more than familiar with it. In fact," he inhales deeply through his nose, "I imagine I was wearing the same one that day I bumped into you at the park last week."

"Right." The day I met Trisha. I avoid his line of questioning. "What was going on with you that day?"

"About thirty minutes before you saw me I told a mother her son didn't make it." How does he speak of loss so easily? "Obviously, it's in the job description, you know? It doesn't make it easy, though. Especially when it's a child."

Is that why Trisha brought him lunch, because he lost a patient? Or is there more?

"That was really nice of Trisha to bring you lunch. You two dating?"

"Wow. You don't like to answer questions, do you?" He pops

71

a stray pistachio from his cannoli into his mouth. "I'll make a deal with you. I'll answer your questions about Trisha, then you have to answer my question."

I slowly chew my struffoli. "And which question is that?"

He raises a brow. "I'd like to know what had you crying this morning. What made you run here to eat this gigantic pile of fried dough?"

It's time. Something tells me Cole is going to be more than a temporary fixture in my life. Even after I screwed things up at The Roof. With him being such good friends with Shawn, we're bound to see more of each other. It'll make it easier if he knows about Paul. "Deal. Trisha first. Are you dating her?"

"I am."

Well, okay. How very evasive and to the point of you, Doctor. "That's nice. She's really pretty." Really pretty, but she'd have to be to land a spot on Cole's arm.

He nods. "She's a great girl. It's casual and new. It's not as though either of us have a ton of time on our hands. Plus, she's never dated Shawn. Do you know how hard it is for me to find females at Bellevue who haven't dated him?"

My head shakes with laughter. "I bet. So she's a smart woman, too."

"I like her. We have fun. Work is stressful." Everything he says is so matter of fact. He licks a smear of cannoli filling from the tip of his thumb. My eyes zero in on his mouth, and my tongue sneaks out, wetting my lips. *Cool it, Samantha.* "Life in general has been stressful since the crash. It's good to have people around you who you can have fun with and enjoy life."

I nod. What would I do without Monica? She's been one of the only people to hold me together since the crash. Otherwise, I'd be an island, distancing myself further and further to shield myself from the pain.

Cole waits, expectant. Right. My turn. I have to compose myself to keep from crying in the middle of the bakery. Maybe I should tell him somewhere more private. No, that would only give me an excuse to cry. I won't cry in front of Cole.

Taking a deep breath, I eye the dessert between us. "This was Paul's favorite dessert. It would've been his birthday today."

He leans forward, his head bobbing as though he already understands, resting his forearms on the table as he asks, "And who was Paul?"

I swallow, holding back my emotions. "My fiancé. He died on Flight 397."

His jaw drops. "That's why you were at the memorial that day," he murmurs. I meet his gaze. He's not asking me a question; he's stating a realization. His hand rubs across his stunned mouth. "I'm so sorry. I wish I'd known that day. I never would have flirted with you the way I did. Not that day, or after when we ran into each other."

"I know." I brush off his apology. "You don't have to be sorry. You didn't know and that's on me."

"Man, I feel like such a prick." His hands form fists on the table.

"Cole, please don't. I kept it from you because I didn't know that we'd become friends. And it's hard for me to talk about. You're the first person that didn't know him that I've had to tell."

"I'm sorry, Sam. I pushed you to tell me why you were sad. Obviously, I didn't expect a fiancé. I thought you would tell me you were having a bout of PMS. I mean, you told me you needed to get out and get dessert." Cole grimaces.

I hate that he feels so badly about the situation. I chuckle through my sniffles. "I wish it was only PMS."

"Apparently, Dr. Rossner's foot-in-mouth disorder has returned. Sorry."

"Stop apologizing. Seriously." I reach over, voluntarily touching him for the first time since the night we kissed. "It was time to tell you. I need to stop avoiding it. I avoided my feelings about his death for a long time after the crash. I'm finally becoming myself again. It's therapeutic to talk about it. At least, that's what Monica keeps telling me."

"Today would have been his birthday?" I nod with a shrug of one shoulder. "And you wanted to have his favorite dessert and celebrate it for him," he says, again more as a statement of fact than a question. "Excuse me for a second."

Cole gets up and walks to the counter. What is he doing? He speaks to Jiovanni who nods and walks away waving his hand. After a moment, Jiovanni returns and passes something across the counter to Cole.

I eye Cole warily when he returns. "Is everything okay?"

"It is now." He pulls his hand from behind his back, producing a small blue candle. "We were missing a candle."

A layer of tears coats my eyes as Cole sticks the candle in the remainder of the struffoli and lights it with a cigarette lighter.

"I'll wait outside. Take your time, okay?"

My fingers itch to grab his hand and ask him to stay with me. I don't want to be alone, but I do need a minute. A minute to give to Paul and compose myself. With a smile and a nod because I still can't answer Cole, he walks out the door.

12

UNDERSTANDING

JIO AND MARIE'S ITALIAN BAKERY—NOVEMBER 6, 1994

HOLY CRAP, she was engaged.

That's why she keeps pushing me away. It's been over two years since the crash, surely she's moving on now. Or she's ready to? *It's not your place to judge her, Cole.* Every patient's family member I've ever had to break the news of death to has reacted differently. There isn't a wrong or right way. I can't judge her grieving. I'm the last guy with room to talk when it comes to dealing with grief. Plus, I'm dating Trisha. What I think is of no concern. Sam and I can be friends. *Friends.* No matter how interested I am in her, I now know the truth.

I peek through the bakery window and see her gathering her things as she waves to the employees behind the counter. Shelving my thoughts about grieving and moving on for when I'm alone, I pull the door open for her.

"You ready?"

"Yeah, thank you. Let's head back."

I pause and take in a deep breath. "Hey, how do you feel about men and women being friends?"

"You just want to be friends?" Sam eyes me, confused. Maybe a little hopeful. Is it that ridiculous of a question?

"Yeah, why not?"

Skeptically, her lip twitches, readying to doubt me. "With no future of anything more?"

"Friends, nothing more. Think you can do that?"

Her raspy laughter is my answer. "I think I'll be okay."

"I'm warning you now, women find me irresistible. Remember Natalie? You're gonna have to be careful. You're not allowed to fall in love with me."

"Trust me, I'm immune to ego maniac doctors, so I'll be safe." She controls her features and very seriously says, "You, on the other hand, might need to keep yourself in check."

A smile is my only response.

"I'm not kidding. Don't go falling in love with me."

My heart rebels at this plan. I'm courting trouble. Before today, the idea that I could merely be friends with this woman was laughable. Now that I know about Paul, it seems like the only answer. If we don't draw the line between friends and lovers now, she'll never open up to me. Why is the idea of not being friends with her so reprehensible to me?

"Don't worry, I've got Trisha. Plus, if things go south, there are a lot of women at work who can distract me." I wag my brows playfully and move in front of her. With a grin, I offer my hand. "Hey, I'm Cole Rossner."

Sam eyes my outstretched hand as a smile forms. Her hand slides gently into mine. "Samantha Cooper. My friends call me Sam."

"Okay, Sam, I realize we just gorged ourselves on dessert, but it's close to dinner, and Shawn and I were going to try out a new diner down on Steinway. Do you want to join us? We can ask Monica, too. I enjoy watching the two of them pretend they haven't already sealed the deal."

Sam laughs. "Oh, I'm sure they totally have."

"Then whaddya say? Come to dinner and help me make our best friends supremely uncomfortable?"

"Sounds perfect."

MAMA'S CAFE

I'M RETURNING TO OUR DINNER TABLE FROM THE RESTROOM when I pause and watch the three occupants.

Shawn, who's probably had one too many beers, talks loudly while using his hands animatedly. "Then the bus jumps a fifty-foot gap, lands on the other side, and drives away like it's nothing." He throws himself back in his chair. "A city bus. Like that's possible."

Sam and Monica break into laughter. Seeing Sam smile warms me. Her agreeing to dinner was a surprise, so for her to not only be here, but to be having a good time...

"Dude, would you stop spoiling the movie?" I swat Shawn's shoulder as I walk around the table and return to my seat.

"It came out this summer, Cole. If you were going to see it, I would think you'd have gone by now," Shawn points out.

"Who has time to go to the movies anymore? I'll rent it when it comes to video."

"Was Keanu as hot in it as he was in *Point Break*?" Monica asks

Shawn's face twists in repulsion.

"Sorry, Mon." Sam's nose scrunches up like a bunny. "I'm gonna have to disagree with you on that one. Give me some Rob Lowe or Matt Dillon."

I snag a roll from the basket in the middle of the table and catch Sam's gaze. "Really?"

"Does that surprise you?"

"I pictured you as more of a man's man kind of girl."

Her brow lifts in question. "Such as?"

"Stallone?" Shawn suggests, and Monica snorts.

"Just because I like kickboxing doesn't mean I'm a *Rocky* fan." Sam frowns, rolling her eyes.

"I'm was thinking *Rambo*. Dude was bad—"

"Shawn," I interrupt. "No. Maybe Mel Gibson? Rugged, funny. Rob Lowe is too pretty. He looks fake."

"Oh, so pretty," Monica swoons.

"There's nothing wrong with pretty men," Sam argues. "But it doesn't mean the ruggedly handsome don't appeal."

"Val Kilmer," Monica suggests.

"Johnny Depp." Sam fans herself.

"Harrison Ford."

Sam leans onto the table, hands flat on either side of her plate. "Patrick Swayze."

"Oh gosh, *Ghost*." Monica clutches her chest.

"I have a feeling this could go on for a while," Shawn groans, rolling his eyes.

"Fine. Do tell, Gomes." Monica feigns boredom. "Who's on your list?"

"Sharon Stone." Shawn's eyes grow wide as he waggles his brows. "She's on fire. Plus, I like blondes," he adds, giving Monica's blonde head a pointed look.

"That woman doesn't play anything but sex symbols," Monica huffs.

"And the problem is?" asks Shawn innocently.

Sam rolls her eyes. "What do you think?" she asks me.

"About Sharon Stone?"

She nods. "Nah, I mean, she's nice to look at, but she'd bore me after an hour."

"Oh, yeah?" Her eyebrow arches, inquiring. "Why do you say that?"

"Unlike Shawn, I want to be able to have conversations with my dates."

Monica giggles. "This is why I like you, Cole. You say it like it is." She claps her hands. "Sam, remember the girl Shawn dated that we ran into a few weeks ago? I was surprised she knew her own name."

"You mean Pigtails who couldn't find the Tic Tacs 'hiding' in her left hand?" Sam sighs, shaking her head. "No one over twelve should try to pull off pigtails."

"Whatever," Shawn scoffs. "You're just jealous I have dates."

"I highly doubt *Dr.* Rossner has trouble securing himself dates," Monica points out. Shawn grumbles at the way she punctuates the word 'doctor'.

I grin. "I'm not complaining." With the exception of the brunette sitting here.

"And what *is* your type?" Sam asks me.

No thought necessary. "Julia Roberts."

"Good one," Shawn agrees. "I can't argue with her, either."

Monica nods. "I love her movies."

"It's the smile and the hair."

"Is that why you're dating Trisha? The red hair?"

Is it? I hadn't considered it. The arrival of our food spares me the need to explain my relationship with Trisha. When the waiter leaves, the topic of conversation shifts back to upcoming movies and plans for the holidays.

WE'RE WALKING HOME AFTER DINNER, THE GIRLS ARM IN arm ahead of Shawn and I as we discuss the Knicks' chances of making the finals.

"This is my turn," I call out to Monica and Sam as I stop at the intersection where I'll turn right to head home, while Sam, Monica, and Shawn will continue straight back to their building.

"Already?" Monica turns. She playfully dances her way to my side and hugs me, planting a kiss on my cheek. "Thanks for the dinner invite, Doctor," she grins. Like Shawn, she may have had a bit too much wine. Shawn throws his arm around her shoulders and tugs her into his side, giving me a nod as he pulls her away.

"Thank you," Sam says softly, stepping around our friends and standing in front of me.

"For what?"

"For dinner." Her hands slide into her heavy coat. "You didn't have to pay. That was sweet. But also for today. For listening."

I mirror her, slipping my hands into my pockets so I won't do anything else with them. Like take her in my arms. *Friends. Trisha. Paul.* I'm gonna chant those things over and over until I look at Sam the way I look at Monica.

"You're welcome for dinner. Thank you for not arguing with me about paying," I mention pointedly.

"I know, I'm stubborn. I gave in, though."

My fingers itch to touch her. I pinch the fabric in my jacket pocket. "Yeah, because I stole your credit card from the waiter."

She laughs and checks over her shoulder. Shawn and Monica have wandered twenty feet up the street, giving us some privacy.

"Alright, Samantha, how do you see this friendship working?" I ask curiously.

"Very easily," she replies. The more we talk, the sassier her tone becomes. "We set rules."

"Such as?"

She tilts her face toward the sky as though in deep thought. When her eyes return to mine, I brace myself.

"Number one: Do not stare deeply into my eyes and tell me how beautiful they are."

I bite back a smile. "What?"

"Uhh, do you and Shawn do that?"

"You and Monica don't?" My brow lifts as I pull my hands from my pockets and cross my arms over my chest. "Are you going to tell me you don't have slumber parties with pillow fights, either?"

Sam chuckles, shaking her head. "Number two: No innuendos."

"You're hardcore." Granted, after learning about Paul, I agree. Just friends.

"I have a feeling I'll need to be with you." She's probably right about that.

"Fine, no innuendos. I have a rule."

"Go on," Sam nods somberly. She's like a Queen giving her acquiesce.

"We have lunch, or dinner, once a month." I hold back the urge to throw in 'breakfast' solely to get her goat since the suggestion falls under the innuendos category.

"Sounds like dating to me," she frowns, skeptical.

"Nope, I'm already dating someone, remember? If we're going to be friends, we need to hang out. Otherwise, we're simply two people who know each other."

Sam opens her mouth.

I throw it all out there. "Look, I could use more friends. I've lived here for over a year, and my social life consists of the occasional date with someone from work and hanging out with Shawn. Show me some mercy." I throw puppy dog eyes her way.

Her smirk deepens like she isn't surprised I did that. "Next meal's on me?"

It's against my man code to let a girl pay, but since we're trying to be friends, I relent, "I'd like that."

"Good. We'll do lunch this week and discuss how funny it is that Monica has no clue how much she looks like Sharon Stone."

"It's a date," I agree. "Now catch up with Shawn and Monica, and be safe getting home," I shout as she moves away. She sends me quick wave over her head.

"Hey, Sam," I call after her. She pivots on her toes and walks backwards.

"Yeah?"

"Any time you need to talk, I'll be here."

She sends me a glowing smile before turning and catching up with Shawn and Monica.

13

ANYTIME YOU NEED A FRIEND
BLOOMINGDALE'S—DECEMBER 17, 1994

"When I agreed to lunch or dinner once a month, I didn't know it would turn into this."

"Don't act like you don't love our *weekly* meals together." Cole opens the door for me with a smile. I roll my eyes. A month ago, I didn't think we'd be able to get over Monica's birthday incident. Now we're catching up weekly and Christmas shopping together. I don't hate it.

"Seriously, Sam, I can't thank you enough for helping me."

"I'm happy to. I needed to shop some, anyway. So, does Amber have a favorite fragrance?"

"I have no idea."

Cole and I walk through a very crowded Bloomingdale's, maneuvering between other holiday shoppers as we pass the fragrance counters.

"She might like CK One. It's super popular right now."

"Isn't that the one with that naked people ad?"

My brow quirks.

"You know, it's black and white, and the girls are all in their bras and the guys are shirtless."

I laugh. "Probably. It's Calvin Klein."

"See. Look at it." We pass the Calvin Klein counter. "They don't even look happy."

My amusement can't be held back. "Okay. No Calvin Klein."

We come upon the accessories. "What about a purse? Every girl loves a good purse."

Cole nods and picks one up from the display. "Are you kidding me? Why are these things $300?"

"Well, that's Gucci, so—" I chuckle. "You're a doctor, right?"

"I'm a resident. I don't make *that* much money."

We continue on through the store, heading for the escalators. "Alright. So, what does Amber like? Does she have a favorite color, or colors she doesn't like? Give me something to work with."

"Maybe I should mention Amber is my half-sister, and I just started to get to know her a few years ago."

My eyes dart to him. "How did I not know this?"

"You never asked," he laughs.

"I'm a terrible friend. Maybe you should reconsider this friendship."

"I'm seriously contemplating."

The corner of my mouth twitches up. "So, is Brett your half-brother or—"

"Uh, did I not mention they're twins?" I stop walking and gape at Cole. How did I—his hand grabs mine as I'm shoved from behind. "You're blocking the shoppers."

"Because I'm stunned still. I don't know if I should feel bad or be offended you haven't mentioned any of this before."

Cole's closed lips twitch. "How about we shop first, talk later."

I step onto the escalator and grab the moving railing, pressing my back against it as I face him. "Fine, but talk about this, we will. Do you know *anything* Amber likes?"

"She's into fashion. Or she was last time I checked."

"Well, that does not help me. She probably has a better fashion sense than I do."

"Ha, I'm sure anything you like she would like."

We get off the escalator in front of the sleepwear department.

"What about a nightgown?" Cole holds up a long, floral, flannel nightgown. It even has ruffles on the cuffs. It looks like something my grandma would wear.

"Do you picture Trisha wearing something like that?"

"If she's cold," he says with a straight face.

"You're so full of it."

"I cannot go where you're going, Sam. If you're suggesting Amber would want something like that." He waves toward the wall of silk teddies, shaking his head vigorously.

"Oh, geez. I'm not saying to picture her like that. I just want you to picture an actual woman, not a seventy-year-old grandma. A woman in her early twenties. And tell me you see her wearing a flannel floor-length nightgown."

"They look comfortable." Cole places the gown back on the rack when I throw him a glare. "I know, I know. I'm not sure I'm cut out for this."

"If you want to get her something comfortable, how about something more like this?" I hold up some plaid lounge pants and a white baby tee.

"But her stomach will show in that T-shirt."

"It's meant for lounging and sleeping, not going out in public." He gives me a look and I laugh. "Okay, okay. You're making this very difficult. Maybe you should go find something for Brett. And I'll find something for Amber."

"Maybe you're right." He looks supremely uncomfortable standing among the hustle and bustle of the Christmas shoppers. "I just want her to be happy, you know? Last year I gave her money because I didn't know what to get for her. I don't want her to think I don't care enough to shop for her."

85

I pat his arm and urge him to leave. "No worries. I have this. I'll find something perfect for her."

AFTER SCOURING BLOOMINGDALE'S, I DECIDE ON A BLACK velvet choker and a black, tan, and forest green plaid scarf. Both seem like safe options. It's cold enough in Pennsylvania for a winter scarf. Hopefully, Cole will approve.

When I'm done, I search for Cole, locating him in the men's department. He's bent at the hips. It's not until I walk around a display of novelty gifts 'perfect for the man in your life' that I realize why.

"Is this what you call shopping?" I ask as he swings a golf club. His club hits the golf ball on the fake grass rug he's standing on and the ball rolls toward a rim with a little flag sticking up from it.

Cole spins on his toes. "Did no one teach you the importance of complete silence on the golf course?"

Laughter bubbles up. "I hate golf."

His jaw drops. "Hate is a strong word, Samantha Cooper."

Wow, the full name? "Yes, and I have strong feelings about golf, *Cole Rossner*."

He straightens, his lips pursed in contemplation as he looks at me. His right eye narrows. It might have twitched. Did I truly offend him? Then a smile curves his lips and he swings the club over his shoulder.

"Good. I hate it, too."

I burst into laughter, walking to his side as he drops the club to the grass rug and picks up the bags at his feet. "I was thinking of buying one for Shawn. Figured he could screw around with it in his office on slow days." He shrugs, picking up a box containing the putting set. "It would save the nurses from his constant attention. That's got to be a win, right?"

"The nurses would love you for it, I'm sure."

"So a win for all of us?" Cole winks as he heads toward the register to check out. "I'm glad I had this idea."

"So, you're aiming to get all of the nurse's attention?" What's up with his dating life? Isn't he dating Trisha? It doesn't matter to me, but how has no one snatched a guy like him up yet?

Cole steps up to the cashier before he answers my question. He politely asks about the sales associate's day, laughing with the blonde about the weather and how hectic the store is the closer Christmas gets.

"Thank you, Sheri." Cole smiles that charming smile of his as he readjusts the multiple bags in his hands.

"Do you know her?"

"Who?" He sends me a confused look. "Oh, the sales clerk? No, I was being nice."

Duh, the name tag. Right. "You're such a good guy." Most people shopping at Christmas time are ornery and snippy, ready to leave the lines and crowded stores. Leave it to Cole to be polite.

"Says the girl who's helping me buy presents for my sister because I'm hopeless at it." Cole smiles, knocking into my side with his hip. "How about you let this nice guy buy you lunch as a thanks?"

"I never turn down free food."

MON PETIT CAFE

"So—" I drag the word out, contemplating how to ask questions about his siblings. "Brett and Amber? They're your half-siblings?"

"Yeah." He shifts his napkin and silverware around on the table like he's uncomfortable. He hadn't originally given me the impression it would be a difficult topic to talk about. "We, um, it's a long story."

My fingers trail up and down the condensation of my water glass. "If it's too personal, you don't have to tell me."

He shakes his head. "The short of it is we have the same father."

The day I met Amber and Cole at the memorial, he'd said *her* parents died on 397. I assumed he lost them, too.

"I'm sorry I never clarified that when we talked about Brett and Amber before. My dad married their mom."

Like a roundhouse to the chest, the realization cuts off the function of my lungs.

"It was our dad and their mom who were on the plane that day."

Why is it that all I want to do is tell him I'm sorry when I know those words will do nothing for him? Instead, I reach across the table and grip his hand, sending my understanding and empathy through my touch.

"Until the crash I struggled with the concept of him being my father. It's ... well, it's a story. You want to hear it?"

"If you feel comfortable enough to tell me, I'd love to know more about you." I, of all people, know about needing time to share personal stuff.

"It's kind of a made for television movie type of cautionary tale." He chuckles wistfully and I retreat my hand to my side of the table. "My mom was a small-town, sheltered, only child who, as she would tell it, went wild when she went off to college. I am the byproduct of a one night stand she had after a night of too much drinking."

Well, that's not what I expected. I have so many things I want to ask, but I won't pry, so I wait.

He sighs. "You may have noticed I don't drink much. One beer, if anything. Now you know why."

"Seems like an understandable reason."

"She was—is—a great mother. For most of my life she gave me everything I needed, but when I started thinking about my future and college, she began acting weird. I'd had a fascination with blood and guts forever. She was disgusted by it. I swear she'd nearly faint at the sight of blood when I scraped my knees playing sports."

I laugh lightly.

"Imagine my surprise when she sat me down at sixteen to tell me she knew my father and he wanted to meet me."

Wait a second. "You never knew him?"

Cole shakes his head, his teeth scraping his top lip as he shrugs. "She raised me as a single mom, never told me anything about the man who fathered me." His voice wavers. It's only a slight crack, but I can see the emotions roiling within him. I can feel them as though they are mine.

"A doctor. That's the first thing she told me about him, as though his job title explained everything about me. My love for science and school, and my desire to be the best in class because I wanted to get into the best programs for college."

He pauses, pushing back his chair and sinking his hands into his hair. "Anyway, I met my dad for the first time when I was nearly seventeen. We'd lived a few hours apart my entire life, by the way. I met him and I hated him."

"Because he didn't step in to help her with you?" I speculate, completely understanding how that must have felt to him as a teen.

"Would you believe I would have preferred it if that had been the case?"

His disgusted laugh takes me aback.

"He didn't even know about me, Sam. My mother was so ashamed about the pregnancy, she dropped out of college and ran home, never even telling the frat boy she'd drunkenly slept with once what happened." Cole sighs heavily. "I hated him because he cared. He was beside himself with worry and compassion for me, and for her. I know it must sound crazy, but at the time I was so angry. I hated her for keeping this magnificent man from being my dad. I hated him for being the type of guy who slept with a girl at a party and not known anything about her. He invited us to dinner at his home. He was nothing but accommodating. He did everything right. Then I saw his family."

"Brett and Amber?" Their names are barely a whisper from my lips.

"They were eight." He blinks a few times, as though he's seeing his siblings as they were so long ago.

"My dad left when I was eight."

Cole stiffens. A crease forms between his eyebrows.

I didn't mean to say that, but I guess I should expand. "One day he decided he didn't want to be a dad anymore." I shrug. It's not something I dwell on. "I don't know why I told you that."

"Do you ever see him?"

"Not really. I've probably only seen him a handful of times since he left." I drop my eyes to the table. "He moved to the west coast. Arizona or Nevada, somewhere over there. I stopped waiting for him to come back a long time ago."

"Man, this is a heavy conversation to be having over lunch."

"Heavy conversations over food seems to be our thing." We share a small smile. Images of Cole as a teenager meeting a family for the first time that he didn't even know existed crowd my mind. His discomfort, his isolation, his longing. "So, it was your dad and their mom who died in the crash?"

His Adam's apple bobs as he swallows hard and nods.

"When—"

"You know, I think Amber will like the scarf and necklace. They seem like her style," he interrupts me.

Even though he hasn't finished the whole story, I give him a pass. He can take all the time he needs to divulge his life to me. I have a hard enough time talking about Paul. I can't expect him to share his dad with me.

14

HEAD OVER FEET

MONICA & SAM'S BUILDING—DECEMBER 31, 1994

"Well, now the party can begin."

Sam's raspy laughter comes from behind me as I walk through the threshold of her and Monica's apartment. Her hand presses into my back and I turn, leaning into her and giving her a quick hug.

"Happy New Year," I offer, looking at her flushed face.

"Happy New Year to you. How was Pennsylvania?"

"It was good. Great actually," I loop my arm around her neck and pull her with me as I make my way toward Shawn who's talking to a paramedic we know from the hospital. "It was great to get away from the hospital for a few days. How about you? How was Christmas?"

"It was good to spend it with my mom and Jamie. You'd think after dealing with New York winters, I'd be a pro, but I keep forgetting how cold Vermont is." She smiles and it punches me in the gut. I missed her. "What did Amber think of her gift?"

"Honestly, I think she suspects you had a hand in it. She loved everything. Oh, and my mom loved that fuzzy blanket you forced me to buy her. You're my new personal shopper, Miss Cooper."

She eyes me curiously. "Why would Amber think I had a hand in it?"

"I probably talked about you a bit." A bit is an understatement, and both Mom and Amber picked up on it. "She got all giddy thinking we were a couple at first."

Sam eyes me, ready to scold me. "Cole."

"Don't worry, I set her straight. Apparently, she finds it hard to believe guys and girls can be friends, too. Is that something you women are taught at a young age? All men want to date you?"

"You make us sound conceited."

I burst into laughter. "Not at all. You know what I meant. Is it a trust issue or something? 'Men only want one thing, and friendship isn't it.' " I fumble with my explanation.

"That's because that's typically the case. I'm still a little leery of you," she teases. "At our age, no man ever shows interest in being *just* friends."

"I think I've done a good job of proving to you we can hang out and be platonic. I don't think we needed those rules you forced upon me."

Sam's face twists, her lips parting—

"Cole, my man!" Shawn yells over the crowd noise as he heads our way.

I drop my arm from around Sam as Shawn knocks into me, nearly bowling me over as he hugs me. "Whoa, you've had a few drinks already, haven't you?"

"Who me?" His arm remains around my shoulder. "It's the last day of the year, buddy. I'm celebrating. Nineteen ninety-five, baby."

Wow. My boy is wasted, and it's only 10 PM.

"Hey, Kev. What's up?"

We shake hands. His eyes flick to my side, scanning over Sam in her short dark blue dress and black tights.

"Have you met Samantha?" I ask, somewhat reluctantly. The

guy isn't as bad as Shawn, but I know he makes the rounds in the hospital dating pool.

"Samantha? No." Kevin smiles as he steps closer and offers her his hand. "It's a pleasure to meet you."

"You, too." Sam shakes his hand and smiles politely.

Kevin asks her something, but I miss it all thanks to Shawn who yanks at me. "Come get a drink and make the rounds with me. There are a lot of available ladies here, man."

I throw Sam a covert 'help me' grimace as I reluctantly allow Shawn to pull me away. "I'm on shift at 8 AM, so I'm not drinking tonight."

"You're no fun. At least let me introduce you around."

"I'm not interested, Shawn."

He clucks his tongue, shaking his head. "Well, I am. Be my wingman."

We wander out of Monica and Sam's apartment and into the one next door. Several of the residents on their floor agreed to an open-door party crawl. Judging by the decor in this loft, it's occupied by someone with an affinity for New Age chic. Travel posters cover the walls and colorful silks are strewn over the chairs and tacked at the one window in the unit.

"This is Shea's. She's into yoga and meditation and has a crap ton of hot girlfriends."

"Why is it you live in a building teeming with single girls perfect for dating and I'm just now hearing about it?"

"Because I don't share?" he suggests as he throws himself into a group of girls standing by the food.

I roll my eyes. He's such a dog. Without warning, a hand grabs my arm and pulls me into the fray.

"SAVE ME?" I BEG, GRABBING SAM'S ELBOW AND PULLING HER from a couple guys once I return to her apartment.

A relieved smile washes over her face as we step away. "I think *you* saved *me*," she hisses. I look over my shoulder, checking out her admirers. "What am I saving *you* from?" she asks, poking me in the side.

"Apparently, single doctors are in high demand," I reply beneath my breath as I steer her toward a darker corner, maneuvering her body in front of mine as cover. "Shawn brought me to Shea's."

"Oh my gosh, say no more. She's sweet, but Monica and I went to dinner with her and her friends once." Sam makes a face like she spent the day herding cats.

"That bad, huh?"

"Let's just say once was enough."

I laugh. Somewhere in the apartment, a high-pitched voice raises above the din.

"Forty-five minutes till midnight, everyone."

Sam sighs. "I kind of hate this part."

"The countdown?"

"Yeah."

She doesn't elaborate, but she doesn't have to. I've spent the last four New Year's Eves without a date. That moment when the clock strikes midnight and everyone searches for their dates to kiss in the new year is awkward at best. If I weren't so superstitious, I'd merely grab a girl and plant one on her, but some traditions have meaning.

"I've got an idea. Follow me."

I drag her into the hallway and two doors down to Shawn's apartment.

"Hey," Sam frowns as I open Shawn's door. "Why didn't he open his place up to the party?"

"I dunno, but we're lucky he didn't." I wink, grabbing her hand and pulling her in before anyone sees us.

Sam closes the door and leans against it, watching me as I cross the room to Shawn's oversized entertainment center. "What are we doing in here?"

"Ringing in the new year."

Her eyes roam the apartment before reluctantly landing on me. "And how exactly do you plan on doing that?"

"By playing Mario Kart." I wave a controller. "Why else would I have brought you to a secluded apartment?"

Sam's laughter fills the apartment. "Well played, Mr. Rossner."

"Grab us some drinks and raid his cabinet for something to eat while I set this up."

Sam rummages through Shawn's things as I plug in two controllers and locate the Mario Kart disc, popping it in the game system. I kick two bean bag chairs closer to the television and drop a controller onto each one before I flip off the main lights in the apartment out of habit. Shawn and I prefer to play by the light of the television. It lends a sort of arcade feeling to the play.

"You ready?" I ask Sam as I plop into the blue chair, wiggling back and forth until it's perfect.

She hops onto the green bean bag beside mine. "Buckle up, Rossner. You challenged the wrong girl."

"Have you played this before?" I ask as the main screen pops up.

She smirks at the TV. "Maybe a time or two."

Her quick clicks as she picks a character and kart beg to differ. Luckily, I'm a bit of a pro.

"Pick the course. Lady's choice."

Sam scrolls through, like she knows exactly which course she wants.

As the countdown begins, my foot nudges Sam's. "Don't let your road rage get the best of you, Supergirl."

The corner of her mouth turns up. "I make no promises."

The green light signals, and Sam and I both slam our buttons, propelling our race cars forward.

"Tell me your favorite New Year's memory," I ask as I'm steering Bowser around a sharp corner.

"Don't you try and distract me. I have an older brother. I know your tricks."

"Ha! I wish I'd thought of that. I was honestly asking you a question, you big cynic."

A turtle shell flies from out of nowhere, knocking my kart spinning. Sam chuckles as her very predictably chosen Princess Peach driven kart flies around mine.

"There's no time for questions. Princess Peach is trying to concentrate on winning."

I bite my tongue. She's not playing. Recovering from my spin out, I deftly work Bowser back into view of Peach as we round the final turns. I'm so close. Maybe I could catch her, but I glance over, watching her profile in the flickering light of the television and my thumb lets off the gas.

Peach crosses the line first, and Sam jumps up, pumping her fist in the air. "Yes! Did I mention I'm a sore winner?"

I can't even be mad. Her face, illuminated in blue and green from the game, is so stunning I'd lose again simply to see it. She always wears this solemn face, like someone who's dealt with the pain of the world and fears not ever finding happiness again. As she gloats, I see true glee written on her face. I haven't seen that look in the two years since we met.

"Did I mention I'm a bit of a competitive freak?" I counter, immediately clicking the controller so I don't have to watch Princess Peach walk into the winner's circle and receive her little first place medal. "Rematch. Pick a course," I order with a grunt, scowling at her self-satisfied grin.

"Maybe you should pick a course. I'll go easy on you next time."

I clear my throat. "Ghost Valley it is."

This time the match isn't nearly as close. I smoke her.

"Did you let me win?" I ask as I cross the finish line first.

Sam leans back, shrugging. "Jamie and I hate that course. It's so dark, we never play it."

"Should we break the tie?"

"Bring it on."

And we do. We break the tie, then go on to even it up again and again until I've lost track of how many games we've played. At one point, I toss my controller onto the carpet in frustration when my kart gets hit time after time with one obstacle or another.

"Anger issues, Doctor?"

"Says the girl who nearly knocked my head off the last time I won." I laugh, dragging myself out of the bean bag and reaching for the thrown controller.

"You were *gloating*."

"Are you kidding me?" I sit up on my knees, completely forgetting about the game in session. "You're complaining because *I* was gloating? Have you looked in the mirror lately?"

"I never said I was perfect."

I grab her ankle, yanking her halfway out of her bean bag chair. "You're—"

"The champion! The winner! The victor!" she provokes between giggles, her eyes wide and locked on mine.

"The giant pain in my butt," I shout back at her laughing face as organized yelling seeps through the walls.

"Eighteen."

"Seventeen."

I lean up, hovering over Sam, and state the obvious, "Countdown time."

The smile on Sam's face fades as she looks into my eyes.

Behind us, the music and timer continue running on Shawn's big screen. Our little animated kart racers sit still, stuck in their spots, forgotten by us. I consider asking her if she wants to run into the hall and join the merriment, but I don't want to. I like this moment. Me and her. Two friends sharing the beginning of a new year.

"Ten."

"Nine."

Sam pushes herself up from her prone position half on the floor, half on the bean bag to sitting inches from me.

And I feel it. That deep pang within my heart, the longing and sadness I push away all the time. By the look on Sam's face, I bet she feels it, too.

"It's moments like these that I miss my dad the most," I whisper out of the blue. He should be here. Her fiancé should be here, too. No amount of time will change that.

Sam's eyes glisten and she blinks away the moisture before releasing a breath.

"Five."

"Four."

We count down with the crowd out in the hallway and next door. Our combined voices barely a blip on the radar.

"Three."

"Two."

"One."

"Happy New Year!" our friends shout.

The echoes of cheering, noisemakers, and "Auld Land Syne" being sung nearly shake the walls.

I rise to my knees and lean toward Sam, my fingers touching the long silky strands of her dark hair. She sucks in a breath, but doesn't move.

"Happy New Year, Sam," I breathe against her cheek as my lips graze her smooth skin. I pause there, part of me wanting to skim across her cheek and find her lips before I come to my senses. Friends. We did the kissing thing, and it didn't end well.

"I think you're the best thing to happen to me in a long time," I say, not only for her benefit, but for my own. I don't want to lose this friendship we've built. If I made a move again it could ruin everything. "I'm honestly glad we're friends."

"Friends." She nods fervently and her eyes shy away. "Me, too. Me, too." Sam pushes off the bean bag and I move out of the way. "I should go find Monica. Wish her a Happy New Year."

"Yeah, we better show our faces out there, or else they might get the wrong idea."

She lets out a nervous laugh. "Smart thinking."

Getting to my feet, I wait while she slips her shoes back on, flipping the television off and plunging us into darkness.

"Oops." My hand searches for hers in the dark, taking hold and leading her toward the door. "Okay, I have a crazy idea."

"Uh oh. What's that?"

"Since this was such a perfect friend date for what is typically a couples' night, what do you say to doing Valentine's Day with me?"

"You don't plan on spending Valentine's Day with Trisha?"

I'm surprised it's taken her this long to ask about Trisha. "We're casual at best. I have more fun with you, *and* there are no expectations," I tease.

"Oh wow. You know how to charm a lady," she chuckles. "So, an anti-Valentine's date?"

"Exactly. I mean, unless you've made a New Year's resolution to jump back into the dating pool?"

"Ha. You're a funny guy. No, actually I hadn't thought about Valentine's Day yet. What do you have in mind?"

I crack Shawn's door because standing in the dark with Sam feels a bit awkward, especially when we're talking about Valentine's Day.

"Talk about putting a guy on the spot. Can I have a few weeks to think about it? I promise we'll do something fun and completely unromantic."

"Deal. If you need my input, feel free to ask. Since it's not a date, it's not like you need to try hard to impress me."

"You don't need to be impressed, huh? It's a wonder you don't have guys lined up to date you." I knock into her shoulder as we finally step into the crowded hallway.

"Oooh. So, that's how it's gonna be? Alright. Alright. Just for that, I'm going to be rating this anti-Valentine's non-date."

Challenge accepted, Samantha Cooper. Challenge accepted.

"I probably should have prefaced this whole plan with the fact that I might not actually get Valentine's Day off." Hazard of my career. "But we can still go out on whatever day I have off near then, just like all the other couples of the world who plan big fancy events."

"Sounds like a plan. Monica and I have spent Valentine's Day together for the last two years, so I'll have to break the news to her gently."

"I'm sure Shawn will be more than happy to pick up her broken pieces."

"If she lets him, I'm sure he will."

"She's definitely going to let him, at some point. I can't believe he hasn't worn her down already."

"He probably has, but she's the kind of girl who wants her men to work for it."

Does Sam have any idea how accurately that statement reflects her?

15

THIS IS HOW WE DO IT
BLARNEY ROCK—FEBRUARY 16, 1995

WHEN COLE CALLED on Valentine's Day to tell me he needed to reschedule our anti-Valentine's date because the ER was too busy, I wasn't surprised. In fact, I was relieved. All I wanted to do was finish up my last class, go home, and put on pajamas to curl up on the couch and watch *Sleepless in Seattle*.

Cole granted me my wish, except I didn't plan on being completely alone. Monica still won't tell me where she disappeared to that night, but I have a pretty good idea since she came home around one, tip-toeing past the couch I pretended to be asleep on.

I breathe hot air into my gloved hands as I sit, waiting outside Blarney Rock for Cole. I pull back my coat sleeve to check my watch. Thirty minutes late. Not the greatest impression of our first non-date, Cole. If he's wanting a good rating, pointer number one would be don't make your non-date wait for thirty minutes in the freezing cold. I should go inside, but it's packed and I'm not in the mood to be in a small space with a hundred other drunk people.

I glance down 33rd, then back to see Cole jogging toward

me. The moment he sees me he grins, and my annoyance slowly melts.

"You are the best date in the world." He nears and I stand from the bench, hugging him as he presses a quick kiss to my cheek. "So sorry I'm late. I got hung up at work."

"I figured. I was about to start docking your non-date rating, but I'll forgive this since they're sick people and all." The minty scent of his shampoo fills my senses as his still-damp hair brushes my temple. At least he had time for a shower.

He eyes me as he pulls away. "You look nice."

"And you look, sporty," I chuckle, taking in his Rangers jersey and blue jeans. This is the first time I've seen him so casually dressed, other than the day he came to the studio. He's always in slacks and button ups.

He nods. "I am."

"Is your choice of outfit a clue?"

"What would you say if I said yes?"

"I'd say I like hockey," I start, not able to tell him I haven't been to a game since Paul died.

"Well, that's a relief because we've got two tickets to see the Rangers play Montreal. Puck drops at 7."

He's so excited, I don't have the heart to tell him this might kill me.

MADISON SQUARE GARDEN

INSIDE MADISON SQUARE GARDEN, WE'RE SWALLOWED UP IN a sea of rushing hockey fans, navigating past food vendors and employees to get to our seats.

"You know, as lovely as you look in that sweater, I think you need something a little more festive." He slows our pace.

Had I known what we were doing, I could've worn my Rangers jersey, though I probably wouldn't have.

Cole grabs my hand. "C'mon."

We veer hard left toward the team store and I tug back on Cole's hand, fighting him. "I don't need anything festive." Do I even want to be here?

"Look around, Supergirl," he argues, and I do. The majority of the crowd is dressed in Ranger red, white, and blue. "You most certainly need some team color."

His eyes scan my outfit again. I like the way his blue eyes look when he takes in my appearance, as if he's trying to hide how much he likes what he sees.

I look down at the light pink mohair sweater I picked out especially for tonight as he continues dragging me toward the store. "I dressed for Valentine's. Had you told me we were going to a hockey game, I would have dressed accordingly."

"Had I told you we were going to a hockey game, it wouldn't have been a surprise," he counters, squeezing my hand. "Pick something."

I groan his name.

He releases my hand as we reach a rack of ladies tops. "My treat," he says from over the rack as he walks around it.

I narrow my eyes. He is not going to buy me a jersey.

"C'mon, what else is a guy supposed to buy for his favorite anti-valentine?" He flashes a charming grin as he holds up a women's cut jersey that matches the one he's wearing. "We could be one of those cute matchy matchy couples."

"Yeah. No." I finger through the rack as Cole laughs. "How about this?" I hold up an oversized sweatshirt that would be perfect for throwing on at the studio on cold days. Might as well be practical about this.

Cole grimaces. "That looks like it will swallow you whole."

"Perfect, I'll take it." I grin, heading toward the long line of fans waiting to check out. "And I'm paying, by the way."

"Nope. My idea, my treat." He snags the hanger from my fingers.

"Cole, this is ridiculous." I try snatching it back, but he holds the hanger out of my reach. "I don't want you to buy me anything."

"Can't hear you," he sings, moving forward with the line. He loads up with two foam fingers and some stickers as we wait.

"Are you an impulse shopper?" I laugh when he seriously considers buying a car decal. "You don't even have a car." I shake my head, taking the package from him and hanging it back on the display stand.

"Yeah, I do."

"You have a car?"

"Yeah, I just don't drive it in the city." He shrugs like it's no big deal, but it is. How did I not know he has a car?

"Do you ever drive it?"

"Not lately. Brett uses it more than I do."

"I can help whoever is next," the man at the register cuts Cole off. I try maneuvering around him so I can give the cashier my credit card, but Cole beats me to it.

"Here." We step back into the crowd after leaving the team store. "Go change." He points toward a women's restroom and hands me the bag containing my new sweatshirt.

"You were serious?"

"About you wearing team colors? Heck yeah, I was serious."

I will not stomp my foot like a petulant child, but I want to. I snatch the bag from him and head into the restroom.

When I emerge, Cole looks way too pleased with himself. "See. Now you look like a true Rangers fan."

"If you'd given me a hint before, I could've worn my own jersey."

"You have your own Rangers jersey?"

"I told you." I shrug. Now isn't the time to get all sentimental and weepy. "I like hockey."

· · ·

WE WALK INTO THE ARENA AND I'M FULLY EXPECTING COLE to follow the crowd heading toward the walkways to the upper levels, but like everything he does, he surprises me by walking straight toward the lower seats. I follow him, attempting to keep my jaw from dropping as we maneuver our way into our ninth-row seats, mid-center. What a view!

"Oh my gosh. Jamie would kill for these seats."

"Yeah? Jamie likes hockey?"

"He's the reason I love it so much. We used to watch it together all the time." I peer around us. "Do you watch that new show *Friends*? This totally reminds me of that episode, the one where the guys go to a Rangers game. These seats are amazing. Usually, I'm up in the nosebleed section." With Paul, since it's all I could afford and he never offered to buy them since it wasn't his thing.

A self-satisfied grin sweeps over Cole's face. "Are you impressed then?"

I lift a small smile. "I'll give this portion a nine. You're already down a peg for making me buy this sweatshirt, but I'll give you these seats. These are impressive."

"You know what else is impressive?"

"What's that?"

"The overpriced drinks and dogs. You hungry?"

"I could eat," I admit with a nod. Honestly, I'm starving. I figured we would go to dinner, so I haven't eaten since lunch.

"I'll be right back."

I settle into my seat and look up at the jumbotron. The same screen Paul and I made it onto once during a short-handed goal in overtime. Looking at the screen, I imagine Paul that night, not cheering or looking at the rink, but smiling at me jumping up and down, completely ecstatic after a goal.

I let my gaze drop to my right to Cole's vacant seat, the seat Paul would've occupied. The crowd roars. Music blares. I can almost picture him there. Paul might not have cared much about hockey, but he came for me. I blink rapidly to clear my watering eyes.

How did I let Cole rope me into this?

Who am I kidding? He didn't need to convince me. His ardent smile and near childlike excitement was all it took. If I'm not careful, I'll ruin the night with my stupid reminiscing. I won't do that to Cole. Tonight it's about the Rangers and having fun with my friend, nothing else.

"MESSIER IS A BEAST," COLE SHOUTS OVER THE ROAR OF THE crowd after Messier makes a goal for the Rangers.

My hands ache from the high-fives we exchanged. "Hall of Fame player, for sure."

"And the press conference last year before game six of the conference finals." He leans closer to me as he talks. "I mean, who does that? Guarantees a win, in New York? Imagine how the media and fans would have chewed him up and spit him out had they lost."

"But they didn't," I remind him with glee, the hype around those playoffs was crazy. The sound bites from that press conference have been played a million times. "He promised a win, then he goes on to score a natural hat trick!"

Cole slaps his chest, shaking his head. "That game made grown men weep."

"Are you talking from experience?"

"I might have been a little misty-eyed."

We sink to our seats when a timeout is called. Cole angles his body toward mine, his expression serious.

"What?" I shift in my seat when his stare gets to be too much.

He smirks, his eyes flicking away from my face then back before he speaks. "You impress me, Samantha Cooper. First, you surprise me with your fighting skills, then you prove to be a worthy competitor at Mario Kart, and now you're dazzling me with your hockey knowledge. Shawn better watch out."

"Uh, oh. Is he in danger of being replaced?" I tease.

"Absolutely. I mean, I'll keep him around as a wingman for bar hopping because I'm sure having you around would cramp my style when picking up dates, but let's face it, you're much prettier and you smell way better than Shawn ever does."

"Oh, I don't know. I think female wingmen can appeal to other women. I can talk you up and I definitely have a more trustworthy face than Shawn. I might actually be an asset to you."

"Are you offering?"

"No." My head shakes with resolution. "Just pleading my case. You know ... you'd love my brother. Jamie taught me all I know."

"*That's* why you're so cool." He nudges my shoulder. "I'll have to meet him someday."

"He'll probably come to visit sometime this year. He always does. We'll do dinner or something."

"What's he do for a living? He's my age, isn't he?"

"Yeah. He turned twenty-eight last month. He's in IT, computer stuff. Technology has always been his thing."

"Sounds like he got the brains and you got the brawn."

I laugh. "You calling me manly?"

His eyes warm as he scans over me before he smiles a crooked smile. "I'm saying you could take down Shawn."

"You better believe I could!"

"But I think I could give you a run for your money."

"I don't know. I almost kicked your trash once before."

Cole bursts into laughter and jumps up as a shot on the goal is made, and missed. So, so close. The action on the ice settles. "That's because you took me by surprise."

"Uh huh. I think you're all talk."

"It's a shame we'll never know."

How do I answer that? I pretend I'm immersed in the game.

Is he flirting? Am I flirting? Is he talking in metaphors, or am I reading into things?

I have to ask. "And why is that?"

Does he hesitate?

"First, I'm not sure I could bring myself to fight you. Second, see these hands?" He lifts his strong, gorgeous hands in front of his chest. Oh, what those hands could do to me. *Stop it, Samantha!* Where is my head? "These babies are gold, I can't risk anything happening to them. They're lifesavers."

What am I thinking? I clear my head and snort. "Of course. Your precious hands. And it would be such an ego killer losing to a girl."

"I don't mind losing to a girl. For the right reasons."

The buzzer goes off, signaling the end of the game. I look at the scoreboard. Tied. 2-2. Though, I don't think Cole and I tied this round.

I think he won.

16

TELL ME

FOOD IS OUR THING. I love catching up with Sam over lunches and dinners. I love it when she surprises me and joins me for dinner in the hospital cafeteria when I'm working late nights. I love dropping by her studio, food cart gyros in hand, when my schedule allows. I love how we find time for a nice meal in a restaurant once a week.

It's the best part of my week. Eating with Sam.

Tonight's a 'fancy dinner' night.

"What made you pick this place?" Sam asks as we wait for a table at the newly renovated Greenhouse Cafe.

"I read an article in *The Times* a few months ago talking about the bombing and how the hotel was finally re-opening. They estimate they lost seventy million dollars in revenue while closed, and that doesn't include all the shops and restaurants."

"Wow," Sam shakes her head. "The bombing wasn't that long after the crash. I was still in such deep mourning, I honestly blocked out all the news on it."

I get that. "I just feel like a New Yorker now, you know? It took me a while to get acclimated, but I love the spirit. The way the city picked up the pieces after the bombing and rebuilt." I glance around at the fresh, clean feeling of everything. "This is the first time I've come down to the complex since I moved here. Once they re-open Windows on the World in the World Trade Center, we'll have to eat there. I want to see that view of the city."

"I went up once, actually. It's a great view. So much better than the Empire State Building because it's unobstructed."

"There are so many places in the city I haven't been yet. You'll have to help me play tourist once the weather gets a little nicer."

"I think I could do that," Sam nods as the hostess arrives with the news that our table is ready.

"Okay, tell me about your day," I ask after our drinks are dropped off.

A little smirk appears on her face. "You remember Natalie?"

"The blonde one that hit on me?"

"Yeah," she chuckles. "So, today she tried hitting on this guy some of the girls in class call Squatting Scott. I overheard her telling him how nice he looks when he squats as he was digging through his gym bag. He produced his wedding ring and put it on." Laughter interrupts each word. "You should've seen the look on her face."

"Do you like looking at Squatting Scott?" I goad.

"What? No!" She tries to stifle her throaty laughter behind her hand when heads swivel our way. "First of all, I have more class than that. And second of all, I don't date clients."

"You don't date at all," I point out.

"Whatever. Then I *really* don't date clients. Do you know how awkward that would be? Not to mention bad for business. We'd lose too many clients."

"Because you'd break so many hearts they'd never come back?" I tease over the top of my menu.

She's motivated, smart, funny, and beautiful. I take her in as she sits across from me, the sweater clinging to her curves, the way her dark hair frames her face. Those magnificent eyes that have become my favorite color. Yeah, she'd break all their hearts.

"Exactly." She tips her glass to me before taking a drink, and I shove my thoughts away. "How was your day? Anything good happen?"

"As a matter of fact, I got to hang with my favorite girl today."

"Your favorite girl?" her face scrunches as though she's trying to figure out who I could be talking about. Thanks to Shawn and I, Sam and Monica have heard about most of the women who work with us.

"Yep. Gorgeous little blonde with the largest brown eyes you'll ever see."

Did she bristle at my description?

"And boy does she love me."

"Does she now?" She cocks her brow and takes a sip of her water.

"Absolutely. It's a shame she's only ten."

Sam crumples her napkin and throws it at me. "You big jerk," she laughs.

"It's not my fault I mention a girl and you automatically assume she's my next conquest."

"As if you ever talk about any other kind of woman," she taunts. "Now back to your day. I want to know what's so special about spending time with her."

My face automatically lifts when I picture Celia.

"She's a transplant patient. I can't give you her name, doctor-patient rules and all that, so we'll call her Sunshine."

Sam frowns. "What kind of transplant is she waiting for?"

"She's in heart failure."

Sam clenches her sweater over her heart. "How old was she when she was diagnosed?"

"Actually, she was a normal, healthy child. That's the crappy part of this whole thing. She contracted a virus when she was six and it attacked her heart and weakened the muscles."

Her head shakes with sadness. "How long has she been waiting for a heart?"

"Not long. She's been fighting this for four years, but her heart won't respond to anything. I get to see her quite a bit, which isn't a good thing for her, but for me it's great. For all of us, it is."

"Why do you see her so much? Doesn't she have normal doctors she sees?"

"She does, but when you're talking heart transplants, you're talking life and death. There are a ton of complications that arise for her and her mother. Plus, they're low income, so they don't exactly have access to the medical care you or I might have."

Sam sighs. "That's horrible. So young to be dealing with that kind of problem. I don't know how you do it. Watching kids go through things like this. My heart couldn't take it."

"It seems sad, but truthfully she brightens our day. Shawn has done a lot for her over the past three years, so she's always excited to see him. She has this stuffed lion, you know the kind you buy from the Bronx Zoo?"

"You mean Sultan?"

"Sultan. Yep. Except she changed his name to Shawn."

Sam chuckles. "Lucky Shawn. How jealous you must be."

"Yeah, yeah," I sneer. "Anyway, they roll in today and I'm already dealing with a car wreck involving multiple victims, so I don't get assigned, but when I find the time to take a breath, I go say hi." Celia's sweet face flashes before me. "Sunshine, who really is a gorgeous little thing with blonde hair and saucer-like brown eyes, is lying in bed hooked up to all of the normal machines, resting with two lions instead of one in her arms.

"Her mother keeps Shawn the Lion in her purse at all times, so if there is an emergency she has him for her."

Sam smiles warmly. "Her little security blanket."

I nod. "So, I hug her mom and check the chart; it's not my case, but there's no way I'm not going to double check behind my peers. Her mother is such a strong woman. Years of waiting and hoping, and she keeps on going." I lapse into silence for a moment longer than necessary. "Anyway, I asked her mother about the new lion and she told me my girl insisted on getting him after her last visit with me. His name is Cole."

Sam's smile brightens. "That's really sweet. She must love you."

"That's why I love what I do, Sam. Because a little girl, who's been fighting for her life for years, thinks I'm so amazing that she names her stuffed toy after me and takes him everywhere she goes."

Sam's eyes glisten.

"So yeah, anytime she comes in, it's a good day. We've colored a few pictures together, we've played games. Sometimes, when she's admitted to Peds for overnight observation, I'll eat lunch or dinner with them if I can."

"I'm glad you get bright spots in your day. What you do isn't easy."

"So, you know Mandy?" I ask midway through dinner.

"Mandy from my classes Mandy?"

"Yep," I exhale. Why am I nervous about telling her? "I got to talking to her at Shawn's party the other night."

Sam nods. "Yeah, I saw you two. She's sweet. Brings her younger sister to class sometimes."

"Oh yeah, she told me. For self-defense training. I guess she was attacked on her college campus last year. The sister, not Mandy."

"You two talked about all that at the party?" Sam's forehead wrinkles.

"Uh, not exactly." Here goes nothing. "We went out the other night."

"Oh?" She takes a bite and waits for me to continue.

"Yeah. She's the first girl I've gone out with that doesn't wear scrubs for a living, in probably a year."

Sam swallows her food and takes a drink of water. "That's great. Good choice. I like Mandy. She's one of the few girls I genuinely like that comes to my classes."

"That's good to know. Part of me was worried you'd tell me you hate her."

"What would it matter? I'm not the one dating her."

"You're one of my best friends. It would matter to me if you didn't like someone I go out with. Your opinion is important to me."

"We're best friends?" Sam smiles.

"You doubted I could do it, didn't you?" I bite back my smug grin.

She nods. Her teeth sink into her bottom lip as she looks at her plate. "I'll be honest, I thought your chances were slim."

If not for the way she pushed me away at Monica's party, and for Paul, they would still be slim.

"We've hung out at least twice a week since our anti-Valentine's date, and we haven't caved to the whole boy/girl thing." I stretch my arm across the table for a high-five. "I think we can safely say we've made it to the friend zone."

She fights a grin, cocking her head to the side before reaching up and slapping my hand.

"Way to go, friend," I congratulate her.

"You're ridiculous."

"That's what you like about me."

"Oh? Is that what I like about you?" Her fork hovers halfway between her plate and her mouth. Her lips twist in this way that always gets my blood flowing. I'd like to kiss the smirk right off that pretty little face of hers. But I can't. I care about her too much to screw things up now, and I'm not competing with a dead guy.

Instead, I use humor. "Well, that and my devilishly handsome face, killer style, and access to great hockey tickets."

"It's the hockey tickets. Definitely the hockey tickets."

"That's cool." I nod. "I mean, I'm only using you for the access to hot chicks knowing you provides."

Her head knocks back with laughter. "If I could reach across this table, I'd punch you."

Thank goodness for oversized dining tables.

"Speaking of dating—" The comment hangs between us.

"What about it?"

"Do you plan on jumping back into the arena anytime soon?" I brace myself for the punch she just finished threatening me with.

"You asking for a friend?" she jokes.

I laugh lightly, but her humor won't deter me. "No. I'm asking as a friend," I say solemnly.

Sam's expression softens as she chews on her lip. "I don't know. It's crossed my mind, but I don't know that it will ever happen. I was with Paul for three years, which means I've been out of the dating scene for almost six years." Laughter flits across her eyes. "You know how exhausting dating can be. All the time it takes to get to know someone new, the awkward phase when you don't exactly know where the other stands, the time it takes to learn the other's bad habits and flaws, the expectations, the heartbreak—" She pauses. It all sounds like a bunch of excuses to me, but I'd never tell her that. "I just—don't know that I'm ready to take the plunge. Or that I'll ever be."

Six years. I do the math.

"Whoa, you were nineteen when you met?" Paul wasn't merely her fiancé, he was probably her first love.

She bobs her head. My mind explodes. Nine-freaking-teen. You need to date, Sam. You're pining away for the first guy you fell in love with. I can't say those things. I never would, but I want to. I've never hurt on the level she must have experienced when she lost Paul, though. I can't pretend to know how she should feel.

"What was he like?" I ask to keep myself from convincing her to take the plunge she doesn't seem ready for.

Sam breathes in and out through her nose before she answers. "Driven. In everything he did. School. Business. Pursuing me." She lifts a distant smile, her eyes wandering beyond my shoulder. Her head shakes. "He came from a long line of entrepreneurs. He was in the process of learning the family business. Do you know Lawson Electronics?"

"You were marrying into Lawson Electronics?"

She shrugs like she wasn't marrying into a family worth billions of dollars. The East Village makes perfect sense now.

"It's Paul's father's company. We were two weeks away from our wedding when 397 happened. He was heading to Europe to close an account. The first that he handled all on his own, from start to finish. He was so excited." Sam's voice chokes up and she clears throat.

"Two weeks?" I'm a jerk for asking. My fingers itch to reach across the table and take hold of her hand, but I refrain. She doesn't talk about Paul enough; she needs to let it out. I hate seeing her upset, but maybe this is the corner she needs to turn to move on.

"I'm sorry. I didn't realize the wedding was so close when he —" I stop, not knowing at all what to say.

Sam waves off my apology, the sadness already clearing from her eyes as she takes a sip of her drink. "Of course you didn't. It's fine." She offers me a small smile. "Anyway, are you going to see Mandy again?"

Change of subject. Good idea.

"I am." I rip a chunk of bread from the basket on our table.

"Sunday afternoon. I'm back on nights for two weeks starting Sunday, so we're doing lunch before my shift."

"Ew, nights again?"

"Yeah, they're not all that bad. Acclimating to the time change is the worst part."

Sam blanches. "I need sunlight to survive. I don't know how people work graveyard shifts and sleep during the day."

"Eight years of college and medical school taught me how to be a vampire, I'm used to nights," I tease. Sad, but true. I almost prefer working nights. "Plus, that's when the crazy cases show up. Keeps me on my toes." I waggle my brows.

"Poor Mandy doesn't know what she's getting herself into, going out with you."

"That's part of my appeal." I wink to chase away the last bit of sadness from her face. "Speaking of Mandy, though. Her story about her sister scared the crap out me, and it got me thinking. That could be Amber."

"It's definitely scary. I think like five in every thousand females are raped every year. Living in this city, it's another reason Monica and I opened Pure Kickboxing. It's self-defense, man."

"Clearly, you're not helping my worry." I frown, pondering the effectiveness of rape whistles and mace. She's so reckless, she'd probably spray herself. "Do you think you could teach her some things when she's here next week for spring break?"

"Of course. She could take some classes or I could make time for some one-on-one training, but why in the world is she coming here? Shouldn't she be doing some big college beach trip for spring break?"

I scoff. "Do you honestly think Brett and I would let her go party on the beaches of Florida, all *Girls Gone Wild* style?"

"Let her? She's almost twenty, isn't she? She's her own person. You two need to let her grow up at some point."

"You don't know Amber, Sam."

"Not well, you're right." Not well? She only knows the things

I've told her, and I would think that's enough to prove how little Amber needs a week of booze, boys, and the beach. "But, you can't protect her forever, and I highly doubt she's dumb enough to go all *Girls Gone Wild* on you guys. Not all college spring breaks are like that, you know."

Sure, just 75% of them.

"Really? What did you do for spring break?"

Sam takes a bite before responding and points her fork at me. "That depends on which spring break you want to know about. There was the one where I went to visit my brother and went to one of his frat parties and met Paul, who ironically enough was visiting that weekend, too. And then there was the spring break that I spent at home doing nothing but relaxing, watching *Family Matters* and *Saved by the Bell*. Such a glamorous life."

Right. She had a serious boyfriend in college. Obviously she didn't party it up.

DANCING DAYS

PURE KICKBOXING—APRIL 7, 1995

"I HAVE to go to Ruby's dance thing tonight at NYU with Brett. Will you please come with me? Last time I had to sit there while Brett gawked at the stage for two hours."

I laugh, picturing Cole in an auditorium watching ballet. One of these things is not like the other. "Why isn't Mandy going with you?"

"You'll laugh." Cole rolls his eyes, embarrassed. "I don't introduce girls I'm dating to my siblings. I know that makes me sound like some crazy over-protective parent. I mean, it's only been like, what, two months and a few dates? We haven't made it to the meet the family portion yet."

I smirk. Too bad Mandy is already head over heels. She won't stop talking about Cole when she comes to class. Every time she opens her mouth now, I have to mentally shield myself from an onslaught of female gushing. As much as Monica wants to ban Shawn, I'm this close to banning Mandy. I get it. Cole is all that. Why does she think I'm friends with him?

"Okay, okay. What about Shawn?"

"Shawn?" Do I have a third eye? Cole's stare suggests I might. "You're joking, right? That would be worse than going alone. I'd have to sit there while he nudges me for two hours, pointing out all the hot dancers. Side note: All dancers are hot."

I pretend like I'm debating, but this is something I actually want to do. An NYU dance company performance sounds amazing.

I heave a sigh. "Monica would have to cover my class, so you'll have to ask her."

Cole turns to Monica next to me. He turns up the charm, leaning onto the counter. "Monica, you look lovely today. Have I told you that?"

"You're gonna have to do better than that, Rossner." She doesn't look up from the scheduler.

"Please. I'll make sure Shawn doesn't come to your classes for a week."

"Make it two and we have a deal."

"Done."

"Well, this means I'm gonna have to go home and actually get ready. What time does it start?"

"Seven-thirty. How about I drive to your place and we get a bite to eat in Queens before taking the train into the city?"

I look at the clock on the wall. Three o'clock. "You're not really giving me a lot of time for this now, are you?"

"I'm sorry. I had to bribe Chuck to work a double so I could get out of there early since Brett sprung this on me kind of last minute. I'm heading home now to take a one-hour cat nap. I'm exhausted, but I want to support Ruby. She's like a little sister to me."

It's going to take us an hour to get back to my place and another hour for me to shower and get ready. Dinner will have to happen somewhere in there. "Mon, you okay if I leave now?"

"Yeah, yeah. I've got this. You two have fun. I'll be the responsible one and keep this place running."

"I don't care what Sam says, you're the best, Monica," Cole winks.

What a wise guy. I shift my elbow into his ribs as he straightens at the counter.

"I'll head back with you." He laughs, as he follows me out the door.

We walk out onto Park Avenue. "How are you going to keep Shawn from coming to class? This deal in no way benefits him."

"I'm not, but Monica doesn't have to know that." Cole smirks.

"You have to head home?"

"Only if I want some sleep."

"You could use my couch while I get ready, so you don't have to waste a trip. Unless you need to go home to shower and change or something."

"Do I look like I need to change?"

I look him up and down in his tan slacks, plaid button up, and hunter green sweater vest. He looks handsome to me. "No, you look fine. Just didn't know if you were going to change. Wear whatever you want."

"I showered at the hospital and I brought these clothes in case I didn't get out of there until later and didn't have time to go back to the house. If you don't mind me borrowing your couch for a nap, we can forget the car and eat at McGuinty's since it's near the station."

"Sounds like a plan."

MONICA AND SAM'S APARTMENT

AFTER I FINISH GETTING READY, I WALK OUT OF MY bedroom and open my mouth to let Cole know we can go. I stop when I see him on his side, sleeping on the couch. His arm curls around the pillow his head rests on, hugging it to his chest. I don't want to wake him. To be honest, it's kind of nice to look at him without him fluttering up my insides with his unsolicited flirting and his stupid charming smile. Even without that stupid smile he's handsome. He looks both peaceful and tempting, spread out along the tan fabric like he's missing a piece. I want to be the pillow clutched against his chest, to feel his rhythmic heartbeat against my body and the warmth of his embrace.

I clench my eyes shut. *Get a grip, Samantha.* I need to stop staring at him while he sleeps. It's creepy.

"Cole." He doesn't move a muscle. I inch closer to the couch and set my hand on his shoulder. "Cole, it's time to go."

He inhales through his nose, his eyes popping open.

"Sorry." I smile, apologetic. Must be a pretty sound sleeper. "I didn't want to wake you, but if we want to be on time for Ruby's performance, we need to head out now."

His startled eyes soften as he takes me in. Releasing a heavy breath, he sits up and stretches, arching his back. His arms flex above his head. Dang those muscular biceps. "How long did I sleep for? What time is it?"

"I don't know. Maybe an hour? It's five o'clock."

He rubs his tired eyes before he stands. Poor Cole looks like he could use another eight hours of sleep. "Let's go get some dinner."

TISCH'S THEATER

COLE AND I WALK UP TO 111 SECOND AVENUE. "HERE WE are. Tisch's dance theater. Brett said he'd wait in the foyer for us."

Brett is looking at the door expectantly when we walk through. "Finally," he breathes.

"We're not even late," Cole chuckles and they hug, patting each other's backs before parting. "It doesn't start for another ten minutes."

"I don't want to miss the opener because you know she'd know. Hey, Sam." Brett steps in and presses a quick kiss to my cheek. "I didn't know Cole was inviting you. Ruby will be thrilled to finally meet you."

"It's good to see you again. I'm excited to be here."

"Let's go take our seats." Brett checks his watch for the third time since we walked in.

Ruby is an incredible dancer. When Cole mentioned it was a showcase at NYU, I knew it would be unbelievable, but this girl is like no other. I sit back in awe as she owns the stage, putting the other dancers to shame.

Heavy breathing to my right interrupts the concert. Cole has nodded off. I gently elbow his arm from the armrest between us, waking him. I have to do that at least three times throughout the show. Poor man doesn't get enough sleep. By the end of the concert, tears are in my eyes and we're standing, clapping. I don't even have words. I just want to keep clapping.

"Seriously, bro. She is fantastic," Cole says.

Brett gives Cole a stern look. "How would you know? You slept through half of it."

Cole's face falls with guilt, and I want to stand up for him, but he beats me to it. "I've been on nights, sue me."

"You didn't have to come, you know. I would have understood, and she would have, too."

I smile as Cole slings his arm around Brett's shoulders. "I wanted to. I saw her two solos."

"She had three," I whisper, trying to help him out.

"Well, crap. What was it? I'm sure she was as perfect in it as she was the other two."

"Yes, she was," Brett hisses, elbowing Cole and ducking from underneath his arm. Brett moves with the crowd out of the auditorium and we follow.

Beside me, Cole leans down close to my ear. "Please tell me I didn't snore?"

I chuckle, debating on giving him a hard time, but hold back.

"You were just breathing a little heavy. Most likely, only Brett and I heard you."

"I think I was essentially sleep-watching that whole thing after the first two dances. I'm sorry I wasn't good company. You got to see Ruby, though. She really is ridiculously talented."

"The entire company was amazing, but I couldn't keep my eyes off her. Thank you for inviting me."

"No one I'd rather fall asleep next to more." Cole take three steps before he stops. His face scrunches up. "I mean, at a dance performance ... like a—"

"It's fine," I interrupt him, smiling. "Don't hurt yourself with that cover up, champ. I know what you meant."

Cole slings his arm around my shoulder, tugging me close, and kisses the top of my head. "That's why I love hanging out with you. You get me."

Ruby meets us in the foyer in her black leotard and a little black wraparound skirt, her chestnut hair pulled into a tight bun atop her head. Brett intercepts her before any of us get a chance to say a word. He lifts Ruby off the ground in a hug, kissing her cheek. "I don't know why you're not already making bank on Broadway," Brett compliments Ruby. My heart leaps at the love in his voice. "You were amazing, twinkle toes."

They are absolutely darling, their young love untouched by the world's ugliness. It's so easy to forget what that was like when I first met Paul. How reality can change everything.

Brett walks Ruby over to us with his arm around her waist and a wide, proud grin on his face.

"Hey, hun." Cole hugs Ruby tightly. "You danced circles around all of those other losers. Amazing."

"You were phenomenal," I say.

"Thanks." She looks confused, obviously wondering who I am.

"Oh," Cole jumps in, "Ruby, this is my friend, Sam. Sam, Ruby."

Ruby's eyes flash to me and back to Cole. "This is Sam, Sam?"

What's that supposed to mean? What much does she know about me?

"In the flesh."

His eyes going wide as he cocks his head.

"I've heard so many good things about you!" Ruby reaches out to hug me. "I feel like I know you already."

"Oh." I choke on a giggle. "Well, it's nice to meet you."

"Amber said your kickboxing lessons were fabulous. I'll have to come by your studio. I'm always looking for different forms of exercise. And having some self-defense techniques in the city, well, maybe Brett would get off my back if he knew I could take care of myself."

"Not likely," Brett mutters. Overprotectiveness must run in the family.

"Yeah, sure. Come on over." I smile, feeling a little overwhelmed. How much do these two know about me? I hardly know anything about them. "Monica and I would love a new face. So," I gesture between Brett and Ruby, "how did you two meet? At NYU?"

They share a smile, like they have a secret no one will ever know. Brett answers, "Through paper planes."

Ruby kisses his cheek and regards me. "Let me clarify that. My mom died on Flight 397 with Brett's parents. I lived in California, so after finding out there were two other teenagers my age on the other side of the US who were dealing with the loss of a parent, I wrote Amber a letter. Brett responded, and the rest is history." She shrugs.

"There's a little more to it than that, but basically she won me over with awkwardness and spouting random facts."

Ruby bumps into him with her shoulder and laughs. "Shut up."

I see now they weren't untouched by the world. Instead, they found the silver lining in tragedy. They found each other.

My eyes drift to Cole. He wears an affectionate smile, looking at Brett and Ruby before his gaze shifts to me. I guess Cole's been my little silver lining, someone who understands the loss of 397. His smile warms when I don't look away. I smile back and he pulls me into his side, lightly tapping his head to mine.

"It's so cute, it makes me sick. You guys wanna go grab some ice cream or something?" Cole asks with a straight face.

Brett's jaw shifts from side to side, likes he's contemplating a nice comeback. "And look at you, bro. You and Sam have a story not unlike Ruby and I."

Cole inhales sharply. Next to Brett, Ruby sucks her lips in between her teeth, biting back laughter.

"Oh, we're just good friends," I clarify, but I don't remove my arm from around his back. I don't know why. To prove a point we're confident enough in our friendship? Or to prove Brett can't rattle me? Though, he totally did.

"We were, too. In the beginning." Brett has the audacity to wink at me, so like his big brother. "Ice cream sounds great. Let's go."

"I think I might kill him," Cole grinds out as Brett and Ruby head for the exit.

"He's just like his big brother. Unafraid to push buttons."

"You're blaming me?"

"It must be in the genes. You didn't need to spend your lives together to be the same person."

His arm tightens around my neck, pulling me closer to his side. "Our dad was like that, too. I mean, I didn't get to see it first hand, but I've heard stories."

I peer up at him. I know how important it must be for him to feel a connection to his dad, a man he didn't get to grow up with. "Like father, like son."

"And here I thought our only real shared traits were our eyes and love of medicine." He releases me and slips his hand into mine. I let him as he tugs me to walk faster so we can catch up with Brett and Ruby.

I want to encourage him to talk to Brett more about his dad, to get to know him through his brother's eyes, but it's clear Cole is ready to move on from the conversation. Someday I'll get him to open up to me about his dad.

VESELKA

"So, Sam," Ruby says after we order. "You own a kickboxing studio. Is that what you went to school for? Fitness? Or business management?"

"Actually, I went to school for physical therapy. I was graduating college and looking forward to beginning my doctorate when 397 happened. So now I've just got a bachelor's in science." I laugh. "Which is useful for having a fitness studio, I suppose."

Cole turns in his seat to face me. "I didn't know that."

I shrug. "You never asked."

"Wow, so why not continue to pursue that if it was something you were passionate about?" Ruby asks.

I click my tongue. "Umm, after my fiancé died in the crash, priorities and passions changed. I'm happy at the studio. I still get to work in an environment meant to help people. And working with my best friend is a perk." Enough about me. "What about you? People don't go to Tisch and not pursue a career in the arts. What do you want to do?"

"Well, the dream is to dance on Broadway."

"And she will," Brett inserts.

Ruby laughs. "For as long as my body will let me, then I guess I want to teach. I'd love to have my own dance studio someday and create a place where passions and dreams are cultivated."

127

"Broadway would be crazy not to take you," I say.

"She won't audition, though." Brett gives Ruby a meaningful look, his hand stretching across the table and taking her hand.

Ruby sighs. This must not be the first time they've had this discussion. "Because I'm not ready yet."

"You're more than ready. You could dance circles around those dancers in Miss Saigon."

"You're biased."

"He's biased, Roo, and so am I, but you *are* ready," Cole chimes in. "You should take the leap."

Ruby turns an adorable shade of pink. "You guys sure know how to make a girl feel good." She looks at me. "You'll never need anyone else in your corner with these two around."

I'm beginning to see that.

18

CARNIVAL

SAM ANSWERS the door with a frantic look, but smiles when she sees me. "Hey! Happy birthday!" She hugs me. "Come in. I'll be a couple minutes."

She turns, her hands plunking on her hips as she looks around the room.

"Am I early? Is everything okay?"

"No, no. You're fine. I'm just looking for a ... thing. Relax on the couch or something. I'll be right out." She disappears.

A thing? Okay. I step into the apartment, stopping at the sight of Monica and Shawn standing in the kitchen, coffee mugs in hands. "Whoa, what's going on in here?"

"Happy birthday, man." Shawn lifts his mug my way.

"I thought you had to work today."

"I lied."

Closing the door behind me, I move toward the kitchen counter. "What are you three planning?"

Shawn chuckles and opens his mouth, but Monica punches him in the arm. "This is all Sam, you'll have to wait for her," she says with wide, innocent eyes.

"Okay!" Sam emerges from her room with a black bag slung over her shoulder. "Let's go!"

"You're bringing your camera?" Monica asks. Her tone turns my head. Her eyes and mouth are open wide with surprise. Judging by the look and tone, I gather Sam bringing her camera is kind of a big deal.

Sam shrugs her off, though. "I want to take pictures today." So maybe I'm misunderstanding things.

Monica smiles like she's proud. "Okay. I think that's a great idea." Or, maybe not.

My eyes flick to the black bag Sam's carrying. I'm curious about it, but I hold back from asking.

The three of them move toward the door, Monica and Sam grabbing light sweaters from the coat rack on their wall as I follow.

"Anyone want to tell me where we're going?" My gaze scans the three of them once we're standing beside my car.

"Nope. No specifics," Sam says. "It's more fun that way."

"Oh? I take it you're driving then?" My keys jiggle from my fingertips.

Sam snatches them out of my hand. "Don't mind if I do."

"You have a license, right?"

She skips to the driver side. "Yes, sir."

I open Monica's door for her as Shawn moves around the back of the car, slipping into the passenger's seat behind Sam. This is new. I'm usually the driver.

"By the way," I lean across the middle console, my voice low. Sam finishes adjusting the seat to her needs then looks at me. Our faces inches from touching. I shoot her a flirtatious smile, it's my birthday and I'm light and carefree today.

"Yes?"

"Please feel free to call me 'sir' any time you want."

Flashes of bright red stain her cheeks and she rolls her eyes as she starts the engine. "Maybe Mandy should be aware of that fetish."

"Maybe she already is."

Sam bites down on her lips, her eyes dancing with laughter as she shakes her head.

"Hey, did you get home in time to watch the game last night?" Shawn asks once I turn away from Sam and grab for my seatbelt.

"Heck no. We hit up Stan's last night. The place was crazy. It was amazing."

"You're a lucky dude," Shawn grumbles jealously, and I chuckle.

"It was a good time. Any time the Bronx Bombers can beat the Sox it's a good time. Their bats were on fire."

Monica groans behind me, the noise sounding suspiciously like someone tossing the contents of their stomach. I twist in my seat as Sam shifts the car into gear and pulls into traffic.

"I take it you're not a baseball fan?"

"I could do without it."

"That's blasphemy. You're a native New Yorker and you don't like baseball?" I shake my head as Shawn gasps beside her, his eyes bugging out of his head. She may have lost a few points with that comment.

"The only good thing about baseball is the hot guys in tight pants."

"Like I haven't heard that before."

Shawn laughs. "Ain't that the truth."

Monica's brows pop up. "You say that like someone who has firsthand knowledge."

Sam's eyes flit my way. "Firsthand knowledge of baseball? You guys play when you were younger?"

"How do you think I pick up so many girls?" Shawn bumps his shoulder against Monica's.

"Remind me why I agreed to come today?" Monica groans.

"Because you're madly in love with me."

Sam and I share knowing smirks. We can read the two of them like a book. Why do they keep pretending indifference?

"To answer your question, Shawn plays for the hospital team. And yeah, I played growing up all the way through high school." I turn back to the front. "How have we not discussed this before?" I ask Sam as Monica and Shawn continue bickering in the back seat.

"I think we're going to keep learning new things about each other every day."

"You've got that many secrets, Supergirl?"

She coyly shrugs. "Every girl has her secrets to keep."

"Tell me one?" I challenge. "What's something I don't know yet?"

Sam chews on her bottom lip, contemplating before she whispers, "When I'm home alone I watch *The Young and the Restless*."

Exhaling deeply, I hang my head. "Well, at least you didn't say *General Hospital*."

Her head throws back against the headrest as she laughs.

"You laugh, but my mom loves *General Hospital*. She honestly thinks I spend my days romancing the nurses and falling in love with patients."

"I only laugh because I used to watch that with my mom all the time. Maybe my confession should've been I watch soap operas." Sam glances at me. "Can we still be friends?"

If she only knew how Amber roped me into watching reruns of *90210* with her when she was here for spring break, and how I ended up sucked into all the drama. She wouldn't be asking that question. Not that I'm telling her.

"Don't worry, it's going to take a whole lot more than soaps to tear us apart." The minute the words are out of my mouth I wince. "That was cheesy, wasn't it?" She doesn't have to respond.

Monica and Shawn's laughter confirms I've exceeded a respectable level of sap.

"Would you two like to be left alone?" Monica asks, humor in her voice. "I hadn't realized we were going to be intruding."

"Oh, shut it, Monica," Sam snaps over her shoulder as she changes lanes. She hops on the Belt Parkway, passing Brooklyn. Where is she taking us? "You know, it'll be a lot less exhausting when you stop pretending you hate Shawn so much."

"Who says I'm pretending?"

"Ouch." Shawn scowls.

"Alright, kids, settle down," I throw into the mix. "Where in the world are we going?"

"You'll see in about ten minutes."

I'm not about to spoil her fun, but with that hint I know where we're going. It's adorable the way she keeps glancing my way, a slight smile on her lips, as though she wants to see my face when I realize where we are.

CONEY ISLAND

"Surprise! Monica and I were talking and realized neither of us have been to Coney Island since we were kids. I thought it would be fun for the four of us to let loose today."

"Cool. That does sound like fun," I smile, looking out the car window. The weather is perfect for a day at Coney Island.

We park and make our way toward the boardwalk. Shawn pokes at Sam about her parking skills as we walk. Sam returns his attacks verbal punch after verbal punch while Monica and I let them duke it out, walking ahead of them.

"He's impossible," Monica laughs.

Sam's voice rises behind us. "And Sam's much better?"

Monica shrugs, checking over her shoulder. "Not at all."

We slow as we near the boardwalk, allowing Shawn and Sam to catch up now that they're finally done bickering.

Shawn knocks into me, grabbing Monica and pulling her forward. He promises to win her the largest stuffed animal ever as they walk away. I stop and stare out at the water, watching the ebb and flow of the tide as Sam steps to my side.

"I haven't been here since I was a kid, either," I admit inhaling the briny air. I haven't been near the ocean since the memorial service. "This was a great idea. Thank you."

"You're welcome. It's no biggie. Let's go win you some prizes, birthday boy."

Shaking off my melancholy, I throw my arm around her shoulders. Our hips bump as we walk. "Are you going to win me a prize? I'm excited to see how this is going to go down."

Looping one arm behind my back, Sam holds her camera that's hanging around her neck in her other hand. "If I'm not careful, you just might take home half the stuffed animals in this park."

"You realize it kind of goes against my man code to allow you to win me prizes. I should be the one playing to win your favor."

"Don't get all chivalrous on me now. It'll take all the fun out of beating you."

"No chivalry. Got it," I nod. "One of these days you're gonna have to up your expectations of a date. Lead the way, madam."

"Oh, if this were a date, I'd play coy and pretend to let you win all the prizes for me to make you feel better about yourself."

I laugh. "That's sounds about right." My date with Mandy last night flashes to the forefront of my brain. She's got coy down to a science. I hate it. "Please don't do that with me, ever."

If Sam detects the irritation in my voice she doesn't remark on it.

"Tell you what. How about we have a little competition to see who can win the most games?" I peer down the boardwalk at

Shawn and Monica who are sitting on a bench waiting for us. "We'll include our best friends in it, too," I add.

"Game on, but I must warn you, I might get a little competitive."

"Mario Kart competitive?"

She nods once. "Mario Kart times ten."

"I'm oddly turned on by that."

Sam punches me.

"I'm kidding, I'm kidding," I choke out as I fend her off. Okay, I'm only half kidding. "May the best man win."

We grab Monica and Shawn and head for the amusement park, explaining the bet as we go. When the gates open at noon, we're some of the first people in. It's only the second weekend they've been open this season. The weather is still a bit chilly with the breeze off the ocean coming in. Sam isn't shy about heading straight for the carnival games. She's all business, her steps pulling her ahead of the rest of us. Clearly, she's excited.

Shawn moves in step with me. "Do we have a strategy here?"

"To win."

"Do you think that's the best strategy for me to employ? Unlike you and Sam, I'm trying to win Monica's affection once and for all."

"Then win her some cute teddy bears to sleep with at night. Then you'll be on her mind."

"Is that how you'd win Sam?"

I shoot him a glare.

"I know, you're *just friends*," he coughs, cursing his disbelief beneath his breath before continuing, "but if you were trying to win her over, is that what you'd do?"

"Are you kidding me? No way. She's not that type of girl."

"Who's not what type of girl?"

I pause. I was completely oblivious to my surroundings. Sam and Monica are standing directly in front of us at, I assume, the first game they want to play.

"You are not the type of girl to give in."

She laughs. "What could possibly make you think that?"

It's in my best interest to keep my mouth shut, so I nod toward the colorful game before us. "You picked a shooting game first?" I smirk as the girls look at me. "Somehow, I figure you two as more Whac-A-Mole types."

"Think I've got some pent up anger I need to let out or something?" Sam asks cheekily.

Shawn clasps me on the shoulder. "I wouldn't answer that if I were you," he mock-whispers.

I ignore his warning. "I've got the bruises to prove it."

"Well, then you know I never miss my target. Let's see how good your aim is."

"If you two would cut the posturing, we could have some fun," Shawn sighs as he takes a seat at one of the water guns.

"Posturing? That's a big word for you." Monica pats Shawn on the back as she takes the seat next to him. "Good job, Gomes."

Sam and I continue to stare at each other. Neither one of us willing to back down. Evidently, we're both too competitive for our own good.

"Shall we?" I finally concede, nodding to the seats and taking a step.

"Ladies first." She gestures for me to go.

I snort. Of course she went there. "You know, our competitive nature might be the death of this friendship." I grab her hand and pull her toward the game to cut the bite my words might have had.

"Jamie and I have been competitive our whole lives, and he's still alive."

"Well then, if Jamie can handle you—" I let the words hang.

Sam shoots me a smirk as she sits down in front of a water gun, positioning her camera carefully around her neck.

The attendant, a bored looking guy around our age, explains the rules; shoot water in the hole, make your boat move. First boat to cross the line wins. Simple enough. He makes a final call for others to join in. "Always a winner," he shouts over our heads. When no one else comes near, he readies the game.

"Obviously, the other park goers know better than to mess with us."

The bell signals and Monica yelps. It takes a moment to get the water to arch straight into the small target in front of me, but once I do I stay steady. To my left, Shawn coaxes his boat to move faster as Monica continues squealing. On my right, Sam is leaning over her colorful gun, looking like a pro as she aims her water spray, ignoring the rest of us. My eyes return to our boats. We're neck and neck. My thumb presses the trigger harder, as though that'll make a difference.

"Go, go, go," Shawn shouts.

The boats hit the top of the board, mine and Sam's red lights go off, and the attendant barks, "We've got a tie!"

"What?" Sam shoots to her feet. Man, she's feisty.

"I take it you don't believe in tying?" I ask, dropping my hands from my gun and sitting back.

"All tying means is everyone wins. Not everyone should get a blue ribbon for participating."

Shawn coughs. "No, tying means you two win and we suck eggs." He shoots daggers at Sam and I as he stands. "I think Monica and I are going to go find some individual games. I promised her a bear, and there's no way I'm winning jack playing with the two of you."

I spin on my seat as Shawn and Monica take off. "Dang, you're so hardcore you scared away our best friends,"

Sam looks sheepish with her fingertips pressed to her lips. "So I got a little carried away."

"A little?" I scoff. "Sweetie, I'm afraid to move without asking for your permission."

"I'm sorry." She cringes. "It's easy for me to forget not everyone is as competitive as I am. I promise to keep myself in check from here on out."

"Somehow I doubt that." And I hope she doesn't. Her scary competitiveness is one of the many things I've come to love about her. "Want a rematch?" I ask hopefully.

"Of course." Sam straddles the seat, ready and waiting to begin.

Another couple joins the game, but they're completely out of their league with us. The bell rings and this time my water cannon shoots straight into the hole without missing a drop and my boat hits the top, setting off the red light. I win.

"The gentleman wins," the attendant barks. "Take your pick." He waves toward the wall of hideous stuffed fruit, dogs wearing bowties, and oddly shaped teddy bears.

Sam inhales. Exhales. Then turns to me. "Congratulations, Cole," she says calmly while looking anything but.

"That was for you." I bite back my smile. "Pick your prize."

Sam eyes the wall and points. "I think we need the dog with the yellow bowtie."

"I concur." The dog is the ugliest stuffed animal I've ever seen.

She holds the dog by its shoulders, examining its lopsided smile before tucking it under her arm.

I glance around the strip. "Where to next?"

"Well, since I chose the last game, I'm a fair person. You can pick the next round."

"Whac-A-Mole?"

"Your funeral." She sounds confident, but it's easy to see she's lost a little of the wind in her sails.

I steal the ugly dog from her arm and cover his ears. "Is that your idea of keeping it in check? You're scaring our dog."

Sam laughs and pouts at the same time. My emotions short-circuit. "I don't think you realize how difficult that is for me!" she exclaims. "That was tame compared to what I wanted to say."

"Awe." I take her under my arm, my hand tugging on her hair "Let's go hit some things and make you feel better."

"You always know just what to say to me."

I keep her tucked against my side as we meander down carnival row, her stuffed dog dangling from my hand. This is nice. Walking around with Sam, knowing she's being one hundred percent herself, even when that means pouting over losing a carnival game. No pretense. How refreshing.

"What are you naming this guy?" I make the dog dance before us. I'm glad Shawn and Monica aren't around to see this.

"I think I shall name him Charlie."

"Charlie? Is there a Charlie out there you hate?" I tease.

She chuckles. "Nope. Just felt right."

"Charlie, it is. I like it."

"Alright, Rocky. You ready to put me to shame?" I ask once we're standing before the Whac-A-Mole tent.

"You better not go easy on me because you feel bad about beating me before. If there's anything I hate more than losing, it's winning because my opponent let me."

"As if I would roll over and let you win." I would, but she doesn't need to know that.

Once again, we take our places, each of us grabbing a mallet as the park worker explains the rules of the game. "First person to 150 wins a plush."

"This feels a bit wrong." I lean toward Sam, nodding my head for her to follow my gaze. Each player spot is taken by people significantly younger than us. There's two giggling preteens, a toddler with her mother standing behind her, and a couple of boys no older than eight or nine.

"Show no mercy, Rossner," Sam whispers, conspiring.

The bell rings and music starts blaring before I can respond. The first little mole pops his head out of the hole in the middle while I'm still watching Sam, and I miss him.

Sam's knocking the heck out of the poor guys, their little mechanical voices shouting, "Ouch" with every swing of her mallet. Hard-freaking-core. That's my girl.

That's my girl? I hesitate and miss two more moles as they go berserk, popping up and down all over the board.

"C'mon! Get your head in the game," Sam snips through gritted teeth. "Don't you dare let me win!"

Shaking my head, I attack the game, not that it'll make a difference now. She's thirty, no, twenty, make that ten points from—

"We have a winner!" The siren sounds and Sam's yellow light starts blinking over her scoreboard.

She jumps up and down, then promptly punches me in the chest. "You let me win!"

"Sorry, I was distracted," I drop my mallet. "And no, I didn't let you win. I highly doubt you missed a single guy, while I missed my very first one. So you would have won anyway."

"My arms are killing me from all this competing," I complain after we play every carnival game here twice and win an army of plushes. I'm grateful she started handing the prizes to kids around the park, or I'd be stuck lugging them around. "Want to take a spin on the Wonder Wheel and grab some lunch?" I glance around the park. It's busier now than it was when we first arrived. "And possibly find Shawn and Monica?"

"Yeah. Where are they?" Sam looks around the crowded park. "I'm surprised they've been able to handle each other alone for this long."

"I haven't the slightest idea. Should we look for them or ride the wheel? Lady's choice."

"If they wanted to be found, I'm sure they would have looked for us by now. They knew where to find us. Let's ride."

The line is short, and after five minutes we're sitting shoulder to shoulder in a green swinging car slowly working its way around the wheel as new riders get on and others are let off.

"The last time I rode this was when I was—I think I was eight. I was terrified of the moving cars and refused to get in one with my cousins."

"Really? I've always loved it. I used to rock the car and Jamie would get so mad at me."

I laugh. Her confession does not surprise me in the least. "Have you always been so fearless?"

Sam ponders the thought as she looks out over the park. Sadness flashes across her face before it disappears and she says with a forced smile, "For most of my life, yeah."

"I completely forgot to ask you to dinner tonight," I say, changing the subject. Today isn't a day for being sad, no matter how badly I want to understand that look. "Brett and Ruby are taking over my apartment and cooking for me."

"Do you trust their cooking?"

"Last I heard they're making spaghetti. You can't mess that up, can you?"

Sam arches a brow.

"Okay, so you can mess it up, but I trust them. For the most part. Plus, Ruby specifically asked if you were coming. Evidently, you made an impression on her."

"Well, if Ruby wants me there—" Sam smiles. *I want you there.* The admission punches me in the gut. What's going on with me today? "Brett definitely made a good choice with that one."

That's easy to answer. "If you listen to the story, he'll tell you it wasn't a choice. If I never believed in fate before, I did once he told me their tale."

"Well, that's sweet. You believe in fate, huh?"

I sigh through my nose, looking out at the ocean. "It's complicated. Fate, I mean. I see enough crap on a day to day basis to have a hard time believing the horrible things in life are someone's fate. No one likes to say, 'Oh, being horribly disfigured was your fate.' Yet, give someone good news and everyone's patting them on the back saying how it must be fate." I shrug. Man, do I sound bitter.

Sam nods. "I guess the fate topic is a bit heavy for a day like today."

"Yeah, poor Charlie looks depressed." I pluck the dog from her lap and the sunglasses wearing banana she won me from between us, and press them against the bars to the cage. "Look guys, check out the view."

"It is quite the view." Sam clears her throat. "So, Mandy took you out last night for your birthday?"

"How? How did you know we went out last night?" I ask, a bit confused

"Earlier, in the car. You said 'we' when talking about going to Stan's to watch the game."

"And 'we' automatically means I was with Mandy?"

"You are a 'we', are you not? I guess I assumed that if you were out with your buddies, Shawn would have been there. Plus, it makes sense Mandy would want to go out for your birthday, and since I stole you this morning and Brett has you tonight—"

"We're not a 'we', actually," I interrupt her completely accurate explanation. Well, except for the 'we' thing.

Sam's eyes dart to me. "Since when?"

"Uh, since about one o'clock this morning." I drop our prizes back to my lap. "You were right, though. I did go out with her last night."

"Oh." Sam sits quietly. "I'm sorry."

"No, don't be sorry. I mean, I'm not all choked up about it. She's a nice girl, but it was becoming clearer with every date that she wasn't the one for me."

"Was it a mutual thing?"

"Actually," I flash her a guilty grin. "You can probably forget about her coming back to the studio any time soon."

"Of course, you were the heartbreaker."

"Whoa, now wait a minute. I didn't set out to break her heart. I made it very clear from day one that what we were doing was casual. It was dating, not a relationship."

"And every girl is okay with a hot doctor breaking up with them in a city with so few prospects."

My ears perk up. "You think I'm hot?"

Sam chuckles. "That's the only thing you picked up? This is why I knew you'd be the heartbreaker."

I angle my body toward hers. "What was I supposed to do? Keep going out with a woman who clearly wasn't the one just so I don't break her heart?"

Sam elbows my side. "No, you did the right thing. I'm just giving you a hard time. Mandy was smitten with you. It's always best to end things before they get too far."

"Exactly." The wheel slows up as we come around and we stop midway to the top, our ride almost over. "You know it's frustrating to guys, too. Dating and breaking up, and looking for the one."

"I never said it wasn't. I just think guys have it a little easier. Women get to a certain age without finding the one and they're labeled old spinsters or cat ladies. While men get to be—"

"Heartbreakers?"

"Well, I was going to say 'eligible bachelors' and—"

"Players?"

Sam chuckles. "Alright. I can see we're not going to agree on this, but better to be a heartbreaker or player than an old spinster with cats."

I stare at her. Her cheeks are pink, her eyes clear and bright. Her dark hair was made for a guy to dig his hands into. My gaze wanders lower, taking her all in as though I haven't already memorized every curve and muscle she owns. She's gorgeous, so her argument seems flawed, considering.

"Sam." My eyes return to hers. "You know there's no way you are going to be a spinster cat lady."

"Oh, I know. I hate cats." She chuckles, self-depreciatingly. "I'll be the spinster with dogs."

"You'll be no such thing, crazy woman. The moment you decide to date again, you'll be snatched up so fast your head will spin," I laugh. "Or, maybe you will be a spinster and I'll be a playboy and we'll be the talk of the town as we carry on beneath our friends' noses." I wink. I like this picture much better.

Sam cracks a smile, peering at me from the corner of her eye.

We reach the bottom and the attendant unlatches the cage door, letting us out. With Charlie and Mr. Banana in one hand and Sam's hand in the other, we step away from the ride.

"Time to locate Shawn and Monica, and eat?"

"Yes, I'm starving."

"Agreed." I loop her hand through my arm. "So, you think I'm hot, huh?"

"Don't let it go to your head."

19

CAN'T YOU SEE

MONICA STANDS in the kitchen stirring something on the stove when I walk into the apartment. "Hey." She looks down at the envelope by my side and studies it. "You finally got the pictures developed?"

Flipping it over in my hand, I nod. "It was time. And I wanted to see the pictures I took on Cole's birthday."

Monica doesn't speak as she looks at me, saying a million things with her eyes that she won't say aloud, making her own assumptions about why I developed a roll of film I've avoided since before the crash.

"I'll be in my room."

"I want to see any pictures you took of me," she hollers before I close my bedroom door.

I drop my purse at the foot of my bed, crawl onto the middle, and sit cross-legged with the pictures in my lap.

Okay. I can do this.

Inhaling a deep breath, I open the picture pouch and Paul's face is the first I see, as I knew he would be. He had such a handsome profile with his sharp jawline and perfectly shaped nose. My fingertips brush along his stubble and the little scar hiding beneath as he looks out on Central Park from the park bench.

I flip to the next picture and then the one after that, all of Paul and me wandering around the city during our last weekend together, enjoying the first summer days. I brush the back of my hand across my cheeks, wiping away the dampness.

The three-year gap ends halfway through the stack when the back of Cole in his jeans and leather jacket appears, his hands tucked into his front pockets, standing on the boardwalk as he faces the beach.

Each image tells a story of our day. Shawn and Monica competing in the ring toss with laugh lines framing their mouths. Monica pointing at Shawn with her other fist pumping the air, celebrating her win.

I slow my shuffle when Cole and I fill the photos. I hadn't realized Monica took pictures every time I asked her to hold the camera. I unhurriedly flip through each image. One after another. Cole and I competing for the giant unicorn. Cole and I walking side by side, passing the game booths, my shoulder nudging his. Cole and I eating corn dogs, laughing as I wipe mustard from the corner of his mouth. I stop on an image of Cole and I standing on the boardwalk, leaning against the railing. I'm looking out at the ocean, but Cole ... Cole is looking at me. My heart flutters frantically, heating up my chest. What is that look? I've never seen him look at me like that before.

It's strange to see myself in pictures. I'm normally the one on the other side of the lens. My fingers halt on another photo. Cole laughs as Shawn concentrates on trying to beat that shooting game again without my interference. But they aren't why I stopped. I'm in the corner of the shot, looking at Cole—the same way he was looking at me, like...

No.

Am I...? With a shake of my head, I shut down the thought. I can't go there.

Flipping through the rest of the pictures, I stop on the last one. The four of our faces squeeze together in front of the Astroland Park rocket at the end of the day.

A smile stretches across my face.

My eyes swivel to the black frame on my nightstand. My fingers inch through the air and clutch the photo in my hand, holding it reverently. Is it time? Can I do that to Paul? Three years is a long time to hold on to a ghost. Or is it? Is there a correct amount of time to grieve? Have I surpassed the allotted time? The photo isn't really here for comfort anymore, only a reminder of what was lost. Every day I'm forgetting more of him.

Reaching under my bed, I pull out my shoebox of memories with Paul: Rangers tickets, movie ticket stubs, handwritten notes, the little black box holding my engagement ring. I set the shoebox next to me on the bed. I can do this.

Please forgive me, Paul. I have to do this.

Turning over the frame, I unhook the back and gently pull out the picture of us on the Brooklyn Bridge.

I have to let you go.

With an unsteady hand, I press my lips to the picture before carefully placing it in the shoebox and closing the lid. I take the picture of the four of us and secure it in the frame before setting it back on my nightstand.

I made the right decision switching out the photos. Bittersweet happiness warms my heart, knowing I'm going to wake up every morning to this picture.

"SAM DEVELOPED THE PICTURES FROM CONEY ISLAND."

I shoot Monica a look, but she's avoiding my gaze. Why would she tell the guys? Maybe I don't want to share the pictures with Cole and Shawn.

"Oh yeah?" Cole asks, stretched out in the recliner, his hands folded behind his head. "I want to see them."

"I'll go get them." Monica darts off the couch toward my bedroom.

"Wait." I try to stand, but get tangled in my blanket. "What are you doing?"

"You haven't shown them to me yet. And the guys want to see them, too." She turns to Cole and Shawn. "You guys might not know, but Sam is a fantastic photographer."

"I'm not that great."

"Oh, stop. Yes she is. You guys have to see."

If Monica grabs the whole envelope, it'll include all the pictures of Paul and me. Not to mention all the ones she took of Cole and me that I haven't decided how I feel about. If I bring them out with all of those missing, she'll know I took some out and question me in front of Cole and Shawn about why I couldn't leave them in. She's meddling, and there's no stopping her now.

"What's the big deal, Sammy?" Shawn quips next to me. "You take some nudie pics you don't want us to see?"

Cole throws a pillow from the chair he's sitting in at Shawn's head.

"No, you sicko." I heave a sigh. "It's fine, Monica. They're on my nightstand. Will you just give them to me first?"

Her brow quirks and settles back down. I think my reasoning finally clicks because she nods.

Cole's eyes heat the side of my head, but I don't want to look at him. I'll get enough looks from him after he sees all the pictures.

When Monica comes back and hands me the envelope, I pull out the stack and pick all the ones with Paul off the top and hand them the rest.

"What are those?" Cole eyes the face down pictures in my lap.

I hesitate. There's no reason they can't see them, but I don't want tonight to turn into a pity party for the woman who lost her fiancé. I've made peace with it. Tonight is supposed to be a fun movie night in, but the more I try to hide them, the more Cole will want to know why.

"They're pictures of Paul." I swallow and stand, readying to take them back to my room. "From right before the crash."

Cole nods, but he doesn't offer me a pitying glance. He focuses on the other pictures, letting it go. I could kiss him. But I won't.

When I return from putting the pictures of Paul in my room, the three of them are on the same couch, passing the pictures back and forth.

"Oh my gosh. Do I really look like that when I laugh?" Monica grumbles. "Tell me to close my mouth a little next time, will you?"

"These are so great, Sam," Cole says. "You did a great job capturing the fun we had."

"Umm, thanks. I prefer candid shots. They're the best way to capture what's real."

Standing in the middle of the room, I wait for Cole to see the ones Monica took. What's he going to think? Has he already seen them and thought nothing of them? Was I reading too much into them?

"I wish we'd remembered to take pictures while we rode the Wonder Wheel. And it would have been great if you could have caught Shawn's little temper tantrum on film after we tied that first game."

The pillow flies around Monica's back and knocks Cole in the head.

"If she'd taken pictures when we first got there we'd have proof of how unsportsmanlike she can be," Shawn points out.

"That's why I'm normally the one behind the camera. No proof. Didn't happen."

Shawn and Monica laugh, but Cole doesn't. He's concentrating on the picture in his hands. Or rather, pictures. I take note of the way he flips between several shots. Back and forth. And back and forth.

With eyebrows furrowed, his lips pressed firmly together, his shoulders rise as he inhales deeply. Then his eyes flick up and catch me staring at his reaction. Yep. He's reached Monica's pictures. Stop looking at him, Samantha. But I can't.

He returns to the pictures, and a slow smile spreads across his face.

I have to say something. If I don't, he'll make his own assumptions. What are his assumptions? Why was he looking at me like that? "Monica's a pretty decent photographer too, huh."

"Definitely." Cole taps the photos against his thigh. "It's uncanny how well she captured such ... complex emotions."

Complex emotions? What the heck is that supposed to mean? Are his emotions complex? Does he think I'm complex? Stop freaking out. Why can't I calm the crap down? This is Cole. My best friend Cole. Monica captured us doing our normal daily stuff. Taking care of each other and having fun. His look was a random moment caught on camera. It didn't mean anything.

"Man, I *am* good." Monica steals some of the photos from Cole. "Maybe I should take up photography."

"Why are they all of those two? You didn't shoot any of me?" Shawn leans back on the couch after looking over Monica's shoulder and checking out the pictures.

"You're not nearly as cute to photograph as these two."

I need to stop standing here like an idiot. "I'm going to make some popcorn for the movie. Who wants some popcorn?"

"I'll help." Cole pops up from the couch.

Before I can tell him to sit and relax, Shawn laughs, "How many morons does it take to toss a bag of popcorn into the microwave and hit start?" Cole kicks him as he scoots by. They might kill each other before the night is through.

"Sam doesn't do microwave popcorn," Monica says absently,

still flipping through the photos. "She's got her own air popper and kernels."

I turn on my heel and enter the kitchen. Searching through the cabinets for the popper, Cole's footsteps come in behind me.

Where did I put it? I used it the other day. Why can't I remember where the stupid popper is?

"You okay?"

His voice is close. I jump and swivel around. "Yeah, I'm great. Will you find the kernels for me?" Why are you smiling so big? Cool it. You're making this awkward.

"Uh, sure." He takes a step back. "You mean those?"

I turn to the countertop. The kernels are pushed against the wall next to the stove. "Ha. Here they are!"

Cole steps closer, his chest nearly touching my back as he stands over me. His hands skim my biceps, raising goosebumps, then fall away as he inhales.

"Are you sure you're okay?"

Take a deep breath, Samantha. This is Cole, for heaven's sake. In and out. In and out. Turn around. Smile. And tell him everything is fine. You're overreacting. Stop making it weird.

His chin comes to rest on top of my head. "Sam?"

I freeze and do my best to remain calm. Breathe. In and out. He's been in close proximity before. This is completely normal for us. "Cole?"

"I just—"

He pauses for too long. What is he thinking? Why isn't he talking?

His arms wrap around my chest, pinning my arms at my sides and pulling me against his chest. I exhale, relaxing into him. "Nothing. I just wanted to thank you again for my birthday. Seeing those pictures reminded me how much fun it was. It was great to get away and act like a kid again." He squeezes me tighter.

The rest of the air leaves my lungs. Relief? Disappointment?

What is this I'm feeling? I drop my head back against his shoulder and reach up, rubbing his arm wrapped around me. "It was a good day, wasn't it? It was nothing. I'm really glad you had a good time."

"Hey, Sam?"

"Are we gonna start this movie or what?" Shawn hollers. "Omph!" I'd bet my life that Monica punched Shawn in the stomach.

Cole sighs, loosening his hold on me. "The natives are restless."

Disappointment. Definitely disappointment. "Yeah. Go get the movie started. I'll finish up the popcorn before they start rioting."

He spins me around, his hands clasping my face, and he stares. He *just* stares. His thumbs brush my cheeks. I try to breathe evenly, but it's difficult with him so close. He's never *this* close. Uncertainty glints his eyes as he holds my gaze, his forehead once again creased and thoughtful. What are you thinking, Cole? He leans in and I suck in a quick breath before he plants a kiss on my forehead, holding his lips there longer than he normally does.

"I don't know what I'd do without you." With his lips so close, they graze my forehead as he speaks.

"Ditto," I breathe out.

He leaves the kitchen without another word or glance, and I slouch against the countertop, gripping the edge for support so I don't melt to the kitchen floor.

What just happened?

When I walk back into the living room, Monica and Shawn are sprawled out on either end of the couch.

"Make yourselves comfortable." I hand them each a small bowl of popcorn. "Don't worry about the rest of us."

"We will." Monica's toes dance as she grins. "Thanks."

"I saved the recliner for you." Cole gets situated on the floor. "Since these two losers called dibs on the couch."

Of course, he's going to be a gentleman. "Oh, thanks." I hand him a bowl and step over him.

Shawn throws Cole some pillows and he lays back at the foot on the recliner, tucking a pillow under his head.

Within the first twenty minutes of the movie, Cole has shifted and re-situated a minimum of a hundred times. It's hard to watch. The floor can't be comfortable with its old matted down carpet and thin padding.

"Hey, Cole," I whisper, pushing the footrest back in. His eyes drift to me. "Take the recliner. You look so uncomfortable. I don't mind the floor."

He doesn't hesitate before getting up. We do a little dance with Cole's hands on my hips, trading places. Before I bend down onto the floor, Cole grabs my waist and draws me onto the recliner with him.

I squawk in surprise.

"There's no reason why we can't both sit here," he says into my ear, pulling out the footrest and reclining us back.

I hesitate. Do I stay? It *is* more comfortable than the hard floor. Or do I take the floor? Put space between us. Keep a clear head. That's what I should do.

His arm shifts behind my back, accommodating me in his space and tucking me into his side. His fingers relax on my hip. I've taken too long to decide. Accept defeat. This is my home now. I curl into Cole, positioning my head in the crook of his shoulder and lifting my hand to his chest to rest my head. My knee hooks up onto his leg. It feels like the most natural place to be.

"Comfortable?" he murmurs into my hair.

If I open my mouth to say something, I'm worried my voice will quiver, so I nod instead.

"Good." He sets his cheek on top of my head.

Can I still explain this away as friends getting comfortable and watching a movie? This feels like so much more.

MY ARM IS TINGLY. I SHIFT AS MY SLEEPY FOG WEARS OFF. I'm not alone. I lift my eyelids enough to take in the masculine body under me. Cole.

His arms have me cradled against his chest, and I've wrapped myself around him in my sleep. Cole is breathing heavily, still asleep. I don't want to wake him, but my arm underneath him is numb.

My eyes drift around the empty room like it will give me answers. At least, I assumed it was empty. Shawn and Monica are tangled on the couch making out.

Before I can stop myself, I gasp.

Cole jerks beneath me. "Sam?" he gasps as he pops up, his arm tightening its hold around my waist to keep me from being thrown to the floor. "What's wrong?"

Shawn and Monica startle apart.

"Your best friend is macking on mine!" He follows my gaze to the couch.

"Busted," Cole chuckles.

Monica carefully shifts off Shawn, straightening her hair and clothes as though they get caught making out all the time.

"What? You've never seen two people kissing before?" she asks nonchalantly.

"Don't you play coy with me, Monica Luscombe. How long has this been going on? And why didn't you tell me?"

"Well, there was that one time a few years ago," Shawn confesses, looking pleased with himself.

"I knew it." Cole lowers the footrest and shifts me from lying in his arms to sitting on his lap. "I knew you two had a thing."

My eyes snap to his face. "What? Do you not find this weird?"

"Weird? No way. It's about dang time."

"You're the one always telling me to stop pretending," Monica says to me. "You knew this was going to happen."

"Well, maybe, yeah, but I didn't expect to be in the same room when it did! And how could you not tell me this happened before?"

"Can we not have this conversation right now? And what about you two? Snuggling in the recliner, falling asleep in each other's arms. I think you should turn that finger around, missy."

Cole's fingers dig into my hip as his other hand runs through his hair. I'm on his lap. I'm still on Cole's lap.

"You guys took the couch. The recliner was all we had," I argue, scooting off. His fingers loosen their grip slowly.

"Yes, *that's* the only reason to share a recliner," Monica quips.

"Well, that and epic make out sessions," Cole says. "Unfortunately, we fell asleep before we had the chance to try that one. Why don't you two leave us alone so we can take the recliner for a spin." His hands reach for me and I smack his arm away, glaring at him.

"It was worth a try." He shrugs with a wink, though his eyes lose their playfulness.

"Yeah, it was." Shawn still looks smug with his hair all askew thanks to Monica's hands.

"*No.*" I point at Shawn. "Don't you encourage him."

The guys chuckle. Out of the corner of my eye, Cole stands and stretches with a loud yawn. "I'd love to hang around and get all the scoop on this little thing here." He wags his finger back and forth between Monica and Shawn. "But unlike the rest of you, I have a twelve-hour shift in the morning."

"What time is it?" I look to the clock on the microwave. The neon green numbers light up. "Three? Cole, what time do you have to be at the hospital?"

"Seven."

"Oh, Cole." I walk over to him. "You're going to be so tired."

155

He closes the gap between us and wraps me in a side hug. "Actually, I got a relatively decent nap in there," he whispers in my ear. His nose nudges my hair before he presses a kiss to my cheek.

My stomach flips. Butterflies? Heck, there's a stinking zoo prancing around inside me. He's kissed my cheek a million times and it's never affected me like this before.

I walk toward the door. "Go get some sleep. No falling asleep on the job."

"That's what coffee's for." He looks back at the couch. "See you two later. Let Sam get some sleep." He waves, following after me.

Shawn chuckles and tosses Cole a wave.

"Goodnight, Cole," Monica calls out.

"I can't believe I'm going to be stuck alone with those two."

"He lives two doors down, kick them out."

"If they don't keep quiet, I might have to."

"Crap." Cole lifts his arm over my head, placing it on the door preventing me from opening it. He leans over me, lowering his head toward mine. "Are we really gonna have to put up with them being a couple now?"

I crack a smile. "We'll see how long it lasts. I mean, it was bound to happen, but I didn't mentally prepare myself to watch it happen."

"You poor thing," he says with a shake of his head, his forehead touching mine. "Maybe they'll tame each other."

"Shawn and Monica, tame? Ha, pigs'll fly before that happens."

"We can hear you," Monica sings from across the room.

Cole laughs and straightens.

"I don't care," I sing back as I twist the doorknob.

"Hey," Cole says softly once we walk into the hall, leaving the door cracked behind us. "About your pictures of Paul?"

My bottom lip tucks between my teeth. I knew he'd ask about them eventually. "What about them?"

"I'd like to see them sometime when it's just the two of us. I mean, if you wouldn't mind sharing them with me. I didn't want to say anything in front of them." He nods toward the apartment. "But I don't want to leave with you thinking I didn't acknowledge how hard that must have been for you."

It's funny. It was easier than I expected it would be. I didn't curl up into an inconsolable ball and cry all day. That's huge progress from three years ago. Heck, that's huge progress from even a year ago. "Sure. I guess if you want to, I'll share them with you sometime."

"We never talk about him. I don't want you to think you can't. Especially with me."

"I know." My eyes shift to the ground. Why don't I talk more about Paul with Cole? It's not an uncomfortable topic. Cole, of all people, understands the feeling of loss, but that's not why I like being around Cole so much. He helps me forget. The pain and the guilt, not Paul. Cole makes me feel lighter. I look back up at him and smile. "I'm really grateful for you, Cole."

The smile on his face grows. "Hey, today marks two years since we met."

Two years since we met. Three years since the crash. I'd rather mark our friendaversary. It's easier.

"You mean two years I've had to put up with you," I tease.

"You mean two years of having me on your mind every day." He ruffles my hair. "You don't have to try and control yourself, you know. My ego can handle your fawning."

I snort, holding back my laughter. "Wow, how did you peg me so accurately?"

"You're the best." He chucks me under the chin. How do I take that after tonight? I'm feeling so many mixed signals. You're the best *friend*. Because that's what we are, Samantha. We've been very particular about that word. "I'm on seven to seven for the next three days, then off three. Want to do dinner Thursday?"

"Sounds like a plan. Rizzo's at six?"

"Yeah, sounds good." He backs up and a piece of me goes missing. "Goodnight."

20

FANTASY

31ST STREET BACKYARD—JULY 4, 1995

Sweat drips from my brow. We should have gone to the beach. Whose bright idea was it to throw a Fourth of July cookout during a heatwave in Queens? I look across the yard at Sam. Yep. All her fault. And Monica's. Monica who has disappeared with Shawn, again. Into one of their air-conditioned apartments, no doubt.

A hip bumps into my side. "When are you two going to admit you're hot for each other?"

"Have you been drinking again?" I glance at Amber to my left. She's been making the rounds, chatting up everyone at the party, for the last hour.

"Ha. Ha." She steals a chip from my plate. "You're not fooling anyone."

"Shhh." Balancing my plate in one hand, I grasp Amber's elbow and back away from the food table to keep our conversation between us and not the other party goers gathering plates of food. She giggles like a child.

"We're just friends," I remind her once we're alone.

"Really?" Amber's head tilts sideways. "I think you're more than that."

My gaze strays, zeroing in on Sam hanging out across the crowded yard. She's involved in an animated conversation with some regulars from her studio, but the moment I find her she pauses and looks my way. A breathtaking smile spreads across her lips and that feeling I got two weeks ago when I looked at our Coney Island pictures assails me. I can't pinpoint the feeling any better today than I could then. Chills slide up my spine and fire rolls in my stomach. Pounding in my head and an odd sense of peace in my gut. She sticks her tongue out at me and the odd emotion morphs to happiness. Pure happiness as she laughs at me from across the crowded yard.

"See," Amber whispers in her not so subtle way. I look away from Sam.

"What? She stuck her tongue out at me, so we must be in love? We're friends, Am," I repeat.

"Cole, you're twenty-eight. You're a gorgeous doctor living in New York City and you don't date. What's wrong with this picture?"

"I date."

Amber blows out a deep breath. "Tell me the last girl you dated," she scoffs, her blue eyes pinning me in place.

The last girl I dated? That was ... uh, there was...

"Exactly." She pilfers another chip from my plate. "You're in love with Sam."

I nearly choke on the cracker in my mouth, swallowing it down forcefully as I stare at Amber. "You're delusional."

Mandy. Mandy was the last girl I went on a date with. I should feel bad for not remembering her name immediately, but I don't. Clearly, I suck.

"Oftentimes I am," Amber agrees with a smile. "But not about this."

I allow my eyes to return to Sam. Checking her out as she laughs with her friends.

"She lost her fiancé," I remind Amber needlessly.

"Three years ago."

I know this and I've pushed it out of my mind ever since our movie night last month. Those Coney Island pictures, the way she seemed so flustered. The way she fell asleep in my arms on the recliner. That moment in the kitchen. I almost caved. And now with Monica and Shawn together? It's getting harder and harder to maintain this idea of our relationship being nothing more than a friendship. I should take the leap. I told Ruby to do it, so why can't I take my own advice?

No.

No, no, no.

"I'm not going to be the one who tells her to move on." The crowd noise picks up as a few new guys walk through the back gate. "

"No, you're going to be the one who pines after her. For how long?"

Why is she so furious?

"Am, what's going on with you? Why are you pushing this?"

"Tell me you don't love her, Cole."

This must be what Mel Gibson was trying to portray in Braveheart. The feeling of being stretched out on a rack. It's torture admitting it anywhere other than my head. I inhale deeply, confessing my feelings for the first time. "You know I can't do that."

"Then act on it, big brother. Before it's too late."

Before it's too late?

She's wandering back into the crowd before my brain can think of a response.

"WHAT ARE YOU GUYS TALKING ABOUT OVER HERE?" MONICA asks as she, Ruby, and Sam join the circle of chairs the guys and I set up.

Shawn reaches for her hand, tugging her into his lap. "We're talking about how hot you look in that sundress."

I groan, rolling my eyes. Sam does the same as we exchange a knowing glance before I avert my eyes from hers as quickly as I can.

"How is it that they've gone from zero to one hundred in a matter of weeks?" Sam grumbles as she sits down next to me.

"Don't be jealous." Monica loops her arms around Shawn's neck. "This could be you if you weren't so oblivious."

"What's that supposed to mean?" Sam retorts.

"If you have to ask, that's part of the problem."

Ruby chuckles and covers it behind her hand when Sam glances at her.

I kick Brett's foot as discreetly as possible, and he looks my way. *Say something*, I plead with my eyes.

"What have you girls been doing?" he asks lamely. Great cover, bro. I lean over, grabbing my water bottle from the ground by my feet.

"We've been trying to find Sam a hot date."

Water goes down the wrong tube and I choke. Wait. What? "You what?" I said that out loud, didn't I?

"Right, Sam? Didn't you say you were ready to jump back in the saddle?"

"I..." Sam looks around the group. "I said it was something on my mind. I definitely did not agree to be set up."

"A date? For Sam?" Did I hear that correctly? "She's not dating." My words come out a bit too forcefully as I look at Sam. "I thought you weren't dating." Crap, drink your water and relax, Cole.

"I did. I'm not," she stumbles over her words. "I mean ... it's possible in the future, but I never agreed to anything." Sam glares at Monica. "Monica is getting a little ahead of herself."

"She's ready. She just doesn't know it yet," Monica says. "I'm thinking Daniel would be a great contender to start out. Don't you think, Ruby?"

I choke on my water for a second time.

"The stock broker? He has major potential." Ruby nods enthusiastically. She's in on this, too? Traitor. "A solid eight. You thought he was good looking. Right, Sam?"

Sam stiffens beside me. "Well, yeah, but I didn't say I wanted to date him."

"Whoa. Daniel? That Daniel?" I look across the yard at the guy. It's a July Fourth barbeque and he's dressed for a golf game at the country club.

"Shh, keep your voice down, bro," Brett warns.

"The guy looks so uptight."

"He's easy on the eyes. He's stable. Seems pretty sensitive and respectful." Monica glances Daniel's way. "The only downside is he's thirty and still single. You've got to wonder why. Mama's boy, maybe?"

"Oh," Ruby chimes. "Very possible. I can see that. Perfectly parted hair, polo buttoned all the way up. Practically screams, 'I want to make my mother proud.'"

"Don't I get a say in this?" Sam asks. "What if I don't want to date Daniel? What if I wanted to date Andrew or Jeremy?"

My water bottle slips through my fingers.

Monica's brow lifts. "Jeremy, the architect? Meh, he's barely a seven. Not worth it."

"Which one is Andrew?" Ruby asks.

"The teacher." Monica points him out, standing in the same group with Daniel and a bunch of other Wall Street wannabes.

"Why are they all defined by their jobs?" I inhale slowly. "Do they not have anything else going for them?"

Monica purses her lips. "Would you rather we refer to each by their looks? The hot brunette with the to-die-for body? Or the sexy blonde with the piercing blue eyes?" Her eyes dart to Ruby. "Oh, how about Travis? Muscular biceps, chiseled jawline, gorgeous green eyes? Can you imagine what their babies would look like?"

Babies! What the—? Sam is not making babies with anyone anytime soon. My gaze scans over the girls and I see it. The glittering humor in their eyes. The knowing smiles behind their hands. They're pulling my leg. Or maybe they're saying this all to prod Sam. They must be.

"Oh, Travis." Ruby grins and finds him next to the grill, chatting up another girl. "Sam, he might be the best one. Great gene pool. Perfect ten. Lock that down before he becomes smitten with that redhead."

"Alright, you two. Enough." Sam sighs, pinching the bridge of her nose. "We're done talking about this. Let a girl ease back into this. I will date who I want, when I want. And it won't be decided by you guys at a community barbeque based on some made-up rating system."

"Wait up," Shawn says, holding his hand up. Finally, maybe he can bring some sense to this ridiculous conversation. "Let's hear more about this rating system—"

"Dude!" I interrupt. Figures he doesn't have anything helpful to say.

"Rate us," he finishes, ignoring my outburst.

"You're all psycho." This is insanity. I slide to the edge of my chair and brace my hands on my knees.

"Thank you, Cole," Sam says. "Someone who has a little sense."

"Hey, no one told me there was a family get together in this corner." Brett, Sam, and I turn as Amber walks up behind us. "Just because I don't live in New York with the rest of you doesn't mean I don't want to be included," she pouts as she plops her hands on my shoulders and squeezes a bit harder than what I would consider to be polite.

"We're deciding who to set Sam up with for her first date," Ruby tells Amber. "We've narrowed it down to Travis, the blonde with the buzz cut over there, and Daniel, the one in the blue polo."

"Ohhh reeeally?" The words are sung near my ear as Amber leans over my shoulder and gives me a calculated look. Uh, oh. That look is never good.

"No, we're not," Sam objects as she shoots Ruby and Monica the eye.

"No?" My sister asks all innocently. She should consider theatre, her knack for drama is astonishing. "Sam, there are so many eligible guys here. I should know, I've been checking them out myself." She tweaks my shoulders again.

"Oh my gosh," Sam mutters under her breath.

"As a matter a fact, I not only checked out the guys, but the girls, too." Amber slithers between my and Brett's chairs and grabs my hand. "Come with me. I was talking to Cathy earlier and she so has the hots for you."

"Cathy?" Sam shifts, crossing her leg over the other. "Isn't she the one that lives below Shawn?"

"The blonde with the fake boobs?" Monica asks.

"Just remember you said it, not me," Shawn laughs and nods confirming that Cathy is indeed the amply-endowed blonde who lives below him.

"She's super sweet. Maybe not the smartest girl here, but she's totally your type."

"Cathy's not Cole's type," Sam chuckles.

"I have a type?" This ought to be good.

"Maybe I'm giving you too much credit, but didn't you say you like to date girls you can have an actual intellectual conversation with."

"And what about you?" I counter. "Please tell me you're not going to pick your first date in years based on his gene pool and job title?"

"Hey." Sam lifts her hands, surrendering. "I'm pretty sure I'm the one who nixed every guy they named off. I didn't ask to be set up with half of New York City."

"Yeah, yeah," Amber tugs at my arm again. "You two can discuss this later. Come talk to Cathy before she makes herself available to someone else."

A low chuckle rolls out of Shawn's mouth. "You mean like that?" He nods toward the grill.

"Dang it," Ruby stamps her foot. "There goes Travis and his gene pool."

Sam snorts. And if I'm not mistaken, it sounds smug.

Amber drops my hand and sinks to the grass. "Oh well, plenty more fish in the sea."

"Right. So easy to find the one person in the world who makes you feel complete," Sam says softly. Did she mean to say it out loud? She's staring off blankly.

"Meh," Monica says. "I'm pretty sure Travis is living off a trust fund. Can't trust the trust fund babies."

The girls, other than Sam, laugh.

"Is that the type of comments you two made about me before you gave in to my charms?" Shawn asks Monica, jabbing her in the side and making her squirm.

"Your charms?" I smirk. "Dude, she gave in merely to get you off her case."

"Whatever, tall, handsome doctor who loves kids and does charitable acts," Shawn mutters. "We can't all be as awesome as you."

"If I were rating Cole, I would totally mention his good hands," Amber says with side glance at Sam. "He's my brother, so that sounds creepy. I'm strictly talking selling points I could use to get him a date."

"Thanks, I think." This is the most absurd conversation I've been in in a while. "Granted, I don't need you to help me find a date."

"Pshhh. What do you think, Sam? You're his best friend these days. How would you sell him?"

"Me?" Sam blinks, her eyes widening in surprise.

"No." Crap. Why did I stop her? Stupid, stupid, stupid. Is Sam blushing or is it the heat? "I mean, really? You don't have to answer her."

Sam shifts uncomfortably. "I think Shawn covered all the obvious points."

That's it? Tall, handsome doctor? "I seem to recall you once said I was hot," I remind her, lest she forgot.

"You're never going to let me live that down, are you? Don't forget. I also know all of your flaws. Best friend perk."

"He has flaws?" Leave it to my twin siblings to say that in tandem.

"Nope, no flaws. Thank you and goodnight." I jump up from my chair, lightly knocking Brett upside the head and raising a fist to the others in the circle.

Sam grabs my hand and pulls me back down. "Oh, stop. You know if any of the girls in this circle rated you, you'd be a ten."

"But, of course, we can't do that vocally because it'll just give you a bigger ego," Monica teases.

I ignore her jab. "Any of the girls?" I hold Sam's gaze. Does she realize she's still holding my hand?

Sam lifts a brow, her gorgeous eyes shining in the late afternoon sun. She thinks her answer should be obvious to me. She always purses those pink lips of her like this when she thinks I'm being absurd. My own lips twitch in response, but we remain steady, our gazes locked, until shouts of laughter interrupt us.

Sam releases my hand. Her eyes dart to the loud group. My eyes dart to the five other people sitting around the circle with us. Their eyes are locked on Sam and me.

Crap.

21

JUST A GIRL

31ST STREET BACKYARD—JULY 4, 1995

WELL, aren't they having a grand ol' time over there. Relaxing back in my seat, I shift my attention to our group. All are focused on me. And Cole. When I peer at him, I can't decipher what his eyes hold as he stares at me, waiting. Circling back to what happened before we were interrupted, why they're staring, and it clicks.

My heart races. Was I just holding Cole's hand, telling him he's a ten?

Yeah. I was. *Great.* But he has to know he is. It's more than him being an *attractive doctor.* What a cliché. It's the other stuff Shawn said. Him loving children and putting others before himself. It's the fact that, even though he barely knew Amber and Brett, at twenty-five he took custody of them so they could finish their senior year in their home instead of being moved to Florida with their Gram.

If he were anything less than a ten, I wouldn't consider letting him into my life, allowing him to work his way into my heart. Not because I'm too good for him, but because I need his goodness in my life.

"Remind me why you two aren't dating?" Amber asks.

Cole clears his throat. "And I think we've tapped out on the dating topic for the day."

"Fine," Amber rolls to her feet, wiping the dirt and grass from her cut off shorts. "I think I'll go mingle some more. Life's too short not to be kissing all those hotties."

Cole throws a long-suffering glance at Brett. "She'll be the death of us," he sighs.

Brett stretches and drapes his arm along the back of Ruby's chair. "You've never had to live with her."

"Someday Amber is going to find herself a ten," Ruby says, "and after being her only two constants, you guys aren't going to know how to let another man into her life."

"I kind of feel bad for the guy who falls for her. She's a whirlwind." Brett's words seem a little harsh, but the look on his face as his eyes follow after Amber clearly read as protective.

"He won't be able to be a pushover, that's for sure. She'll walk all over him," Cole agrees.

"As strange as this sounds, you two are making me miss Jamie."

"When's he coming to visit?" Monica asks.

"I don't know if he is. We've talked about meeting up somewhere for Thanksgiving, but we'll see."

Cole clucks his tongue in disappointment. "I really need Jamie to come to the city so I can get all of the dirt on teenage Samantha Cooper."

"Sorry to break it to ya, but I was an angel as a teenager. No juicy stories."

If I have anything to say about it, Jamie will keep his mouth shut or Mom will hear all about the weekend in high school when he threw a rager while she was out of town.

"Believe it or not, I'm more interested in hearing all the embarrassing stories you'd rather keep hidden. Like who was hanging on your walls and what your favorite bands were."

"Pshh, that's all you want to know?"

"Please tell me you had Wham! in your cassette player. I need to be able to picture you fawning over George Michael in all his neon glory."

"Of course, I did. What teenage girl didn't? I had Duran Duran and A-ha on my wall, too. Oh man. A-ha. The lead singer in the *Take On Me* video was so hot. And Simon from Duran Duran." I sigh dreamily.

"Oh my gosh, the *Take Me On* music video," Monica swoons.

Brett groans. "You four are so old."

"Old?" Cole scoffs. "I'm seven years older than you."

"You better watch who you're calling old," I say. "I'm only five years older than you."

"Youngsters these days," Shawn mutters, nuzzling Monica's neck. "They listen to all that grunge stuff from Seattle. What do they know?"

Ruby gasps, "Excuse me. West coast girl over here, and I happen to enjoy that grunge stuff. Mighty Mighty Bosstones. No Doubt. Fishbone." She looks around. "Anyone?"

"You like ska?" My excitement blossoms. "Have you heard anything by Stretch Armstrong? They're a small time west coast band."

"No, I haven't. Wait. You like ska, too? Everyone looks at me funny when I play it for them. Brett always changes it."

I smile. "I knew I liked you for a reason, Ruby."

"Oh boy, that's our cue," Cole hisses at Brett and they both stand.

"Time for food?" The brothers look at each other, nod in agreement, and escape.

"I'm surprised it took them this long," Ruby says.

"I assume you want to get some food, too." Monica untangles herself, getting off Shawn's lap.

"Sure, I want food." Shawn stands. He smiles at Monica mischievously and presses his lips against her ear.

"Get a room," I tease.

Shawn grins, wiggling his brow. "If you say so."

Monica nudges him to follow Cole and Brett. He winks at her as he walks away and she smiles back.

When he's out of earshot, I turn to Monica. "You're really serious about him, aren't you?"

"Heaven help me, yeah."

"I mean, I knew you two liked to push each other's buttons, and the attraction has obviously always been there, but you *really* like him."

Monica smiles crookedly and shrugs. "Guilty."

"I'm happy for you, Mon."

"Thanks." Her eyes follow Shawn with a dreamy gaze. "Now if only we could find someone for you."

"I know Amber asked this and essentially got booed out of here, but now that the boys are gone, can I ask why you and Cole aren't dating?" Ruby asks.

Monica settles into her chair with a satisfied grin on her face, but keeps her mouth shut.

"Umm..." How do I answer this?

"You guys." I look up at an excited Amber rushing our way. I've never been more grateful to see a person. "Guys. Did you know that Antonio is a firefighter? An honest to goodness New York City firefighter." She falls into the seat vacated by Cole as she fans herself.

"Oh, yeah," Monica says, "but he has a major foot fetish."

"You say that like it's a bad thing."

My laughter bubbles over. "If your brothers only knew..."

"Speaking of, where are they? Antonio is going to take me to his precinct and show me around the station."

Oh my gosh. Cole would die. "I bet he is. They went to grab some food."

Amber's face lights up. She's totally thinking of sneaking away from the party without letting them know. "Don't even think about it. They'll kill you. And I can't promise to keep my mouth shut." My loyalty is to Cole, not his not-so-innocent little sister.

Amber eyes me. "I won't leave until they come back."

Ruby gets up and mumbles something about telling Brett not to come back until after Cole does.

"I'm getting hungry. I'm gonna go get something." Monica sneaks away, too.

"Wow, are they really that worried about Brett and Cole making a scene? I'm twenty, not sixteen."

"From one younger sister to another, it doesn't matter how old you are. They'll never stop worrying about you. I'm twenty-five, and my brother would still clock any man who looked at me wrong."

Uncertainty clouds Amber's face. "Can I ask you something?"

Uh oh. I want a good relationship with Amber, but if she asks me anything that will compromise my friendship with her brother, I don't know what I'll do. "Sure."

"Do you care about him?" She looks so innocent. Please, no more Cole questions. I sigh heavily. It's impossible to hold it back.

"I'm not trying to grill you about dating him. I'm asking in general. Do you care about him?"

I can only answer honestly. No matter how she takes my answer. "Absolutely. He's one of my best friends."

Amber smiles, then exhales. "I dropped out of school."

Well, crap. "Do your brothers know?"

"Uh, yeah. No." The way her eyes search the party is enough of an answer. She's dreading that conversation. I quickly decide that this doesn't affect her safety, so I will not be the one to drop that bomb.

"What are you going to do?"

"Besides the money from our parents' insurance and estate, Brett and I inherited some money from our grandfather when we turned eighteen. It's not a ton, but it's enough to live off of for a

173

while." She bows her head, her fingers tugging on the frayed edges of her shorts. "I kind of bought a one-way ticket—"

I wait for a moment, expecting her to finish her sentence. It's clear she's too nervous to continue. "For?"

"Europe."

"*Europe*?" I gasp, and clasp my hand over my mouth, looking around. I didn't mean to say that so loud.

"It's crazy, right?" She blows out a quick breath. "I know it is, or it seems like it is. But it's not. Not for me."

"What will you do in Europe?"

"What any twenty-year-old girl does in Europe." Amber shrugs as though my question is ridiculous. "I'll live life."

I see where she's coming from. Who wouldn't want to be able to drop everything and travel around Europe? I'd kill to be able to do that. But I can't help thinking about the logical side. A beautiful, twenty-something-year-old girl traveling around Europe by herself. That's not safe.

Cole and Brett are going to flip out. I do *not* want to be around when she breaks the news to them.

"Why are you telling me all of this? Shouldn't you be telling your brothers? You're going to tell your brothers, right?"

Amber tugs at her ponytail, pulling a long strand of her blonde hair around her finger and twirling it. "Yeah, I will."

"Oh, thank goodness. Okay. I mean, I appreciate the trust you're putting in me, Amber, but I assume there's a reason you came to me first."

"There is." She bobs her head. "Brett is going to get all worked up over this, but ultimately he'll understand my reasons because we know each other so well. He knows me. Plus, he has Ruby. She stabilizes him whenever he considers falling off the deep end. Not that he does very often."

"Cole, though," she says. There's such weight in those two words. "He's going to be hurt. He's a fixer. He's tried so hard to be what I lost. They both have." Amber blinks a few times, clearing her throat.

"I get it," I breathe. I think Cole has tried to do the same thing for me without even realizing it. No matter how many times I shut down, he's been there.

"I kinda knew you would." The troublemaker light in her eyes returns.

"You won't have to worry about Cole."

"I'd like to tell you to hurry up and go out with Cole because you two are ridiculously perfect for each other, but I'm not going to." She inhales and continues, "I think you need to figure out what you need just as much as I do. So I'll tell you to move forward."

I open my mouth to respond, but Amber raises a hand and stops me.

"You don't have to tell me it's none of my business. I won't listen to you and I'll butt in anyway." She smiles.

I laugh. "I wasn't going to. I was actually going to say, between you and me, I think I'm ready to move forward."

"Really?" Amber lights up, clapping her hands. Gosh, she reminds me of a cheerleader, the way she gets all excited and bouncy over something so simple.

"I can't say who I'm ready to move forward with, because I don't even know—"

"No. I know, I know. It doesn't even matter who you date. You should just date. Cole says so many wonderful things about you. I'd hate to think you're sitting around because you lost Paul. I hope that doesn't sound wrong."

"Not at all." I smile graciously. "I know you mean well."

"My brothers love you, you know. So does Ruby. Besides my gram, they are the most important people in the world to me."

Having them in my life has become such a normal thing. We've kind of created our own little makeshift family in the city.

A bunch of transplants who found each other and created a home.

"I love them, too. And I know I don't know you well, Amber, but as much as the three of them talk about you, I feel like I do. I hope you know how much you're loved."

"Oh, I know. Believe me, I know. That's exactly why I wanted to talk to you first. As much as Brett and Cole think they're the ones who are the fixers in this family, I'm a fixer too. Just ask Brett and Ruby how they worked things out." Amber points to her chest. "I'm asking you to help me with Cole. Will you help talk him out of locking me up after I tell him?"

"I've got your back."

"And you'll have his, too? If you thought he worried about me when I was just five hours away and starting college—"

I don't know how I'll help him, because he's not going to be happy about this, but I assure her, "I'll do my best."

"What are you two huddled up talking about?"

My eyes dart up to Cole hovering behind us. How long has he been there? Amber nonchalantly crosses her arms over her chest. "Girl stuff. Actually, I was waiting on you. I'm going to go out with Antonio."

"Antoni-who?"

"You don't want to know," I warn. "Just say, 'Have fun, Amber.' "

Cole flicks his gaze between the two of us. "Um, okay. Have fun, Amber."

Amber pops up from her seat and hugs me tightly. "Thank you," she whispers. "For everything." She pulls back and gives Cole a kiss on his cheek. "Love you."

"Hey, Am," he calls after her as she walks toward Antonio. "Remember I know a lot of cops. Warn him."

"Monica knows where he lives," I tell him, though we'll keep the foot fetish between us girls. Cole doesn't need to know that.

· · ·

"You forgot the other chair?" Monica scolds Shawn.

"I thought you had it, woman. I could only carry so many chairs."

"You could've at least told me so I could've grabbed it. Now one of us is going to have to sit on the damp grass and it's not going to be me."

They're starting to sound like an old married couple already. Or I guess this is how they've always sounded.

We only have a small patch of grass to work with in this crowd of people waiting for the fireworks to start. Two chairs in a row and one lone chair behind them.

Cole plops down in the lone lawn chair. "It's fine." He grabs me by the waist and pulls me into his lap. "We'll share."

Is it just me, or does Cole like having me in his lap?

"That won't be comfortable for long," Shawn snickers, and Monica elbows him. He looks at her, not understanding why what he said wrong. He's not wrong. My toes barely touch the ground and I'm trying very hard not to put all my weight on Cole.

"We'll be fine." Cole's warm breath runs along the curve of my neck. I suppress a shiver.

Should I protest and make Shawn and Monica share a seat? That would make more sense. They *are* the couple. Except, I don't want to protest. If Cole doesn't mind, I don't mind.

"If my boney butt bothers you I'll happily take the grass."

"You're not going anywhere." His arms tighten around my waist, encouraging me to get comfortable against him.

The fireworks don't start for another five minutes. I could stand until then. I should.

But I don't want to.

I'm tip-toeing a very thin line. The more time I spend with Cole, the fuzzier the line becomes. If I'm not careful, the line is going to disappear and I won't be able to catch myself. My heart doesn't come with a safety net.

It's exhausting denying what my heart wants, but how could I live with myself? What have I done to deserve him?

Nothing.

Cole really is the perfect ten. Forget the obvious stability and good looks. The man brings a sense of comfort to our friendship. He never makes me question whether I can count on him or trust him. Those go without saying. He handles my heart with care in all things. My memories of Paul, my ambitions, my passions. Not to mention, he can match my competitive streak and up the ante.

What have I done? Letting someone as perfect as Cole weave so effortlessly into my life.

As subtly as I can, I shift on his lap. Shawn was so right. This is not comfortable. Maybe if I just...

I scoot down a little on Cole's lap, planting my feet flat on the ground, reclining against his chest.

"That's better." He sits his chin on my shoulder, nestling his cheek into the crook of my neck. His five o'clock shadow tickles my skin and I can't subdue my shiver. His arms fall away from my waist and rest on the plastic armrests.

I laugh and shrug away from his jaw. "Why didn't you say something before?"

"Because you would've moved."

"You can't be any more comfortable than I am." I peer over my shoulder.

"It might not be the recliner, but it's good enough." *Boom!* I jump. "Shhh ... the fireworks are starting."

"You need quiet for the fireworks show?"

The low rumble of his laugh does something to me. *You cannot kiss him, Samantha.*

Patriotic music amplifies throughout the park. Around us, murmured exclamations of awe carry across the gathering. It's fun to hear everyone point out their favorites. Somehow fireworks bring everyone together. Who doesn't love a good fireworks show?

Cole's chin moves back and forth over the top of my bare shoulder. Another shiver works its way up my spine thanks to his stubble. He stops abruptly. He must have had an itch. I refocus on the flashes of color lighting up the sky. A moment later, his chin moves again. This time he lightly skims across my skin from the curve of my shoulder to the base of my neck. His cheek touches against my neck before he switches direction and moves the other way. My insides flip. What is he doing?

His hands, firmly planted on the armrests of the chair, slide to my waist. My breath catches when he loops his index fingers through the belt loops of my jean shorts as his hands splay wide, gripping me tightly.

Holy crap. I'm thinking thoughts. Thoughts I shouldn't have. These are not friendly touches I can explain away as getting comfortable to watch the fireworks. I can hardly breathe.

A machine gun explosion of crackles echoes around us as Cole's lips touch my back. He inhales. His lips so close to my skin, the intake of breath rolls across.

It's not cold outside, but goosebumps spread across my skin. He pulls away, the loss of his heat making my skin feel cold by comparison.

"I'm trying really hard, Sam." His broken whisper tickles my ear. "I'm trying to respect our friendship, but—" His right hand slips from my waist and crosses my chest, gripping the opposite side of my neck. "I'm failing."

He's failing? If this is what failing feels like I don't know if I can handle winning. Though, I'm losing my self-control. After that night in the recliner. Our moment in the kitchen. The night on the dance floor at The Roof crashes into me. My head screams to tell Cole 'no,' to take control of the situation and get off of his lap to sit on the grass, but every other part of me says to let it happen. Let. Go.

His mouth closes on my neck. His tongue touches my skin and lingers for one agonizingly hot moment before he pulls away again. The pounding of my blood and the fireworks are all I hear. If Cole exhales, I have no idea. If he speaks, I don't hear it. My hands grip the side of his thighs, holding myself steady for fear that I might melt onto the ground.

His forehead presses against my back and his hand falls from my neck. Warm air flutters across my skin as he exhales. His hands return to my hips and squeeze once before falling away from my body.

He's stopping? Wait, isn't that what I want? No. Definitely not what I want, but it's what I need.

"I'm sorry."

The words are so faint I barely hear them over the noise around us, but they're his. They're coming from his lips because they skim my back as he speaks.

He curses and shifts beneath me.

Am I supposed to accept his apology? Should I tell him, "Apology not accepted," and turn around to finish what he started? My fists clench, my nails digging into my palms to control myself.

His head lifts from my back and he's on my neck again. His lips press a long kiss under my ear before he touches the tip of my earlobe. Only it's not a kiss. That spot. Nothing makes any sense with his mouth on that spot. He presses his mouth to my ear, holding it, breathing shallow for a few beats.

"I'm sorry. We're friends. I know that. I know we can't do this. I know it, I do."

Is he trying to convince himself or me? I may need more convincing. My rational thought exploded with the first firework. I release a shaky breath.

"What?" I murmur, needing him to explain what happened here. I wasn't stopping him. Did I not encourage him enough?

"You said we're not right." His face nuzzles into my neck again and he growls. "Stupid Amber."

I said that?

I said that. At The Roof. I close my eyes and focus on my heartbeat, steadying my breathing to something marginally normal. He's right. We can't do this. We are friends. I've made sure that's all we'd ever be. We've spent all this time building something worth protecting. And that friendship is all I can hope to deserve. I need to be grateful for only that.

Cole clears his throat and sits back while pushing me forward to the edge of his lap. The maneuver puts space between my back and his chest. I swallow hard and turn my cheek, looking over my shoulder at his shadowed face, partially covered by one of his hands.

He shakes his head. "I'm sorry. I shouldn't have done that." The words are drowned out by the grand finale of fireworks popping all over the sky.

"Stop." I place my hand on his chest and pull his hand away from his face with my other. "Don't apologize. It's fine."

As we stand, folding out chairs and gathering our things, Cole's hand takes mine. "Can we blame it on the heat and the alcohol?" His eyes plead for reprieve.

I'm not stupid. He's hardly had a drink in hours. "I don't even know what you're talking about." Though I know I'll never forget it, I offer him an oblivious smile.

I don't want there to be any awkwardness between us. If his friendship is all I get to have, I will do everything in my power to protect it.

22

STRONG ENOUGH

BOWERY BAR—AUGUST 11, 1995

"So, you wanna head back to my place?"

Does he really think things are going that well? "You know, I've got an early morning tomorrow. I think I'm going to head home."

Rodney moves in, closer than is comfortable. "I'd be happy to ride home with you, so you don't have to travel alone."

No, no. "That's really not necessary."

"You sure?" He closes the gap between us and lowers his voice, "I'd make it worth your while."

Can this date get any worse? Forcing a smile, I take a subtle step back. Run. Don't look back. He's not worth it. "I'm sure you would, Rodney. I'll have to pass, though." Stupid manners.

He works his jaw and cocks his head to the side. "Your loss."

I very much disagree. Very. *Very* much. "Thanks for—" I can't really say dinner. "Thanks for the night out."

"We should do it again soon."

Not if he were the last man on earth. "You know, Rodney, I'm gonna have to say thanks, but no thanks."

BELLEVUE HOSPITAL

Disinfectant and antiseptic waft toward me, tickling my nose as the automatic hospital doors slide open. I spot the front desk in the ER and smile, grateful for a familiar face. "Robin, hi."

"Hey, Samantha. You're here late. Are you here to see Dr. Rossner?"

"If he's not busy. I'll just wait in the waiting room if you could page him whenever you have a minute."

"You came on a good night. It's been pretty slow. I'll page him right now."

"Thanks, Robin." I smile as she picks up the phone.

A few minutes later, the double doors push open and Cole walks through in his green scrubs and his stethoscope hanging around his neck. It never gets old seeing him like this. Something about those scrubs and the air of confidence he exudes in his element.

"Hey, you look nice." He smiles warmly. "What are you doing here?"

"You get off at ten, right?"

"Yeah, why?"

"You wanna grab the train back together?"

He checks his watch. "Uh, you don't mind waiting a couple hours?"

"No, after the night I've had, I could use a couple hours to relax. I don't want to ride home alone."

"I can take a break right now. You wanna come with me and grab a bite at the cafe real quick? You can tell me all about your night."

How do I breach this topic? How is he going to react? Whatever. It shouldn't matter.

"I went on a date."

Cole pushes through the double doors. "I'm sorry, did you

just say you went on a date? With who?"

"Erica, one of the regulars at the studio, set me up with her older brother. She's been telling me about Rodney for like a year now, and she caught me on a good day. If only I'd said no."

"That doesn't sound promising."

"Oh my gosh, Cole." How can I not laugh? "It was so bad."

"Do you want something?" We enter the cafe, his hand settling on the small of my back.

"No, thanks. I just ate."

"Right. Date." He shakes his head, the muscle in his jaw flexing. "Why don't you get us a table and I'll grab a club and coffee. Would you believe I didn't eat earlier? Might as well have something since we're slow."

"You got it."

"Okay." Cole takes a seat across from me at the corner table I chose. "Tell me about this date."

He makes 'date' sound like a death sentence, which in all honesty it kind of was. Taking a deep breath, I settle into my seat. "Okay. So, since Rodney lives in Tribeca I agreed to meet him in the city, that way he wouldn't have to come all the way to Queens. We met at the Bowery Bar. Have you ever been?"

Cole nods.

"It's pretty good, so we were already starting on a high note. Until I arrived. You know how guys will sometimes bring a girl flowers or chocolates before a date?"

He nods again, his brow arched and his mouth curved up on one side, clearly amused.

"He brought me a Beanie Baby. I realize those are a fad right now, but c'mon. Do I look twelve?"

Cole coughs, slapping his chest as his face turns red. "Crap, warn me next time," he chokes out, grabbing his water and taking a long sip. "Please tell me you're joking."

"I wish I was. He said with how much people are collecting them now, they'll be worth a fortune someday, so I should thank him." I take a second to breathe my frustration. A humorless laugh escapes my throat. "The entire dinner all he wanted to talk about was himself, which you know, I was kind of okay with, but there was hardly any room for me at the table because his ego nearly took up the entire booth."

"Well, that's not surprising. Guys like to talk themselves up, especially when they're out with a gorgeous, successful woman. Was he a lawyer? They have huge egos."

Gorgeous, successful woman? I can't answer him right away. What was Rodney's job? Cole thinks I'm gorgeous.

"Um, he's in some sort of sales. Insurance or commercial real estate. I'll be honest, I stopped listening after he told me he spent five-thousand dollars on his watch. But, get this, he tried to pay for dinner with three different credit cards. Every single one of them was declined. I was so embarrassed for him until he didn't seem the least bit concerned. And he didn't bring any cash with him, so he asked me to pay and said he'd fork over the bill next time. I'm sorry, next time?"

Cole chuckles, though he's clearly not amused anymore. "And the girl who set you up actually likes you? Are you sure?"

Right? I laugh. "*That's* not even the worst part. He then proceeded to pick his teeth at the table with a golf tee he found in the front pocket of his khakis."

"And there goes my appetite." Cole pushes his mostly eaten salad away. "This sounds like an episode of that old show— What's it called? The one where they film people doing stupid things and practical jokes. Mom loves watching the specials they air." He snaps his fingers as he looks into space thinking. "*Candid Camera*. Dude, it had to be a fake date."

"It might as well have been *Candid Camera*. I thought dates like this were exaggerations in movies. Rodney tried convincing me to go home with him. When I declined, he tried coming home with me. Told me he'd make it worth my while." I cringe, shaking the memory away. "I don't know why I agreed to go on this date."

"Why did you?" he asks after a moment of silence. "I mean, why'd you pick some stranger to be the first date?"

My hands run down my face. "I don't know." I groan. "I guess I thought the pressure would be off if it was a blind date, someone I didn't know. He wouldn't expect more from me than one date. I couldn't handle all the choices Monica has been throwing at me. And Erica is nice. I figured with the way she talks about her brother, he had to be decent enough to test the waters. All it did was make me want to hunker down in my apartment forever."

"Monica's been throwing choices at you?" The tic in his jaw starts back up again. "I thought after the Fourth you'd nixed the idea. Why didn't you tell me?"

"Because ... I don't know. The date was set up yesterday. I didn't think about it." Lies, lies, lies. "I never nixed the idea completely. I just didn't want Monica and Ruby to be the ones to make the choice for me."

Cole leans back in the booth. "What about me?"

Blood drains from my face, and what happened to my heartbeats? Did they stop? Oh gosh, I don't have a heartbeat anymore.

"I mean, I know a lot of single doctors here. I get you didn't trust Monica and Ruby, but you can trust me. I wouldn't let you go out with some teeth-picking punk who can't remember his wallet."

"You would want to set me up on a date with one of the other doctors at this hospital?" I don't believe that for once second.

"Uh, sure." Cole shrugs, his eyes looking everywhere but at me. He's full of it.

"Okay," I call his bluff. "If you can promise he'll be better than Rodney, which won't be difficult, I'll think about it."

Beep, beep, beep.

"Well, shoot, we'll have to finish this conversation later." Cole gives me a frown, then winks. He shifts in the booth, glancing down at the pager he wears almost constantly, whether on shift or not.

He inhales sharply, "Code blue? Oh, no." He slides out of the booth quickly. "I've got to run. Sorry. Are you—"

"I'll hang out and wait for you to get off. Go." I shoo him off. "You're needed."

———

I haven't seen Cole since he left the cafe. Normally, he'd at least show his face to come get another patient, or bring a chart to the front desk. I look at the clock by the TV. It's 10:30. He should've been done by now.

I approach Robin, who's been all over the place since I sat back down to wait. It's supposed to be a slow night. "Hey, Dr. Rossner was supposed to get off at 10:00. Do you know what's going on?"

Tears well up in Robin's eyes. "He had a code blue."

"Yeah, he mentioned that." I know it can't be good, but that was almost two hours ago. "What is that?"

"Cardiac arrest."

My heart clenches. "Did he lose a patient?"

Robin nods. "Let me take you to him."

23

I'LL STAND BY YOU

BELLEVUE HOSPITAL--AUGUST 11, 1995

TWO LIGHT KNOCKS sound on the door.

"I need a few more minutes."

The door cracks open, letting a strip of fluorescent light shine into the dimly lit room. I should have locked it. I swing my legs from the bed and sit up, squinting.

"It's me."

Sam? How long has she been waiting on me? What time is it? I tear my gaze away from the drab grey wall that typically puts me to sleep within five minutes when I'm in here and focus on the door.

"May I come in?" She peeks in through the crack. The subdued sadness of her voice tells me she knows what she's walking into.

"Her mother wanted me to have him," I explain, holding up my left hand.

Cole the Lion. My fingers dig into his shaggy mane; his little stuffed body is barely larger than my palm.

Sam's eyes droop and she closes the door behind her. Her soft footfalls approach me.

"I lose patients, Sam. I'm a doctor, it's not uncommon. We

saw it coming. Her heart kept deteriorating and there aren't nearly enough people on donor lists in this country to cover the need. You don't give up hope, but as a doctor you know how to face the facts."

The mattress squeaks, dipping as she sits beside me. Her hand rests on my back. "Just because you saw it coming doesn't make it any easier. It's okay to feel the loss, Cole."

"Why does this one hit me so hard? Why do I feel so empty?"

Her breathing comes out shaky, like she's fighting tears. "She was important to you. You cared about her. Took care of her on a regular basis. I would wonder why if it didn't impact you."

"She was ten. It was senseless. She got sick, then she died four years later of heart failure. What is that? You get on a plane for a vacation, and you crash and die. Senseless. All my knowledge, all my training—" I yank my hair, wanting to pull every strand out of my head in frustration. "What's the point? I couldn't save her. I couldn't save my dad. I couldn't do anything."

Sam's hand curls around my shoulder, tugging me closer, and she sniffles. "No one could've saved your dad, Cole. You can't blame yourself for that. Is that what you've been doing all of these years?" Her voice cracks. "There's not enough medical training in the world to save the people on that plane."

"I couldn't mourn him. I didn't have time." Why? Why is this coming out now? My eyes land on Sam's hand resting on my thigh. The heat of her arm around my shoulder seeps through my scrubs. Her touch spurs me to speak. To confide. To confess.

"There I was, being told of the plane crash. Being told my father has died and all I could see were Brett and Amber's faces. I lost a man I barely knew. They lost both their parents. Their mom *and* their dad.

"Do you have any idea what that felt like? The teenage siblings I'd only had a few dinners with over the course of their entire lives had become orphans in one moment. I pushed any sadness I had away because who was I to feel something like that?

Not when they were facing what they were. Not when all those other families were facing their losses. Not when you were mourning Paul."

Her tears fall onto my arm. "You had every right to grieve. Just because someone's loss seems bigger than yours doesn't mean your loss is any less significant. Your pain is not irrelevant. Grief is grief."

"I could have grieved, you're right." I nod, taking her hand in mine and squeezing it tightly. "I hate myself, Sam. I threw away six years. It wasn't his fault he wasn't in my life. My mom made that choice. I shouldn't have blamed him for having a family, but I did." I'm dumping every ounce of the crap that is my family on her, but I can't stop.

"Do you remember when I told you I hated him? I hated him so much that I gave him two dinners then cut him off?"

She's silent as she nods against my shoulder.

"I pretended I didn't have a father through the rest of high school. I went on with life as though he'd never shown up. Then I ignored his requests to get to know me after I turned eighteen. I was so stupid. I didn't know I wouldn't have another thirty years to get to know him."

"Cole, you couldn't have known," she whispers.

"I applied and did my internship at his hospital in Allentown so I could get to know him. I got two years, but it wasn't enough." My throat tightens. "It wasn't enough, Sam."

Sam slides off the bed. A low sob releasing from her own lips as she stands before me. My hands reach for her hips, pulling her between my legs as I press my face against her chest. Her arms go around my back, and I let the tears I should have shed three years ago come. She lets me. She holds me, her head resting atop mine, her hands rubbing across my back as she soothes and shushes me. Her soft voice murmuring little phrases of commiseration.

"Of course it wasn't enough time." Her fingers thread

through the hair on the back of my head. "I'm so sorry, Cole," she sniffles, her arms tightening. "I'm so sorry."

Waves of emotion overwhelm me. Anger at Celia's loss, anger at mine. At my father, at a pilot, at a mechanic who might have missed something crucial that could have saved 397. Everything pours out and into Sam's chest.

The pain crescendos into one resounding thought: I can't do this. I can't lie to myself anymore. I drag myself away from her embrace, sitting back as my hands move up, cupping her face. She stops murmuring as we stare at one another.

"I can't." My thumbs wipe at the moisture on her cheeks as I catch my breath.

"You can't? You can't what?" Her voice is barely above a whisper.

The weight of years of not mourning lifting as clarity shines through. I know what I need. What I want. "I can't set you up with some doctor. I don't want to. I'm not going to." I count my heartbeats waiting for Sam's reply.

"Why?"

"You have to ask why?"

"I need to hear you say it."

"Words won't be enough." Her eyes flare as I pull her face to mine, my lips covering hers. My mouth sighs into Sam's. Her body sinks into mine. No words necessary here.

She whimpers against my lips and I smile. My hands release her face, trailing down her spine and holding her tightly as I stand, never letting our lips part. The way her entire body presses against mine just about sends me to my knees.

"And now you know why there's no way I'm setting you up with anyone else," I point out.

"And now you know why I didn't tell you I was going on that stupid date," she counters.

"Because you're hot for me?"

"What gave it away? Was it the kiss? Dang it, I knew I

should've held back." She tilts her head, a sweet smile playing on her lips.

Man, how have I managed to hold myself back since our first kiss? "So, about that whole hunkering down in your apartment forever."

"I think I can make a few appearances."

"Think you'd consider trying to date again?"

Sam taps her lips. "Hmm..."

"Let me rephrase that." I pull her arms from around my neck and take her hands. "Go out with me, Sam?"

"Okay," she breathes, smiling wide.

"Okay?"

"Do you need more enthusiasm?" She brings her hands to my face, and her fingertips stroke the stubble on my jaw, her mouth nearly touching mine as she says, "yes."

"Come back to my place tonight." The words pop out before I can stop them. "I mean, not for—I just don't want to let you go. Not yet. I'm feeling all kinds of burned out right now, and I'm afraid if you go back to your place, this—"

She stops me with another kiss. "Let's go."

N TRAIN

THANK THE LORD FOR EMPTY TRAINS AND HOT CHICKS. My hands can't be tamed. The moment the train doors close, I pull Sam into my lap and attack her lips. Her hair, which was so perfectly styled for her date earlier, is a wreck thanks to me. How is she feeling right now? If it's half as good as I feel, I'd say she's about to explode. My tongue traces the length of her slim neck, and then my lips replace the moisture with kisses. Man, she smells so good, her skin tastes so good.

"Do you know how hard it's been to resist kissing these lips since Monica's party? How badly I wanted to kiss you since the day we met?" My mouth drags across her cheek and finds her lips once again.

Her breathing is shaky when she says, "In the beginning? Yeah, it was a bit obvious." She smirks against my mouth. "But not again until recently, right?"

"Sam, I walked away from you at the memorial cursing myself for not getting your name, and there hasn't been a day since then when I haven't wanted you. All you had to do was say yes."

She looks like she's going to cry. "I didn't know."

I tug on her hair lightly and frown.

"Well, after the party I had a clue," she clarifies.

"You play some serious hard ball, Samantha Cooper." I press a kiss against her neck, sucking her skin between my teeth until she shakes me away with a laugh. "Admit it, you hated me in the beginning."

Her head shakes. "I've never hated you, Cole. If anything, you scared me. That's why things went so wrong that night. Why I pushed you away. There's always been something about you that felt like home." She holds my gaze, peering at me with her piercing hazel eyes. "Our meeting was poor timing. I wasn't ready. That's all it was."

I love her. Period. I've loved her for months. She doesn't feel like home, she is home. I won't tell her yet, though. She's not ready.

"Isn't there some saying about people meeting at the wrong time and letting fate work it out?"

"If not, it's sounds right." She smiles.

I cover her smile with my mouth once again. Her fingers grip my hair, pulling my head whichever way she wants as our kisses go on and on. My mind wanders places it shouldn't when we're in public. She's driving me crazy and all we're doing is kissing.

"Just so we're clear," I ask between kisses. "You're ready now, right? Because I'm so beyond ready."

Her laughter is mumbled under her breath. "Cole. I don't know how else to show you I'm ready for this, for you. I never took you for someone so insecure."

"Oh, Supergirl, I assure you I am not insecure." My hand sneaks under her shirt. The pad of my thumb caressing its way up her ribcage until I'm toying with the elastic band of her bra. Teasing her. "I'm very, very secure in my abilities."

She sucks in a breath as my thumb slips beneath a gap between her skin and the material at her breast bone. I linger for one moment, loving the way her riotous heart pounds at my touch, then retreat. "I'd be happy to show you if you're not sure."

Sam playfully knocks me in the chest. "Your abilities were never called into question, but thank you for the clarification." She bites my bottom lip, sucking it into her mouth.

Drawing her as close as physically possible, I devour her. Taking everything she's willing to give me. Finally.

This is the longest train ride ever. The two-block walk to my apartment is the longest walk ever. The rest of the night, however...

24

I LIKE IT, I LOVE IT

COLE'S PLACE--AUGUST 12, 1995

FALLING to the bed in a sweaty, exhausted heap, I release a gratified exhale.

I can't believe that just happened.

Clamping a hand over my mouth, I stifle a laugh. My skin tingles, a lingering reaction of Cole's effect on my body.

He rolls to his side and wraps his arm over my waist, pulling me close.

"Wow. We... I guess—" Cole falters, a charming grin twisting his lips. His face flushed, his hair damp.

Sucking on my bottom lip to curb my smile, I tuck my chin to my chest. I have no idea what to say right now. I can't meet his eyes. That was unexpected in the most satisfying way possible. And all I want is to do it again.

"I think it's safe to say I've lost the bet on being able to remain just friends with you." He draws little swirls along my hip and across my lower back.

"So, does that mean I win?"

"I'd say you just did." His voice drops an octave as his body scoots closer, the ridges of his body caressing my sensitive skin.

I shake my head into his chest, biting back a grin. "Nope, definitely not insecure."

Cole laughs as he rolls on top of me and buries his face in my hair, inhaling deeply. "I wondered if I was ever going to be able to do this." His lips and sigh brush against the sensitive skin behind my ear.

A shiver rolls down my spine and I tilt my head to give him better access. "I'd be lying if I said it never crossed my mind," I whisper shakily.

"Yeah? Are you saying you thought about us?" He nips at my earlobe, sucking it between his plump lips. "Like this?" His tongue traces the outline of my ear and my eyes flutter closed.

"Maybe once or twice." My breath quivers on my exhale. I equally need my space and never want him to stop. So many emotions shred through me. No one has ever touched me this way, except for Paul.

Cole's head pops up, leaving my skin wanting. "Only once or twice?" He frowns, propping himself up on his elbows.

"Aww, that's cute. You thought I was serious."

"I'm serious right now."

He wants serious Sam. Can I be that for him? I can't even process the idea of whether this should've happened. "More times than I'm willing to admit, and that's all you're getting out of me, mister." I thump his chest with my pointer finger. *Stop being so awkward, Samantha.*

His smile fades, his eyes pierce mine. What did I say wrong?

"I don't know exactly what this was tonight, but I want you to know it isn't a one-night stand." His eyes delve into mine like he's attempting to read my thoughts. "You know that, right? I don't do that. I'm not that kind of guy, and even if I was, you would never be one. Our friendship is too important to me."

What friendship? Didn't we just smash that to smithereens? If this doesn't work out, we'll never be able to go back. Oh gosh, what did we do? We shouldn't have—

"Sam?" He kisses the corner of my mouth.

—but, I love the way his lips feel. "I know, Cole. It's important to me, too."

———

I JOLT AWAKE. WHAT IS RINGING? I SEARCH FOR MY ALARM clock, aiming to hit the snooze button. My hand connects with a warm body. Startled, I look over to the right side of the bed. Cole. I'm at Cole's house. Oh, crap, I'm at Cole's house!

"Cole." I nudge him. He grunts and blindly reaches for the phone on his nightstand. I squint at the time on his alarm clock. 3AM? "Who is calling this late?"

"Hello?" he answers drowsily.

A frantic female voice shouts on the other end, but I can't tell what she's saying. What if it's Amber? Oh gosh, I hope everything is okay.

He clears his throat and rolls over to me. "Monica," he tries to interrupt her. "Monica," he says louder.

Monica? Shoot! I didn't tell her I wasn't coming home. More freaking out spews from the phone. She's probably worried sick and I won't hear the end of it.

"Here. She's right here."

"What!" I hear *that* loud and clear.

Cole looks apologetically at me. "It's for you." He hands over the portable phone. Instead of rolling away, he snuggles closer, his lips touching my bare shoulder as he chuckles. "I can't believe you forgot to tell your warden you were sleeping over."

Because I didn't realize I was going to sleep over. When did we fall asleep? Taking a deep breath, I put the phone to my ear. "Hey, Mon."

"Why didn't you tell me you weren't coming home? You went on that blind date. I don't hear from you all night. I thought you were dead in a dark alley, and now you're at

Cole's? Wait. What are you doing at Cole's at three in the morning?"

I don't want to have this conversation while I'm half-asleep, nor do I want to have it in front of Cole.

"I know. I'm sorry, Mon. The date went horribly. I stopped by the hospital afterward to take the subway home with Cole. I should've called to let you know I wasn't coming home."

"But why aren't you coming home?" She pauses. "Oh my gosh. Samantha Lynn Cooper! Did you...?"

"I'm gonna go now. I'll see you tomorrow."

"What? No. You can't leave me hanging. If you don't tell me, I'll imagine all kinds of things."

"Goodbye, Monica." Hitting end, I hand the phone back to Cole and drag my fingers through my hair. I groan. "That's going to be a fun one to explain in the morning."

"Can I come with you? I want to see her eyes bug out." Cole pulls me toward him and I flip over to my side, facing away. He looks so hot all half-asleep, his hair ruffled. I can't think straight. His body curves around my back as his arm snakes around my waist. He breathes in and presses a kiss to my neck. "It could be worse. You could have to deal with Shawn."

COLE SNEAKS UP BEHIND ME AND LATHERS MY JAWLINE with kisses before he sits down across from me at his kitchen table. His hands run across my shoulders as though he still can't get enough. "Thank you for last night."

How am I supposed to respond to that? Which part exactly is he referring?

"At the hospital," he clarifies as though he knows what I'm thinking. Is my face giving me away? "I—" He takes a sip of the coffee he poured himself. "I don't know what came over me. It's like everything sort of came to a head."

"Cole, you don't have to thank me for anything." I reach

across the table and take his hand. "I'm glad I was there. I know losing that patient wasn't easy. And I wish I'd known you were carrying around all that guilt. Guilt that never should've been."

"You wish you'd known? *I* didn't even know." His shoulders curve inward as he hunches over his mug. "Before you, I ignored my loss most of the time. I focused on work and Brett and Am..." he trails off.

"So, I remind you of your loss?" Where is he going with this?

He throws his head back and laughs. "And here I go putting my foot in my mouth again. No. No, you don't remind me of loss. You..." He inhales through his nose, closing his eyes. "You remind me of home. When I heard your voice last night I had this urge to let it all go. You do that to me. You make me want to share everything. I've never felt that way before."

My heart pounds against my chest. Is he going to say something I'm not ready to hear, something I'm not ready to say back yet? Please wait, Cole.

I pull my hand back. "Tell me about your dad. What was he like?"

Cole straightens, his eyes regard me with silent questions. He takes another sip of his coffee and smiles. I'm redirecting and he doesn't understand why.

"Smart." He sits back in his chair. "He was an amazing doctor. I was extremely lucky to be able to learn under him, son or not."

I curl my fingers around my mug and bring it to my lips.

"He liked classic rock and James Bond movies. He was a lot like Brett—he loved the outdoors—but also a lot like Amber. He was brash and confident the way she is. It's what made him a good doctor. He once got into a patient care argument with a premiere surgeon ten years his senior, and when most doctors would have caved in, he didn't. He held his ground and in the end the diagnosis he made was the right one."

"He's sounds pretty amazing." I peer over my mug. "He sounds a lot like someone I know."

"I hope to do him proud. It's why I work so hard, why I studied my butt off in college and gave up all the parties and most of the dating after my first two years. At first, it was to prove myself to him, to make him kick himself for not being around me while I was growing up. Then, once I met with him again before medical school, I wanted to be just like him. Since the crash it's become my goal to continue his legacy."

The microwave beeps and Cole stands.

"I'm starving." He pulls bacon from the platter in the microwave and stacks it on a paper plate. "You know, I've been considering changing my name to Pratt."

"I think that would be a great way to honor him. How would your mom feel about that?"

"She knows. She doesn't hate him or anything. She blames herself for keeping me a secret for all of those years. She said if I choose to change it she will support me."

He plops the pile of crunchy bacon in front of me. My stomach growls. "Brett and Amber signed off on it, too. Actually, Brett's reply was, 'It's about high time you admit to being related to us.'"

I chuckle. Sounds like Brett.

"Do you want some eggs?"

I crunch on a piece of savory bacon. My mouth is so happy. "This is good."

We sit across from each other, the crunching of bacon the only sound for long enough to make things even more awkward.

Cole clears his throat. "I work until ten again tonight, but I'm off tomorrow."

Plans. Right. It'll be Saturday. Are we a couple now? Does this mean date night? "Okay. What do you want to do?"

"Well, do you want to come over tonight? Or—"

Oh geez. This is going to be a thing now. Am I ready for this to be a thing? Can I handle being alone with him again tonight. Samantha, chill. This isn't new. We always hang out when he's not working. But—

I need space so this can all sink in.

"I can't tonight, but what if we go on a double date with Shawn and Monica tomorrow?"

His expression dulls. "Oh. Sure. Yeah, let's do that. Hey, doesn't the fall festival start this weekend in the park?"

"Hmm, I don't think that starts until October."

"Oh? Well, okay, are you willing to do something outdoors tomorrow? I've been cooped up for way too long. I could use a day in the sun." He studies me much too closely. "With my friends," he adds.

Friends. Is he saying that for my benefit? Or is he pushing back? I don't want him to know I'm having so many conflicting emotions about last night.

"I'm up for anything." I smile.

"I tell you what, you talk with Monica and you two make plans. Whatever you ladies want to do will work for me, and you know Shawn will be happy to follow her around wherever she wants to drag him."

"Okay. I'll talk to Monica." Oh gosh. Monica. I want to go home and face her about as much as I want to talk about last night with Cole.

He glances over to the clock on the microwave. "I should get a shower." He scratches his head, rubbing the back of his neck. For the first time this morning he actually looks as awkward as I feel. "Um, you're welcome to grab one first, if you'd like. I assume you have to go into the studio. I guess Monica opened?" His words shoot-out like rapid fire.

"Oh, um, yeah. It's okay." I stand and clear the dishes off the table. "You get ready for work. I'll head home and we'll figure out tomorrow. I'll call you."

"Sounds good." His hands flit about before he stuffs them in the pockets of his athletic shorts. "I'll mention it to Shawn when I get to the hospital."

Stop being awkward, Samantha. You're making this worse.

After I put our dishes in the sink, Cole walks me to the door. "Are you going to be okay with your dad ... and your patient?"

A shadow crosses his face. "Yeah. I mean, I wish I could tell you more about him. I wish I could've introduced you to him. I wish I'd had more time, but I got Brett and Amber." He stands before me for a few beats before he wraps his arms around my shoulders, pulling us nose to nose. His forehead touches mine as he smiles. "And I've got you."

I smile through my uncertainty. Please let us not screw this up. I bridge the gap and kiss him, letting my lips linger. Kissing him once, twice. He needs to know I'm still here. I don't regret last night, but... What am I feeling? What does all of this mean?

He draws in an unsteady breath against my lips. "Are *you* going to be okay?" His hands rub up and down my biceps.

He knows me too well. Dang perceptive Cole. "Me? Yeah. I'm great." I pull back and force a smile. "I'm just tired." I rub my eyes and wave him off. "I'll call you tomorrow morning to let you know the plan. Okay?"

25

DON'T TAKE IT PERSONAL

BELLEVUE—AUGUST 13, 1995

"HEY, Am. What's up with you? I've called three times now. Is Hope giving you my messages? Call me back? I know you hate us checking up on you, but we want to hear about school. And know you're okay. Love you."

I hang up the phone as Shawn rounds the corner coming my way. I brace myself for the inevitable questions.

"You and Sam?" He leans his elbows on the nurses' station, a knowing smile begging me to deny his words.

"I'm trying to work on charts, man."

"Didn't you just get here?"

"A couple of hours ago, yeah. I have a first-year shadow coming in at two, so I figured I'd clean up the paperwork trail I left last night before she gets here."

His smile fades. "You have Celia's chart in that pile?"

I nod.

"I'm sorry you had to be here for that. Robin left me a message, said you called it."

The sadness I was hit with so abruptly last night lingers in my chest. I clear my throat. "I'm glad I was here." I'm glad I could try my best to save her life. I lost, but maybe next time I won't. It's more fuel for my fire to specialize in peds surgery. More fuel to help me push for organ donations worldwide.

"And Sam was here?" he asks uncertainly.

"Shawn," I warn without looking up.

He sighs "Fine, I thought we could do lunch."

I glance at the patient board. It's a slow day. "Sure, let me finish this up."

He drums his fingers against the countertop as I complete my last chart and check the time. Two hours, that might be a record.

I stack the charts for medical records and let the desk know I'll be in the cafe.

"Hey, were you able to speak with the Gleason's yet?" I ask when he seems content to follow me with a look that clearly says he's waiting for details about last night. Not gonna happen, man.

"Yeah, I left them before I came to see you. Got them all set up with the clinic and transportation. Hopefully, we can find more financial support for him."

"Good."

I spy a few first-year residents arguing over a patient chart and slow my pace. As we pass by I turn. "Anything I can assist you three with?" I ask straight-faced.

The residents, two bright-eyed females and one overly confident guy I haven't worked with yet, become flustered. "Uhhhh—"

"No, sir. No."

"We're fine, Dr. Rossner. Just discussing the merits of different treatment plans before we present to Dr. Shriver."

"Ahhh." I nod. "Dr. Evil. Go with cost, speed, and effectiveness."

"I'm sorry?" the blonde asks. Is it Reynolds?

"Shriver prefers the most cost effective treatment that will take the least amount of time while still being the most effective. We need to save the hospital money. That means efficiency in time of care, but you always need to consider what's best for the patient. Ultimately, they come first."

"Patient comes first, but they want us to be cheap and fast." Cocky resident says, his face twisting in thought.

"You got it." I bob my head in a salute and turn away.

"Cheap and fast?" Shawn chuckles under his breath. "That blonde was totally checking you out."

Was she? "I didn't notice."

"I suppose that's Sam's doing."

My eyes roll. "No, that's professionalism. Aren't you happy with Monica? Why are you paying attention to the women around here anyway?"

"We're dating, Cole. I'm not dead."

"Don't screw her over, Shawn. It could get messy." The implications punch me in the gut. Last night. Sam and I. Monica and Shawn. Things don't go right and my life could blow up in my face. I should have thought it through more before allowing myself to jump straight into bed. Last night I had no will power. Being around her finally wore me down, I couldn't stop myself. And I don't regret it.

I just hope she doesn't.

———

"Pure Kickboxing, this is Sam."

God, I love the sound of her voice. "Hey, gorgeous."

"Cole." She sounds startled and fumbles with the phone. "Sorry. Hey, what's up?"

What's up? It's a far cry from her usual greeting. Maybe I'm being paranoid. I'll go with paranoid. After last night this is bound to be confusing. We should have discussed it this morning.

"Well, Shawn had an idea, and I know we usually ignore his ideas, but—"

She chuckles in agreement.

"This one isn't too bad. How do you two feel about heading into Brooklyn and doing a little karaoke tomorrow night?"

"You're joking, right?"

"You said you'd be up for anything." And this is laid back and simple.

"And now I'm cursing myself."

Monica's voice raises in the background. Good thing I can count on her to say yes, Shawn made that perfectly clear when he suggested it.

"Your boyfriend wants to go to a karaoke bar tomorrow night," Sam grumbles.

Monica bursts out laughing. "We're in!" she shouts into the phone.

Sam sighs heavily. "I guess we're in." I try not to laugh at her pitiful agreement as she continues, "But I make no promises of getting up on that stage."

"Oh, yeah you most certainly will be getting up on that stage." My resident shadow steps into the hallway and glances around expectantly. "Hey, I need to run, but I'll see you tomorrow night. Seven?"

"Yeah, yeah. I'll be ready."

I wanted her to stop me from hanging up and tell me she wants to spend the day with me still.

UNION DIVE

SAM HAS AVOIDED ME SINCE SHE LEFT MY PLACE FRIDAY morning. Her not wanting to come over last night wouldn't be an issue if she'd made some effort to get together today. She wasn't doing anything. Shawn unknowingly confirmed that when I called to him this afternoon and he'd just returned home from hanging with the girls at their place.

It wouldn't be an issue if she hadn't seemed so distant yesterday morning. If she hadn't seemed so awkward when I knocked on her door tonight. What happened between us was unexpected, I know she must be as shell-shocked by it as I am. But it was exactly what I'd hoped for since the day I met her. Why do I feel as though in her mind it was a mistake?

"Finally," Shawn huffs as a waitress in a micro-mini and painted on black top leads us to an empty table after a forty-five-minute wait. I push my aggravation with Sam and our situation to the back corner of my mind. This is us. Cole and Sam. She's one of the most important people in my life; surely I'm overthinking things. It'll be fine.

"I'm so hungry, I could eat a horse," Monica hisses.

"Dude, when you said dive bar, I assumed it would be some little unknown place in Brooklyn. I didn't realize you meant *Union Dive.* I didn't expect this kind of crowd."

I pull out Sam's chair. She seems a little ill at ease. "There isn't any amount of money that could get me up on that stage in front of all these people."

"Would you two stop whining. This place has killer food and —" Shawn pauses as the crowd around us claps enthusiastically at something going on at the stage. "Great singers," he finishes.

A woman takes the stage, her brightly dyed red hair reminding me of flames under the stage lighting. As she welcomes everyone, I slide my chair closer to Sam's, in pretense of seeing the stage better, and casually set my arm around the back of her chair. Did she flinch?

"See anything you want?" I ask, close to her ear so she can hear me over the emcee. Leaning in wasn't a bright idea. Flowers and honey fill my senses and I have the urge to press my nose under her ear and breathe her in.

"Huh?" She turns to me, eyes wide. "Want? What do I want?"

Yes, Samantha, what *do* you want? "The menu," I tap the

sticky bound menu sitting on the table before her. "Anything look good?"

"Oh, right." Her eyelashes flutter before she looks down at the menu. "These burgers look delicious. Are they any good?" she asks Shawn and Monica.

"Yeah. The burgers and wings are my favorite." Shawn reaches over and points out his usual order.

"As always, let's get the night started with a little Sinatra," the emcee calls out, and the crowd cheers as a well-dressed man in his fifties weaves through the tables and chairs toward the stage. "Everyone welcome Bill to the stage."

I squeeze Sam's shoulder. "How much you wanna bet he sings "New York, New York"?"

Sam lets out an explosive laugh and clasps her hand over her mouth when realizes how loud she was. "Sorry. That would just be so cliché."

I'm staring at her red face when the telltale first notes of the classic fill the bar. Her head falls back on my arm as she chuckles. "Of course."

The arrival of another skimpily dressed waitress causes Sam to sit up, putting space between us once again. Her guard back up. What is this?

"You guys ready to order?" the waitress asks, standing a bit close to my elbow considering my arm is draped around Sam's chair.

Shawn orders a pitcher of beer for the table, bleu cheese burgers for Monica and himself, and an order of chili cheese fries. It sounds so good I order the same. Good thing I got a run in this afternoon.

"Regular burger for me." Sam hands her menu to the waitress. "And onion rings."

"Got it. I'll be right back with your pitcher."

The Sinatra wannabe finishes up his song to thunderous applause as the entire bar joins him in belting out the last two lines. Shawn and Monica are singing at the top of their lungs. The table next to us is standing, arms thrown around each other, swaying and singing. I suppose I can call what they're doing singing.

I glance over at Sam. She's looking around the place, a look of amusement mixed with disbelief on her face. Oh, why not. I give into the crowd and finish off the song with them. *It's up to you, New York, New York!*

"He was amazing," Shawn laughs, turning back to the table and pouring four cups of beer from the pitcher the waitress dropped off while we were too busy singing to notice. "There was this old guy last time we were here, he must have been eighty, and he sang "Let's Get It On" and it was fantastic."

Monica lifts her cup into the air between us. "To being young and living life."

Shawn smiles wide, holding his next to hers. "To best friends and lovers," he adds as he turns and kisses Monica's cheek.

I glance at Sam as we both raise our glasses. "To finding happiness," I toast, my eyes holding hers meaningfully.

Sam inhales through her nose. "To letting go."

A new singer takes the stage as a classic *Queen* song comes on. Can't ever go wrong with *Queen*. The guy opens his mouth and I take that back. You can go wrong. So, so wrong.

"Hey, Sammy," Shawn shouts over the music. "What song are you gonna sing for us?"

"In your dreams!" she hollers back.

"Aw, sorry, I'm a taken man now," he winks and I choke on my beer. "Don't worry though, I'm sure Cole has enough for the both of us."

Rolling my eyes heavenward, I turn to Monica. "Whatever did he do to win you over?"

"I ask myself the same question every day." She rolls her eyes, but she's looking affectionately at Shawn who kisses her.

"You two should do a duet," I suggest, changing the subject

away from anything to do with Sam and I. "Show us how it's done."

"Yes. Yes, I think that is a great idea," Sam agrees, sparing me a quick glance. "The veterans need to share their talent with us."

Shawn shrugs, sharing a look with Monica. "We're on the list, so I think we could make that happen."

"On the list?" I ask.

"Yep." His brow lifts purposefully. Oh, crap. I bet they aren't the only ones at this table on that list, but I'm not warning Sam. He can deal with her wrath when the time comes.

THE MUSIC AND CROWD REMAIN ONE NOTCH ABOVE WHAT we can talk through, so I sit back and listen to the performers. Shawn and Monica turn their chairs toward to stage, scooting close to one another and chatting. I watch them. Who would have thought? They look like a couple in love. I give Sam a sidelong glance. She's also staring at our best friends as the melody of a well-known love song comes on.

My fingers brush her bare shoulder as I lean over. "They seem perfect for each other, don't they?"

"I look at them now and I forget that they haven't always been together." Sam smiles meaningfully.

She turns her gaze to me and I want to swoop in and kiss her. I want to tell her we're perfect for each other, too. I want to ask her to not let what happened between us the other night scare her.

"And that they're two of the biggest flirts we know?" I ask, making a joke instead of addressing the elephant in the room.

She laughs lightly. "Yeah, that too. And they're probably the only two people in this world who could handle each other."

"We have some new residents at the hospital, and I have to say as hard as they try, not one of them has been able to get him to turn his head their way. I think he may be done for this time."

"He better be, or I'll kick his trash. I have a feeling Monica is pretty smitten."

The arrival of our food denies me the opportunity to answer. We dig in. Starving.

"So good," I moan after my first bite.

"Have I ever steered you wrong?" Shawn asks. I give him a look. "When it comes to food," he clarifies.

Sam pulls her burger away, humming in satisfaction, ketchup smearing the corner of her mouth. I'm tempted to lick it away for her, but I hang onto my sanity and wait to see if she notices it herself. She swallows and inches her tongue out, licking the red smudge away.

"Cole?"

Something hits my shin and I flinch.

"Cole?"

Crap. Shawn's saying my name. I remove my gaze from Sam's mouth, from her tongue, and shift in my seat.

"Where's Cole?"

My name again. It's not coming from Shawn's mouth. What the—?

"Cole, they're calling you," Monica asserts.

My burger drops to the plate and I turn to my supposed best friend. "Really, man?"

His reply is to halfway stand and wave his arm over his head. "He's right here. He's coming."

As I'm standing, Sam says, "If you put my name on that list, Shawn Gomes, I will murder you in your sleep."

"I wouldn't have dreamt of it. I've heard you sing, remember."

Monica's giggles follow me as I move toward the stage.

Fifty percent of the bar is drinking and talking, not paying attention to what's going on onstage. The other fifty percent follow me as I move. Lucky for Shawn, I'm not shy. He knows that already from a few of our outings when I first moved to the city. I take the mic from the deejay next to the steps who whispers my, or more accurately, Shawn's song choice. There's only one song I sing when I'm forced to. Shawn's a snake. My gaze flicks to Sam. What is she going to think of this song choice? I could change it, but I know it by heart. I'm good at this song.

And it's rather meaningful in the situation we find ourselves in right now. Here goes nothing.

26

YOU OUGHTA KNOW

COLE STANDS BEHIND THE MICROPHONE, his hand wrapped around it like he's not nervous at all. Well, I'm nauseated just looking at him on the stage. Alone. Under the spotlight. I can't believe he actually got up there.

Shameless starts to play through the speakers. Garth Brooks, huh? I never pegged Cole for a country man.

As soon as his mouth opens and he starts to sing, my nerves diminish completely. Slowly, my jaw drops and the air escapes my lungs. Cole's deep voice carries the melody like he's sung this song a million times before. Who knew that voice would come out of that man? It's mesmerizing and a dang good thing I'm sitting down because I'm feeling a little lightheaded.

I know Cole can't see me with the lights shining on the stage blinding him, but it feels like he looking directly at me. My heart races, absorbing the lyrics. It's just a song, but it feels like so much more. We're so much more.

"Did you pick the song?" I ask Shawn during the guitar solo.

"Sort of."

"Sort of?"

"It's his go-to song. You know, he isn't a country fan, but one of his friends from med school was and got him hooked on Garth. So I picked it, knowing he can sing it."

With the end of the guitar solo, Cole picks back up and I turn my attention to him. The bar is silent, all eyes on Cole. I'm beaming, knowing I get to call him mine. Wait. I do, right? Or maybe we're not quite there yet. It doesn't matter. Cole is hot, owning that stage, singing like I'm the only one in the room, and when he comes back, I get to be the one to kiss him.

The music fades and Cole stands there like he didn't just sing that heck out of that Garth Brooks song. Everyone in the bar gets to their feet, clapping and cheering. Okay, so maybe I'm the first one. Whatever. He deserves it.

He makes his way back to us, nodding at people as he goes by when they compliment him. When he reaches us, looking all modest and humble, I toss my arms around his neck, jumping into his arms.

"Oh my gosh." I don't hold back. I plant one on him right in front of everyone. It's not until Shawn whistles and Monica loudly clears her throat that I come back to myself.

I plant my feet on the floor, loosening my arms around his neck. "You were amazing! Why have you been keeping that voice from me all this time? Did you not want to rub my terrible voice in my face?"

His hands grip my hips, keeping me close. "I make it a habit of not using my secret powers for evil." His voice maintains a touch of the accent he sang with.

I smirk, teasing him. "If you'd sung for me before, you might have won me over a long time ago. I'm speechless."

Cole steps closer. "I'd be happy to sing for you whenever you want, but I hope I don't need it to win you over." His strong hands give my hips a little squeeze before he lets go of me completely, stepping back as he looks at Shawn. "You, my friend, owe me for that ambush."

"I think I just did *you* a favor." Shawn looks at us with a mischievous grin.

Right. I attacked Cole in front of everyone. Maybe I should've controlled myself a little bit better.

Cole and I sit down. My burger is officially cold, but I don't even care. It was just a distraction while watching Cole. Nothing was going to take my eyes away from him. He didn't just own that stage, he owned my heart.

"So." Shawn gestures to Cole and me. He sits back and drapes his arm along the back of Monica's chair. "Is this, like, a real thing now?"

Why didn't Cole and I have this conversation before tonight? This question was bound to come up. I don't want to be the one to answer it, but how can we not be a thing? After the night at the hospital, and his house, and tonight. I know he feels it, too.

Hoping Monica will cut him off, I spare her a glance, but she looks just as interested in the answer.

"We discussed this already," Cole says between clenched teeth.

"No. I asked, you avoided."

"Shawn." That was a warning, clear as day. Cole's chin juts out, perturbed.

"I think what Cole is trying to get across is that—" I peer at him, gaging his reaction. "We haven't really established what this is yet, but it's something." I smile, the admission freeing me.

Blue eyes snap to my face, and they're not as warm as I expected. What did I say wrong? Have I misinterpreted something? If I spend that night with him ... If I kissed him in front of one hundred other people, in front of our best friends, and I was wrong...

Cole pushes a hand through his hair as he scoots his chair back. "I'm gonna use the restroom. Excuse me."

He's getting up and walking away? Right now? I turn and see the confused looks from Monica and Shawn. At least I'm not the only one who read the situation wrong. Except now I want to excuse myself and hide in the girls' room.

Shawn finishes off the pitcher of beer he ordered. "Are you sure you don't want to sing?"

"I'll pass." I don't even want to be here anymore. I nibble on my onion rings, but they make me nauseous.

"I'm sure he just had to pee really bad," Monica offers. Yeah, perfect timing, Cole.

"Yeah," I mumble. "Probably."

What did I do wrong? Should I not have kissed him? I know things have been a little strained, but that was inevitable. This is new territory for us. Am I conflicted? Yes, okay. Was I not hiding my confusion well enough? If not, Cole must understand how this might be strange for me. Two days ago we were platonic best friends, and now we've muddied the water. Heck, it's a freaking swamp now. But, not only that, doesn't he understand what a big deal this is for me? The steps I've taken for him?

"You know what? I'm gonna take off." I drop a twenty on the table. "Should cover my portion. Monica, I'll see you at home."

"What? No, I'm not letting you go home alone. Shawn," she leans in and kisses him on the cheek. "I'll call you later."

"You're going to leave me here?"

"You're his best friend. You can deal with him," I quip and stand, slinging my purse over my shoulder. "And let Cole know not to bother contacting me. I *won't* be available for him." I make my way through the bar to the exit.

27

HURT
BELLEVUE—AUGUST 30, 1995

"Have you called her yet?" Shawn asks as our paths cross in the hospital hallway.

I don't have to clarify who 'her' is. He's asked me the same question every shift we've worked over the last two weeks.

I grab his arm, pulling him to the side. "Has she said something to you?"

"Oh, no." He tugs free of me. "I'm not getting in the middle of this, remember?"

"Then why do you keep asking me if I've called?"

Shawn slaps my back. "That's me taking your side, man. You're miserable at best. Call her."

I've always considered my relationships private. I hate sharing the details, but at this point Shawn *is* in the middle of it, like it or not.

"What's the point? I can't keep getting jerked around by her. We tried friends and I know it seems like it worked, but it was a ticking time bomb." I wave to a nurse flagging me down at the end of the hallway.

"Maybe that's because you're not meant to be friends," Shawn points out.

I frown. "Exactly."

"You're a doctor and you're this stupid?"

"You're pushing the boundaries of our friendship, Shawn." I sidestep him, ready to walk away. "She's stuck in the past. She doesn't want a relationship."

"Then talk her out of that mindset. Dude, the girl is in love with you and you're in love with her. Everyone but the two of you can see it as clear as day."

I look up and spot two nurses and an x-ray tech now waiting for me. "I've got to run."

Shawn sighs, shaking his head. "You hurt her at the bar."

I hate him for that. For reminding me that I let my pride get in the way of being an adult. "I know." I nod, already walking backward, away from Shawn.

"And?"

"And I love her, so I'll make it up to her. If she'll let me."

28

DON'T SPEAK

PURE KICKBOXING—AUGUST 30, 1995

"Great job today, everyone. I hope to see you all again next time," I huff, getting my breathing under control as I grab my water bottle.

"You haven't been that tough on a class since ... ever." Monica follows me from the back office up to the front of the studio. "Do you think maybe you should not take your aggression out on the paying customers."

"They come here for a workout, not to be babied, Mon."

"I know. I'm just saying. Ever since the karaoke bar, you've been harder and harder on your classes."

I sift through the schedule, looking at the names for my six o'clock class. "They'll thank me for it later."

"Maybe you should call Cole."

I snort. "Fat chance. I'm not the one in the wrong here."

"Look, I get it. He was a jerk, but don't you think maybe you should hear him out? It's been two weeks."

"Why?" I look up. "What do you know? Have you talked to him?"

She takes a step back with arms raised. "No, just in talking to

Shawn, he says Cole hasn't been himself at work. I think this little fight is really getting to him."

"Well, if he cared enough he'd call."

"Don't be so prideful."

"Monica, he *humiliated* me. I never thought Cole was capable of that." I hold back the tears threatening to surface. "He walked away. He can come to me if he's sorry."

"In all fairness," she eyes me uneasily, "he went to the bathroom. *You* left the bar and told Shawn to tell Cole not to bother calling you."

"He should know it was only because I was upset and wanted him to know."

Monica shakes her head at me. "You're *such* a girl. Be a woman and tell him how you feel. You owe him that much."

I hate it when she's right.

29

ONLY WANNA BE WITH YOU

MONICA & SAM'S—SEPT 2, 1995

WHEN I ROUND the corner of the stairwell and walk into the hallway to my apartment, a guy stands in front of my door. His hands are shoved in his pockets, his foot propped up against the wall behind him. Well, it's not just any guy. It's Cole. His head turns my way. His expression lifts. It's not so much a smile as it is relief. I know because I feel it, too. Only mine's mixed with hurt.

Taking a deep breath, I hesitantly make my way down the hallway. As I approach, he pushes himself off of the wall and waits for me. I don't say anything when I reach my door.

With my back to my apartment, Cole steps away, all the way until he bumps into the wall across from my front door. His hand goes to his neck, rubbing it the way he does when he's stressed. "Sam." My name is barely a whisper as he shakes his head. "I miss you."

Those three words tear me in two. I wanted him to be here when I got home. I wanted to see his face and know that he misses me as much as I miss him, but I'm still so hurt. Can I admit my feelings to him when I feel this way?

We can't leave things the way they are. I unlock the door and crack it open. "Want to come in?"

He inhales. "Please."

Cole closes the door behind him as I make my way to the kitchen, dropping my purse on the countertop and leaning my hip against it. "Do you want anything to drink?"

"I'm okay. Thanks."

The space between us lengthens the longer we stare. I want him to apologize, but from the look on his face it doesn't appear he's ready to do that. Is he waiting for an apology from me? Does he even realize what he did wrong?

"You humiliated me at the bar. I know it was weird and we hadn't established anything after we ... after that night, but excusing yourself after I put myself out there in front of our friends was not cool."

"You were humiliated?" he asks evenly.

"When I told Shawn and Monica we were something, you looked at me like you'd never seen me before, and then got up and walked away. How was I supposed to feel?"

"Oh, I don't know." He leans against my front door. "How was I supposed to feel about the way you held me at arm's length after we spent the night together? I swear, I felt as though I had to beg you to see me."

"So, you were trying to get back at me for needing space by humiliating me?" Unbelievable. "Cole, that night was confusing. I needed time to wrap my head around it. I didn't mean to make you feel like I was distancing myself."

Cole pushes off the door and steps closer to the kitchen. "Shawn bugged the crap out of me after that night, trying to figure out what happened between us. I didn't say jack. But at the karaoke bar, I sing a freaking song, and you're kissing me and telling our friends we're an item or 'something.'"

Air-quotes? Really? The nerve of this man.

"I don't do that, Sam. I don't justify my relationships to people. Especially since we hadn't discussed it ourselves. You pissed me off. I'm sorry if I hurt you by walking off, but—" He lowers his head, slapping his forehead and cursing.

I try so hard to keep from yelling at him. "I don't even know what to respond to first. I wasn't trying to *justify* our relationship; I was trying to offer you an olive branch! I know I was being weird. That night drudged up a lot of different emotions for me, emotions I don't even know how to explain to you!" Okay. I fail. Not yelling is impossible. "And you honestly believe I only kissed you because you sang a *freaking* song? Cole, I kissed you because for some stupid reason I thought the words you sang were directed at me! I wanted you to know once and for all that I don't regret this." I gesture to the expansive space between us. "Obviously, I was wrong in doing that."

Cole's palms press against his closed eyes as he chuckles. "The words *were* directed at you. Every. Single. One." He lets out another string of curses and paces in a circle. "You put a dent in my fragile ego, okay?" He drops his hands and lifts soft eyes to me, his lips curving into a rueful smile. "I was a little—crap. I was hurt."

"I'm sorry." I exhale my animosity and shut my eyes. "Next time you're hurt or I bruise your fragile ego, it'd be nice if you would talk to me instead of walking away."

"I'm sorry. You couldn't get out of my house fast enough that morning. And I get that, I do. But when you blew me off about coming over the next night and wavered on spending my day off with me—" He shrugs. "I couldn't figure you out. Then you made that flippant comment at the bar saying if I had sung to you a long time ago, I could have won you over." He exhales. "Apparently, I snapped."

We're so dumb. I chuckle softly. "Cole, I was *trying* to be playful, to break the tension. I see where you could've misinterpreted everything. I didn't mean to hurt you. The other night when I woke up, it hit me. I was waking up next to someone that wasn't him for the very first time. You realize that, right? You're the only person I've been with besides Paul. That's a *huge* deal for me. To let someone else in. This kind of stuff isn't something I take lightly.

"And it wasn't that I was upset you weren't him. It made me realize I liked who I was waking up next to, and I felt equally guilty and elated. I want to be able to enjoy our firsts without the past looming over me.

"But then, yes, I worried that we might've rushed things and we'd ruined this because we weren't thinking clearly. I was once terrified of getting close to you, and now I'm terrified of losing you, Cole. There were so many conflicting emotions running through me afterward, I didn't know how to react to that. I didn't know how I was supposed to feel. I didn't even know what I was feeling. I just knew something life changing had happened between us. And being a woman, I thought too much."

Okay, shut up, Samantha. You've said enough.

"I can't compete with your dead fiancé."

"I'm not asking you to."

He lifts a hand. "Wait, don't get mad at that. Let me finish, okay?"

I close my mouth, breathing through my nose as I nod. Cole holds out his hand for me to take and leads me to the couch.

"I can't compete with Paul, and I don't want to. I'm not saying you should forget him or anything like that. I've never been in the position you were in. I've never loved and lost someone like that. I don't know. That night, us being together, it wasn't a mistake. It was right." His hands squeeze mine tighter.

"Maybe we took things a little faster than we should have, and maybe we should've talked about our feelings and discussed dating first, but honestly why would we? We're adults. We know what we want in our lives. We've hung out at least once a week for the past year. We've essentially been dating all this time." He pauses. "Well, without the benefits," he grins, in what I suppose is his attempt to bring levity to the moment.

"Every time I look at you, I see the woman I wanted from day one. There was a connection between us at first sight, and for the last three years I've gone from feeling that connection, to being turned down, to pushing away my feelings after I learned about Paul, to wanting to rip my hair out because you refused to move on.

"As your friend, I wasn't going to be the person who told you to start dating. But, as the man who was falling for you, that's all I wanted to do, but couldn't. I couldn't tell you what I wanted because I care too much about you to hurt you, and everything I knew about you told me if I pushed you to move on, I'd lose you. But, now here we are, and I have to tell you that I'm in that spot. That spot where I have to make this clear. Sam, I need you to move on from your past, or I need you to tell me to move on from you. Because you either want something here," Cole taps his chest. "Or you don't. It's that simple."

"I'm scared," I whisper. Cole's hand returns to mine, wrapping around my fingers as though he's trying to infuse strength into them. "I'm scared of what you make me feel. I'm scared that we'll screw this all up and we'll never be the same. I'm sorry I questioned what happened that night, but it wasn't because I don't care enough about you. It's because I care too much."

"Will you answer a few questions? Just give me a yes or no, nothing crazy."

I bite my lips and their need to say too much. "I can do that."

"Are you ready to move forward with your life?"

I close my eyes, breathing deeply. It's time. "I think so."

"Are you interested in moving forward with me?"

I pretend to think about it. When Cole's face falls a fraction, I chuckle, "Yes."

He eyes me with a chiding smirk. "Are you willing to be a little scared? To take a chance, knowing the reward is so much greater than the risk?"

He makes that sound so easy, like we aren't making a decision that will affect everything about us. But if Cole is willing to risk it all, I am, too. "Yes."

His lips stretch into a wide smile. "You're not sure, though. I can see it in your eyes. You always squint when you're thinking too hard. You're scared that we'll never be the same, aren't you?"

I hate being so transparent around him. "Maybe."

His fingers toy with mine. His index finger trace over my knuckles and the back of my hand, racing my already unsteady heart rate. "You're right. We won't ever be the same. If we do this, there's only one way I see it going. Like I said before. I know you, you know me. I can see my future when I'm with you. I'm not interested in a fling, or a few years followed by an amicable break up where we promise we'll be friends but we never call."

Nervous laughter slips out. I don't want that either, but I gently remind him, "Baby steps, Cole." I lace my fingers in between his.

"I'm not asking for forever today. We can take things slow, or as slow as we can be considering our past together. I'm merely telling you that if we pursue this, I'm going to work my hardest to make this last."

"Me too. From here on out I won't keep anything from you. You won't have to question how I feel."

Relief rushes across his features. "I have one more yes or no question for you."

"I feel like I'm back in college." I prepare myself for his last question. "Hit me."

"Will you have lunch with me tomorrow? Oh, and can I kiss you now?"

That's an easy one. "That's two questions, but yes and yes, please."

30

ROLL TO ME

MONICA & SAM'S—OCTOBER 16, 1995

THE BIG GESTURE. That's what this is. She's going to love it. Shawn assured me she would. Monica was giddy as she helped me set it up. Even Brett and Ruby threw their two cents into the planning. It's a lot considering we've only been officially dating for a month and we're supposed to be going slow. I tap on Sam and Monica's door lightly.

Monica answers the door. "Perfect timing."

"Hey," I whisper back as she waves me in.

"She's almost ready. Doesn't suspect a thing." She checks over her shoulder toward Sam's bedroom. "I told her I wanted to do breakfast."

"Perfect. Thanks for helping, Mon." Sam's voice turns my attention. She's singing. Monica shakes her head, laughing. "Is she dressed?" I'm already gravitating toward the music. Toward Sam.

"Would it matter if she wasn't?" Monica laughs winking mischievously. "Yeah, she should be decent. Just doing her make-up, I think."

Using the toe of my shoe, I push open Sam's cracked bedroom door and lean against the frame, my arms crossed over my chest. Two things hit me. One, I'm struck by how she makes me feel with one look. One month of dating and I still take a deep breath each time I lay my eyes on her. Especially when they're catching her backside shaking away to the beat of her radio. Two, contrary to what Shawn has teased in the past, Sam's voice isn't all that bad. She's belting out the lyrics to that angsty chick song Amber likes. How have we known each other for a few years and I've not heard her sing? She hits a high note. I cringe. Maybe I spoke too soon.

Sam spins away from the mirror, fist to her mouth like she's holding a microphone, and screams when she spots me in the doorway.

"Hey, rockstar."

"Oh my gosh! Cole." Her hand flies to her chest. "What are you doing here?"

"I came for the show," I grin, straightening.

She marches forward and punches me in the shoulder. "Jerk." Standing on her tiptoes, she curls her fingers around my shirt collar and presses a kiss to my lips. "Well, hopefully you got an earful 'cause you're never getting another show again."

My hand slides easily around her back. "Never is a long time."

"I'm a pretty competitive person, in case you haven't heard. You might not want to challenge me."

I throw my head back with laughter, my hold tightening. "God, you're adorable."

"It's why you can't resist me." She gives me another kiss. "Back to my first question. What are you doing here? Monica and I are about to head out for breakfast. You want to come?"

"Actually, I'm here to kidnap you."

"Oh yeah? And take me to a land far far away?"

"Close."

"For real?" She smiles, excitement lighting her eyes. "I was just kidding. Where are we going?"

"Are you done getting ready?" I sidestep her question.

Monica pops in behind me. "She's ready."

Sam looks are her, questioning. "You knew about this?"

"Maybe." She holds up a duffel bag. "Everything is packed and ready to go."

I release Sam reluctantly, bowing low. "Madame, your bags are packed and your driver awaits. You ready to take a little trip?"

Sam stares back and forth between Monica and me, shaking her head. "You packed me a bag? When did you even do that?"

"I raced while you were in the shower" She's so proud of herself. "You can thank me later." Monica winks, exaggeratedly.

Sam's head continues shaking, like she can't believe we went through the trouble, as she smiles. "I can't believe you two, but what about the studio?"

"I've got it covered," Monica assures as she hands me Sam's bag. "You two go and have fun. Don't think about work."

"But how long are we going to be gone?"

"Hopefully long enough to de-stress."

Sam beams, clapping her hands. "Eee! Let's go!"

A weight lifts. Part of me worried she'd say no. Part of me keeps waiting for her to tell me she's not ready to be with me. I take hold of Sam in one hand and her bag in the other as we head out.

"My camera? Is that a hint?" Sam asks excitedly as I open the car door for her.

"Perhaps."

Running around to the driver's side, I throw her bag in the back with mine and slide into my seat. She's shifting things around and opening the bag with her favorite guilty pleasure breakfast I left on her seat, along with her camera. I lean across the console and press a kiss to her cheek.

231

"And an asiago bagel with strawberry cream cheese? You're *really* trying to butter me up. Are you trying to top your birthday at Coney Island? Because I think it's working."

"I'm trying to make your birthday a special one." With a smile, I crank the engine. "So, four days with me. You ready for this?"

"Four whole days? I don't know. That's an awful long time to spend alone together. You might decide I'm not worth it after you discover the rest of my flaws."

"If your singing didn't scare me off, nothing will."

"I'll hold off on punching you, but only because you're driving."

We pull onto the interstate for our hour-and-a-half drive toward Danbury, Connecticut. Destination one: Candlewood Lake. I'm content with fighting traffic and listening to the radio as Sam eats her bagel. Once she's done, she shifts in her seat. Her head swiveling around as she bites her lips.

"You're going to put a permanent wrinkle in that forehead of yours if you keep scowling," I tease. "Stop trying to figure it out."

The back of her hand goes to her forehead as she casually brushes her hair out of her face. "I can't help it. Where are we going?"

"We're taking a road trip."

"Yes, but where?" Her shoulders lift and drop in an exaggerated sigh. If I look at her face right now I'll see a pout. I'd bet my life on it so I maintain eye contact with the road. Her pretty pout will break me.

"Everywhere, Sammy." I shoot a side glance her way as I use Shawn's nickname for her. "We're going everywhere."

"Sammy, huh? Can I start calling you Coley, then?"

"Uh, no." My head can't shake fast enough. "As a doctor, all I hear is colon."

Sam's lips twist with disgust. "Good, so we're in agreement on that."

"How about studmuffin?" I suggest.

"Or snookums? I think it suits you well."

"Wow." That's horrible. "I don't think so. I mean, I guess if I can call you sugar plum."

"There are worse things. Snookums and Sugar Plum. We're like the next Bonnie and Clyde."

"Well, when you put it that way." I laugh.

"Next stop, bank robbery!"

"Anywhere you go, baby, I'll go." She has no idea how much I mean that.

She bats her eyelashes, a warm smile curving her lips. "You're so romantic."

"You have no idea. Wait until later, after the bank robbery we'll hit up a convenience store, then I want to find an overpass."

"An overpass?"

"Absolutely, we need to tag a little 'Snookums and Sugar Plum Forever.' Isn't that what all the notorious criminals do?"

"Oh, right," she laughs. "Yes, but it has to be in a heart. With a plus sign and an equal sign. That's how all the cool criminals do it."

"You've got it."

ROAD TRIP

"I FEEL LIKE WE'VE SPENT BARELY ANY TIME TOGETHER THIS last week. What's been going on with you?"

"We talked every day," she laughs. "I don't think there's anything you don't know."

My hand slides from the gear shift to the knee she's tucked up under her. "No, I called you each night to say goodnight. We didn't talk about our days. Tell me about work, or what you ate—"

Her face scrunches up in amusement. "What I ate?"

"Yeah." I massage her knee. "I want to know about your life, Sam."

"Aww," she coos, her hand covering mine.

After a few beats of silence. "So?"

"Hmm?"

I shake my head. Does she not believe me when I say I want to know everything? That I'm interested in every aspect of her life right down to the tiniest detail? The more I know, the easier it is for me to break down the wall she maintains. It's not large, but it's there. The wall that keeps her from being able to completely move on, even though she says she wants to.

"Didn't you and Monica check out that new Mexican restaurant this week? You never told me how it was?"

"Oh, Sol? It was all right. I wasn't super impressed. Not enough flavor. I don't know that I'd go back."

"That stinks. I was hoping we might have a new date place."

"We live in New York City, snookums." She's barely able to say the nickname without laughter.

"I can't believe I actually kind of like that," I interrupt.

"It's ridiculous." Sam laughs harder. "And as I was saying, we live in New York City, I don't think we're going to run out of places to go on dates."

"And yet we always end up going to the same places, don't we?"

"Because they're our places," she says meaningfully. "But you know I'm up for trying new things. When we get back we'll try someplace new."

———

"You know, this is my first road trip in ... I don't know how many years." The corners of Sam's mouth turn up as she stares out the passenger's side window. "I've always loved road trips, taking the scenic route just to drive through small towns

234

you wouldn't normally visit. So much to experience and appreciate along the way. We used to take road trips when I was younger. My mom, Jamie, and I. Little family vacations. It's all my mom could afford." She pauses, and I glance her way. Her expression falls as she runs her nails along her bottom lip. "Paul hated road trips, couldn't handle being in a car for more than an hour. He felt like they were a waste of time when flying could get you there so much faster."

I could sell myself here, but I won't. I love road trips. Mom and I took weekend trips all the time growing up. I want Sam to fall for me without my having to push her. I want her to see me, not compare me to him.

Her head swivels. "Sorry, I didn't mean to bring him up. This is our trip." She reaches out and wraps her hand around my bicep, squeezing it once.

"Hey." I remove my left hand from the steering wheel and cover her fingers on my arm, patting them once before returning it. "You can talk about him, Sam. I hope you know that."

"I know. And thank you."

She inhales, but says nothing more. Does she not want to share her past with him with me? It's hard to think of her almost marrying another man, being in love with another man, but he was her past. I'll listen, even if it almost kills me to hear it.

"So, we're heading north. Have crossed into Connecticut. Hmm ... Oh, we're near Candlewood Lake." Sam twists in her seat, grabbing the camera case she stashed behind my chair. "Please tell me we're driving by the lake? I'd love to grab some fall foliage shots."

No discussion about Paul. Cue taken. I move my right hand from her leg as she messes with her camera, switching hands on the steering wheel.

"You're smiling in an awfully mischievous way, Dr. Rossner."

"Am I?" I suck in my cheeks, but the smile lingers.

"What are you up to?"

"Fine. I thought we'd go on a little foliage field trip."

"A foliage field trip," she tastes the words and looks out the window. We're surrounded by orange and red leaves.

"Monica and I were talking a couple weeks ago when I was waiting on you to finish getting ready to go out. She pulled out one of your photo albums. The one with Madison Square Park Garden on it. With all your scenic pics."

"Oh." Sam sinks into her seat, nervously pulling on her bottom lip.

"You're not mad at her, are you? I mean, I wish you would have shown me. You've got a great eye."

"I'm not mad." Her mouth twitches from side to side, contemplative. "Just—I don't know. Photography is an intimate part of me. It's one thing for you to see me taking pictures. It's another to see the outcome. It's hard for me to share them with people. That probably sounds silly to you."

We should stop the car and have this conversation face-to-face. Since we can't, I reach across and pull her hand away from toying with her lip. Bringing her hand to my mouth, I kiss the pads of her fingers. The tips that were touching her lips. My bottom lip tingles, thanks to the residue of her peppermint chapstick lingering on her fingertips. And now I want to stop the car on the shoulder just to kiss the breath right out of her.

"It's not silly at all," I manage to eke out, shaking thoughts of devouring her lips away.

"So she showed you my pictures and you planned this trip?" She tilts her head away from me. She's uncomfortable.

"Pretty much." I give her her hand back. "She told me that other than Coney Island, you hadn't taken pictures since before the crash. I was thinking it's time for you to get back to that part of you."

Sam's shoulders relax as she breathes out, nodding and accepting. "This is really sweet of you. Thank you, Cole."

I pull off Interstate 7 and maneuver onto Candlewood Lake

Road. The drive is a small detour on route to our next destination, but it brings us along the eastern shoreline of the lake so we can see all the beautiful homes, water, and some fall color.

"Oh my gosh, look at the trees across the lake. Can we stop somewhere?"

Her excitement is contagious. "Of course we can. I was going to pull into the marina up ahead."

A few minutes later we're climbing out of the vehicle and walking toward the boat docks. The lake is huge, the largest in Connecticut. I spent a few weeks in the summers here with a buddy growing up. As teens we explored the entire coast of the lake. I smile at the click, click, click of Sam's camera. She's all but forgotten me standing beside her as she captures what she sees.

"I swore one day I'd have a vacation home of my own here." I breathe in the clean fall air.

"Really? Did you spend time here growing up?"

"Yeah, my best friend Todd had a place. A couple of the surgeons at the hospital have homes here. It's a popular place for New Yorkers to summer."

"I can see why. It's beautiful, but still close enough to make a perfect weekend trip," She agrees hiding behind her camera again.

"Is that something you'd be interested in?"

"A home on the lake?"

A home on the lake *with me*. I want to add those two all-important words. "Yeah, are you a beach or lake girl?"

She lowers her lens and looks at me like I should know this answer already. "You're talking to a girl who grew up in a town near several lakes. I'll take the fresh water over salt any day."

Such a good answer. We mesh so well.

"Let's drive through and find our future home," I tease when she finally slides her camera strap over her head, leaving it dangling at her chest.

"Hold on." She looks at me deadpan. Did I take it too far?

"Are we talking home home or vacation home? Because those are two very different things."

"Vacation home. I think I'm a city boy forever." Crap. What if she hates the city? I shuffle through my memories. Other than traffic woes, she's never hinted at not liking living in the city.

"Okay. Good. Then we can talk. Hypothetically speaking, of course."

We drive along the lake, taking detours down streets here and there looking for the perfect, vacation home.

"What are your requirements?"

"Well, hypothetically speaking, if someone were looking for a home in Connecticut, I feel like one would have to stick with the classic Colonial or Victorian style. Throw in a front porch, and you're set."

"Hmmm, I agree with the front porch. Growing up in Pennsylvania there were so many old homes. I kind of found myself scoping out something more modern. All straight lines and glass. Maybe that's the doctor side of me, wanting something neat and clean?"

Sam chuckles. "Definitely the doctor in you. It must be the artist in me, looking for the more historical architecture."

"Something we disagree on. It's about time, huh?"

"I'm pretty sure this isn't the first time." Her eyes light up. She's so ready to prove me wrong. "Ska music? Oh, and I think I recall someone saying they didn't like gyros. The nerve."

I reach over, covering her mouth. "Shhh, you're misremembering."

Her raspy laughter bubbles up behind my hand. Her tongue sticks out, licking a streak up my palm.

"Dang, Sugar Plum, you fight dirty." In more ways than one.

"How do you feel about a little hike?"

"It's a good thing I've got my comfy shoes on." She wiggles her ankles, bobbing her feet up and down.

"It'll take us about forty minutes to drive up to Cobble

Mountain. It's a little climb to the ridge, but once we get up there I hear there's an amazing view of the mountain ranges."

COBBLE MOUNTAIN, CT

"FINALLY, I CAN KEEP UP WITH YOU PHYSICALLY." I LAUGH, dragging Sam up the ridge of Cobble Mountain.

"Okay," she breathes. "How can I kick circles around you, but this climb is killing me?"

"Hiking is just a different beast." I stop and allow her to catch her breath.

"I guess I'll scratch Mount Everest off my bucket list."

The view spread out before us when we reach the crest is worth the sweat.

"I'm so glad I didn't leave my camera in the car."

"Snap away. I'll be over here." I release her hand so she can do what she loves.

I lower myself to a boulder and rest my elbows against my knees. "This view can make a person feel so small," I comment as the snapping of Sam's camera continues.

"It's funny. I love the city, but capturing the millions of people there reminds me I'm just one more person in the big city. Being in places like this make me feel alive."

"It's Heaven on Earth."

I turn myself full circle on the boulder, scanning the valley below, the trees, the sparkling reflection of a river in the distance—

"Hey." My hand goes up, blocking my face as I turn and find her camera focused on me instead of the scenery.

"Don't get all camera shy on me now."

I lower my hand. "You're supposed to be taking pictures of the scenery, not me. Nobody wants to see me."

"I do." Sam shifts her camera and lifts a sweet smile. "Don't forget. I take pictures for me."

"Is this what it means to date an artist? Everywhere we go you'll be capturing me?" I give her the best bedroom eyes I can manage.

"Sounds about right. How else will we capture the memories?"

I tap my temple wordlessly.

"You've got that much faith in your brain, huh?"

"Nah, I've got that much faith in the fact that I never want to forget these moments."

Sam bites back her smile as she holds my gaze, her eyes conveying thoughts I can't decipher. "When these moments turn to memories, you'll have to tell me how you remember them. I'll capture them with this." She holds up her camera. "You can capture them with words."

"C'mere." I reach for her waist when she ventures close enough to grab. Pulling her close, I steer her onto my lap. "Put down the camera and enjoy the view," I whisper, wrapping her tight and kissing the back of her exposed neck.

"You want words?" I ask after a few minutes of silence.

"I want all of your words."

I turn her chin with my finger. "I'll give you three. I'm in love with you." I pause. "Okay, that's five, but true nonetheless."

Her inhales and exhales tremble against my chest, her back pressed so close. Please say something.

She doesn't move.

"Does that terrify the living daylights out of you?"

"No," she breathes, twisting in my lap. She blinks, moisture coating her eyes. "No ... I think I love you, too."

My hands plunge into her hair. "Let's see if I can remove the think from that statement." I growl like a possessive caveman as my mouth descends on hers.

SEVEN FALLS STATE PARK, CT

ONCE I TEAR MYSELF AWAY FROM SAM'S LIPS AND WE HIKE down from the ridge, we make the twenty-five-minute ride to our next stop. We drive our way up from Kent along a one way stretch that dips and weaves through a bounty of red, orange, and yellow.

"The Appalachian Trail runs along Seven here," I point out a few hikers as we go, reminding her of the hike Brett went on after his high school graduation.

We pull into Seven Fall State Park so Sam can take pictures of the cascading waterfalls of Kent Falls Brook. It's a perfect day. I've missed being outdoors lately.

"I'm starving," I admit almost reluctantly. We're lying on a blanket from my trunk listening to the sound of the water, my ring finger and pinky laced with hers. I hate breaking the moment, but our hike burned through my early morning breakfast and it's now late in the afternoon.

We pick a small cafe where we sit in the corner and stare at each other over club sandwiches and homemade chips. I'm giddy, reveling in the fact that I told her I loved her and she replied favorably.

"We have one more stop to make and then we're done for the day," I explain as we wait for our check.

"Already?"

"I know, it's early." Our waitress returns with my credit card and to-go cups. I sign the check. "You ready?"

My eyes drift to our connected hands as we walk to the car. I'm so content. This is the most relaxed Sam has been since the night we first kissed.

"Where to next, snookums?"

"Ha, it's cute because you're saying it, but don't get too comfortable with it, okay?" I squeeze her hand.

Her laughter resonates in her throat. "Dangit, so you're

telling me I'm going to have to come up with a different nickname for you?"

"Well, due to our future criminal activity, we probably should have aliases lined up."

"Ah. Yes. Aliases. Good point."

"The whole point of today's trip is where I'm taking you next. Where we're going next, *and* where we're staying tonight." That's not a suggestive hint at all.

"Oh yeah? What's so amazing about it? It'll be hard to top the places we've already been."

"You love history. How about a historical covered bridge?"

WEST CORNWALL COVERED BRIDGE, CT

It takes us all of twelve minutes to reach the West Cornwall Covered Bridge, but Sam's excitement reminds me of those commercials where the kids call out, "Are we there yet?" every mile of a family vacation.

It's a scene right out of a postcard. The red wooden bridge spanning the Housatonic River with its little square windows and gable roof.

"Oh my gosh, I have an idea for the perfect shot. Pull over."

Sam hops out of the car with her camera thrown around her neck and climbs down the hillside.

"Where are you going?" I ask, watching her not so carefully maneuver over the rocks. Me being a doctor might come in handy if she's not careful.

"Just down to the river. I want a shot from the rocks."

———

"One of the nurses was telling me about this place," I explain to Sam as we pull into the bed and breakfast where we're staying for the night.

The sunlight is waning and I can see Sam is conflicted as we pull our bags from the car. Her desire to shoot the spectacular view at odds with leaving me. Walking around the vehicle and meeting her by the passenger door, I take her bag and press a kiss to her forehead.

"Why don't you take some shots of the building and sunset while I check us in?"

Her smile is immediate.

"Did you get some shots?" I ask when she wanders into the lobby ten minutes later.

"A few. It's a gorgeous sunset out there with that fall backdrop."

"The employees were giving me all the history of the area and suggesting restaurants for dinner. I thought we could get showered up and check out the little town."

"Sounds perfect."

We walk to the king suite on the second floor I reserved for the night.

"I love how quaint it is." Sam walks around the room, studying the artwork and antique furniture.

"I got this room because of the private bathroom." This is my first B & B visit and I was a bit put off by the idea of sharing restrooms with strangers. What is this, college? I've been there, done that. "You want to shower first?"

"Yeah, I could use some freshening up."

. . .

Why does my arm hurt? I open my eyes to a dimly lit room. I groan and attempt to roll over, but a body pressed against my side stops me. What?

The fuzziness of sleep subsides. Sam. I'm with Sam, on vacation, not at the hospital.

"Sam? Baby?" I whisper as I shake her gently.

She groans sleepily, but doesn't move.

"You fell asleep," I raise my voice. "Sweetie, you hungry? We should get up."

Sighing and stretching, Sam pries her eyes open one at a time. Once she gets a look around the room she says, "Why didn't you wake me?"

"Why didn't I wake you? Why didn't you wake me? You took a shower. I guess I fell asleep."

"Oh right." She smiles lazily. "You looked so comfortable. I didn't want to wake you, so I joined you."

I check the clock. It's a quarter past ten. So much for dinner and romantic walks around the town. "You hungry? I have protein bars in my bag, I think other than that we might be out of luck."

"Protein bars it is," she yawns. "Then back to bed."

I agree wholeheartedly as I dig out water bottles and bars. Evidently hiking and being outdoors tires us out.

31

DOWN BY THE WATER

FALLS VILLAGE INN—OCTOBER 17, 1995

MY EYES open to the morning light filtering through the blinds. My head rolls to the side and Cole is sprawled out with his arm propped above his head. With his lips slightly parted, his breathing shallow and even, I have the urge to press my lips to the corner of his mouth to wake him. Instead I wait, appreciating the view. I could get used to this.

This man.

Goodness, this man.

I don't even have the words. I didn't think my heart could ever feel this way again. His patience, his thoughtfulness, his compassion. I can't wrap my head around how much I love this man. More than I did when I woke up yesterday. What did I do to get so lucky with him?

I can't believe he planned this road trip for us. The time it must have taken to find these beautiful spots and plan the route perfectly. I can't wait to find out what he planned for today.

Scooting across my side of the bed, I mold myself around Cole's solid frame and rest my head in the crook of his arm. Gosh, these muscles. I could stroke them all day. My hand creeps up the ridges of his abs and he stirs, inhaling deeply. My fingers crawl higher, landing over his heart and my palm lays flat, feeling the rhythm of his heartbeats.

Cole's arm falls from above his head and wraps around my shoulders, drawing me closer. He exhales with a groggy morning voice. "Good morning."

What is it about morning voices that make them so dang sexy? I peek up at his face. "Morning."

He lifts a crooked smile and stretches, his back arching with a sated sigh. I want to wake up to this man every morning. Cole reaches across his chest, encircling me in his arms, and buries his cheek in my messy hair. "I love waking up next to you."

"That's funny. I was just thinking the *exact same thing*." My smile stretches wide. I roll on top of him, propping myself up on my elbows. "Breakfast?"

His hands splay out on my lower back, gently massaging the dimples above my waistband. "You're dragging me out of bed already?"

"A woman needs to eat. You don't want hungry Sam on your hands. She's not pleasant."

"I'll happily take any type of Sam in my hands," he offers suggestively.

I swat his hands away and roll off him, though it's not without a fight. "Food. I need sustenance. I'm withering away."

Tugging my hoodie around my neck, I wait with Cole for our breakfast on the back porch of the inn. A whiff of the sweet and savory fragrances of the kitchen drift our way through the back doors.

"It smells amazing."

"Hopefully, it tastes as good as it smells."

"I feel like you can't go wrong with crème brulée French toast." Digging my hands in the front pocket of my hoodie, I ask,

"So, what's the plan for today? You still gonna keep me in the dark?"

"Today it's up to you. Where do you want to go?"

"Really? Anywhere?"

"Within a reasonable distance," I counter.

"Seriously?" Excitement builds inside me. I know just the place. "Rhode Island. Newport."

"Well, that was easy."

I smile. "We went there once when I was little and did this walk along a long cliff that had a bunch of mansions by the ocean. I've been wanting to go back and take pictures for a long time, but you know how life gets crazy."

"Let's go for it."

PROPPING MY FEET UP ON THE DASHBOARD, I FLIP THROUGH the atlas and find the right page. "If I'm reading the map right, it should take us about three hours from here."

"That's not bad."

"Not bad at all."

"What kind of road trips did you take with your mom and Jamie?"

I look up from the atlas. "Well, it actually used to be all four of us. My mom, dad, and Jamie. We'd go up and down the East Coast every summer, stopping in different cities each year." Huh. Those memories came out of nowhere. "Man, it's been a long time since I've thought of those trips and the I Spy games Jamie and I'd play with my dad. And the license plate game, seeing if we could find every state before the trip was over. Thirty-one states. That was the record," I mumble.

I breathe away the memories, sitting straighter in my seat. "After my dad left, my mom didn't want me and Jamie to feel like anything had changed, even though everything did. So she did what she could to scrimp and save for our summer road trips. We could never afford to go very far, but she'd set aside at least a week and we'd go all over the New England states." I peer at Cole, confessing with a meek smile, "Rhode Island has always been my favorite."

"My mom and I did the same thing, only it was just the two of us. We stuck to the places we could easily explore on long weekends."

"Being able to escape only a state away for a few days and finding hidden gems, there's something magical about it. Road trips aren't glamorous trips to Fiji or Paris, but the good memories are all the same."

NEWPORT, RHODE ISLAND

"WE SHOULD BE ABLE TO FIND PARKING NEAR THE FORTY Steps. That's where we're going to begin the walk."

Fresh ocean air assaults my senses as soon as I step out of the car. I know I said I was a fresh water girl, but the sound of the crashing waves and the open air are so calming and refreshing. Taking a deep breath, I take Cole's hand. "C'mon, let's get started."

"I don't know if anything beats the rocky New England coastline. I'm not sure how I've missed coming here. Mom and I spent a lot of time in Maine and Massachusetts. She'd love it here."

"We only went to Maine once. I don't remember it that well. I'd love to go back, though."

We stop at an observation deck, overlooking the ocean, and I peer over the edge at the tall rocky cliffside. "We're just as high as I remember, but it's even more beautiful than I recall."

"If you prefer this area, I suppose we could find a summer home here. You know, hypothetically."

Right. Hypothetically. I muffle my laughter with a closed mouth. "You're really set on this summer home."

Cole gives me a look as if to ask, 'Why wouldn't I be?'

"I dunno. This is kind of far from the city, but I don't think you can go wrong with anywhere up here."

"Ask me why later," he says cryptically as he tosses his arm around my shoulders and pulls me close.

"Okay..." I nod to the stone pathway. "Let's keep walking. This mansion up here is incredible."

"As opposed to all the dumps we've been seeing?"

Laughter tickles my throat. "I know. What could be better than what we've already seen? Have you ever heard of the Biltmore? It's in North Carolina."

"No. It's a house?"

"Yeah. The biggest in the US. I've never been, but my dad showed me pictures from when he visited it. This one totally reminds me of it. The stone, those rooftop points. I mean, look at that architecture. I have to get some close up shots of this place. C'mon."

We walk straight up through the lawn to the French chateau style mansion. It's like walking into a Jane Austen novel.

"Forget modern architecture, this place is amazing."

"You and your straight lines and glass." Shaking my head, I knock my hip into his. "Sorry, babe. Modern doesn't a hold a candle to this kind of detail."

My finger clicks at every angle and detail, finding too many perfect shots. This place is an architectural gold mine. I could use this entire roll on it. Dang it. Do I have enough film to hold enough pictures for the rest of the trip? When was the last time I bought film? I turn to Cole who's dutifully holding my bag. "Can I look in there? I need to make sure I have an extra roll."

"There's more in the trunk. Monica made sure you were well stocked in case you got trigger happy."

Flipping open the side compartment, my fingers find two new rolls. "Oh, I could kiss her."

"I'll gladly be her stand in."

"I bet you would." Biting my lip, I slowly inch away before turning and bolting across the grass toward the Cliff Walk.

"Oh, that's how it's gonna be?" he calls out. Cole quickly catches me, looping one arm around my waist and heaving me against his body. My squeals can probably be heard for miles.

Carefully, I hold my camera to the side and lift onto my toes to meet Cole's lips. No matter how many times we kiss, I can't control the butterflies. It still feels surreal being more than friends.

"We need a picture of us together," he suggests when I finally drag my lips from his. "Would you be willing to hand your precious camera over so someone can take one?"

"Let someone else use my camera? Blasphemy!"

"For the memories," he reminds me.

I let out an exaggerated sigh. "Fine. For the memories. But if they break my camera, you're buying me a new one."

"Deal."

Cole stops a family of four and asks the mom to take our picture. With the backdrop of the Ochre Court, Cole draws me to him and molds my back against his chest. His arms drape across my shoulders as he kisses my temple, then presses his cheek to mine.

"Smile pretty for the camera," he whispers in my ear. "Though it's not possible for you to do anything less."

I snort and hope the woman takes more than one picture because that look was not my most flattering.

"Okay, we have to stop at The Breakers and tour the inside." I point as we walk up the coastline. "This mansion up ahead. I begged my mom, but she didn't go for it."

My mouth drops when we walk inside.

"I'm digging this Great Hall. What do you think? Can we incorporate this into our little summer house?"

"Only if it looks exactly like this." My head tilts back as my eyes climb to the expansive mural of the sky on the ceiling.

"Noted."

Cole and I practically get lost in the mansion, absorbing the marble walls, high ceilings, and intricate detail of the moldings and pillars. Gah, I wish I were allowed to take pictures of the inside. My fingers itch to pull out my camera. This is every photographer's nightmare. Words could never do this kind of detail justice, but I guess I'll have to leave that up to Cole in the future.

"Okay. So that was amazing, but can you imagine living in a place like that? It would take five minutes just to get from one end of the house to the other. Not to mention the cleaning." I groan. "But I guess the Vanderbilt's had people for that."

"It's unreal. I'd like something bigger than our little Queens apartments, but that would be overwhelming. Do you think they rang bells when they were looking for their kids? A horn, maybe?"

Laughter rushes from my mouth. "A horn. Definitely a horn."

"I don't think I'd want to play hide and seek with you to find you in our home." Cole chuckles before adding, "Hypothetically."

I can't tell if he keeps saying hypothetically for my benefit or if he wants to keep this hypothetical. Do I want to keep this hypothetical? "I'm very good at hide and seek. You'd never be able to find me."

"Granted, ringing a bell would be kind of fun. Very Pavlov's dog."

My shoulder nudges his. "Enough with the bell ringing." Our poor children. Wait. Where did that come from?

The ocean crashes against the cliff, misting us as we walk.

"Oh man, that's cold!" I jog to get ahead of the waves curling over the railing. "Save the camera!"

Cole catches up with me. "Okay, the beach in October isn't exactly warm. We should come back in the summer. I bet we can find some great beach rentals. Bring Shawn and Monica, Brett, Ruby, Amber. Maybe we could get your brother to come."

"Oh, yeah. I like that idea. It would be so much fun! But maybe not Jamie, unless you don't mind him hitting on Amber. He's shameless."

"I'd hate to have to murder your only brother."

I burst into laughter. "We'll reconsider the guest list."

———

AFTER HOURS OF TRAILING DOWN THE CLIFF WALK IN AWE, Cole and I make it back to the car.

"If Ruby doesn't already know, I'm gonna have to ask her to do some research. I gotta know more about these mansions."

"Ruby likes to research, I take it."

"She retains information like no one's business. Brett says if she's not dancing, he knows to find her at the library on campus. It's her second favorite place."

"I guess I can see that now. She does know a lot of random facts." I buckle my seat belt. "We should walk down Thames Street. There's a ton of shops and historical homes and places to eat. We could grab some dinner there."

"I'm game. Newport is winning me over. I'm so glad this is where you picked to spend the day."

Cole's hand in mine gets me emotional. I haven't been this content in so long. We're peering in shop windows and talking about the historical homes. It's nothing really, and yet, it's the happiest I've been in years.

We stop at a corner shop. "Hand blown glass? How cool is that?"

"We need to go in. Amber loves blown glass. I wonder if I could pick her up something for Christmas in there?"

"I'm sure we could find something she'll love."

"It'll probably be easier than the Bloomingdale's shopping trip." He winks. "You'll forever be my Amber present picker-outer."

My chest puffs out as I strut into the little shop ahead of him. "I'll wear that badge proudly."

We walk out with a teal and white swirled dish Amber can put jewelry in. "Good choice," Cole says.

"You're welcome."

———

"So, let's pick a place to stay tonight," I suggest as we're walking back to the car after dinner.

"Already done."

"Oh, yeah? You've got something up your sleeve?"

"I didn't until this afternoon when you referred to it."

"The Castle Hill Inn?" I ask, mixed with hope and shock. He simply nods and smiles, his teeth glowing in the moonlight.

"Cole, that's too much. Really. That place is so fancy."

I know he's a doctor and all, but he's spent enough money already. I hope he doesn't think I need things like that to be happy in this relationship. Knowing him, he probably wouldn't even let me chip in if I tried. I'd probably offend him.

He opens the passenger door for me and presses himself close, keeping me from sliding into the car. "This is your birthday trip. Nothing is too much. I like seeing you happy."

"You know I'd be happy with a little motel. We had the cute bed and breakfast last night. We don't need to go all out every night."

"Tell you what, next trip we take we'll stay at cheap motels and eat at dives. Deal?"

My lips spread into a smile. "Deal." Before ducking into the car, I give him a quick kiss.

As we pull up to the inn, I nearly gasp. It's dreamier than I remembered. The idyllic gray mansion sits atop the cliff on the edge of Newport overlooking the Atlantic. It encompasses all the charm and class of New England.

After checking in, I throw myself on the fluffy bed. This bedding must be meant for royalty. It's so soft. I snuggle into the pillows. He can't make me leave this spot if he tickles me until I pee my pants.

"Don't you dare lay down. You know what happened last night. C'mon." Cole grabs a fluffy blanket and my hand, pulling me from the bed. Dangit. "Let's go cuddle under the stars out on that fancy lawn of theirs."

Okay. He's got me. That does sound dreamy. "Yes, sir." I salute him and he smacks my butt, shooing me out the door.

COLE FINDS AN ADIRONDACK CHAIR AND PULLS ME INTO HIS lap before throwing the thick blanket over us.

"This is what I hate about the city." I lean my head back against his shoulder. "You can never see the stars." His warm breath blows over my cheek.

"I do miss the stars. Being out here makes me forget why I love the city so much, but I guess there are pros and cons anywhere you live. You always want what you can't have."

"So true." His arms encircle my waist tightly. Like bands of steel, I imagine he will never let me go.

"About the whole summer home thing." I grip his arms wrapped around my waist and use my fingernails to doodle above his elbows. "You wanted me to ask you later."

"Oh, yeah." He shifts his legs beneath me, stretching them out. "Can I get serious on you here?"

"Does that mean I have to be serious, too?" My lips twitch with a smirk he can't see.

Cole's fingers poke my side. "As long as you know I'm serious, Sugar Plum, you can do whatever you want."

I squirm away from his fingers. "Okay, okay. I'll be serious, too."

His warm lips find my neck and I melt into him. He's found my weak spot.

"Okay," he says after pressing two kisses to my skin. "Obviously, my job is never going to be your typical eight to five type of job. My hours will be more consistent as an attending, but they'll still be all over the place. It's the hazard of emergency medicine.

"Family is extremely important to me. I want a place where I can get away and make memories whenever I can. That's something I know my dad wished they'd done more of." Cole inhales deeply, releasing a long breath before he continues. "You know they'd been putting off that trip to Paris for years. He told me the week before the crash he wished he'd made more time for Brett and Amber, and their mom. I'm not going to be that guy.

"Sam, I know I keep saying hypothetically to you, but you should know I'm not talking hypotheticals here. I want to know how you feel about these things. I want you to know what I want for my future and I want to know if it lines up with what you want." He twists me around on his lap. His face is barely visible by the light of the moon and stars, but I can see the whites of his eyes clearly focused on me as he says, "I want my future to be with you. I know we're going slow, and that's fine, but I want to be sure you know exactly where I stand."

These are things I knew. Deep down I've known how serious Cole is about us, but hearing him tell me brings a whole new level of meaning. If there wasn't a potential future for us, there's no way we'd risk our friendship. My heart flutters nonetheless.

I bring my hand up to the side of his face. My fingers brush the underside of his jawline, his stubble tickling my skin. "Cole, your future sounds pretty amazing. I'd be crazy to turn something like that down. I think the one thing Flight 397 taught me is to live with no regrets. I haven't been heeding that advice very well. It's time I start."

His eyes close as the fingers on my knee dig a little deeper. "Let me make sure I heard you right. You're saying you wouldn't turn down the summer mansion on the lake. Right?" The whites of his eyes flash in the dark, as he looks at me. He must be wearing the cockiest grin right now.

"I'd be even crazier to turn down the summer mansion."

"And you're cool with me using a bell on our six children?"

I choke. "Six?"

"Five?"

"How about three, and we'll talk."

"But the bell's a go?"

"As long as it's a pleasant-sounding bell."

He grabs my face and pulls me a breath away from his lips. "Good. As for the number," he pauses, kissing me deeply before continuing, "if they're ours, I don't care how many we have."

His touch lures me to a place where everything is perfection. I want to memorize this moment, so it can never be taken away. I want it to become untouchable.

32

TILL I HEAR IT FROM YOU

COLE'S PLACE—NOVEMBER 21, 1995

SAM ROLLS her eyes as I finagle the key in the lock, pushing on my apartment door. She's reminded me a million times that I need to call the super and have him fix this stupid lock.

"I know, I know," I respond before she can give me crap about it again.

The lock gives. Sam breathes a sigh of relief as she squeezes past me into the apartment.

"You grab your stuff. I'll go pee," she calls out already shutting the bathroom door.

Dropping my mail on the counter, I head to my room. I'm tossing some clean underwear and socks into my duffle when Sam steps out of the bathroom.

"Almost done."

"It's fine." She sits on the edge of my bed.

I glance at my clock. "I had no idea grocery shopping would take us so long. I have to be at the hospital in a little over an hour."

Sam laughs. "It wouldn't have taken so long if we'd made a list and stuck to it."

I pull out an extra set of scrubs and add them to my bag

along with jeans and a sweater for Thanksgiving since I plan on spending the next two nights at Sam's.

"Yeah, yeah. I want to make a good impression on your brother. I can't help it."

She removes the T-shirt I threw in my bag. "And you figure cooking him ten side dishes is the way to impress him?" She neatly folds my shirt and replaces it in the bag. Her need to be organized is a ridiculous turn on.

"First, it's not ten dishes." I zip my bag. "Second, yes. The way to a man's good graces is always through his stomach."

"We're making two different types of stuffing, four vegetables—"

"You counted them off at the store," I interrupt. "I think it's important for us both to have our traditional dishes. This is our first Thanksgiving together, we need to test out the recipes for the future."

"There's only three of us, Cole." Her head cocks to the side, her dark hair falling over her shoulder, begging me to sink my hands in.

"That means lots of leftovers. My favorite." I hold my hand out. "C'mon, we have groceries in the car, and if you keep sitting on my bed looking gorgeous, I'm going to be late for work." I wink, pulling her up.

We walk into the living room and Sam inhales sharply.

"What?"

"When was the last time you watered her?" she whines. I love the way she refers to my one plant as a girl. She bumps into my arm as she walks into the kitchen and fills a cup with water.

"My doubles last week killed me, I didn't have time," I offer as an apology. Sam mutters under her breath.

The light on my answering machine blinks on the counter. Since I'm waiting ... I press the message button and pick up the mail pile while Sam fawns over the little plant she gave me a few weeks ago after deciding I needed more life in my place.

"Yes, I'm calling from First Charter Bank about our new—" The machine beeps as I hit delete.

"Dr. Rossner, this is Dr. Rushdie from Seattle Presby. Dr. Bannon forwarded your paperwork to me in hopes I'd consider you for a fellowship in peds. I'd like to find the time to talk with you—" I hit the skip button and check over my shoulder at Sam who's standing next to my plant. Staring at me, straight-faced. Fabulous. That's going to start a conversation.

"Cole. Hey, call me as soon as you get this. It's important," Brett sighs through the line, sending my heart rate accelerating. "It's about Amber."

My hand seizes the phone and dials Brett's dorm.

"What's wrong?" I snap the instant he picks up. Sam's at my side in a flash, her hand wrapping around my arm.

"Uh, nothing. I mean, she's fine—"

"Crap. You had me freaking out."

"But," Brett continues. I inhale. "Have you checked your mail today?"

"My mail? What's this about?"

"Check your mail," he says calmly.

As though she heard Brett, Sam releases my arm as I reach for the mail beside the phone. Her head bobs into my line of sight, her eyes silently questioning what's going on. I lift my shoulder in a half shrug. There's a coupon mailer, two utility bills, a credit card application, and an envelope addressed to me in boxy penmanship. I study the worn envelope. There's no return address and a ... what the heck?

"I have a letter with a Paris postmark." A beat pulses in my temple.

"Open it."

My finger slides beneath the seal. I tug a slip of paper out. Before I read the words, I know who wrote them. But, Paris?

Dear Cole,

I'm a coward. I should have spoken to you in person. I should have talked with you and Brett face-to-face, but I couldn't. I didn't want to face either of you if you didn't understand.

I quit school.

The phone slips from my shoulder, hitting the counter and bouncing to the floor. Sam bends over and picks it up. She says something to Brett. I hear her voice, but my mind is too numb with the words on the paper to register what she says.

I quit school and I decided to backpack Europe. Right now I can picture you both yelling at me. Your face is probably ten shades of red. Take a deep breath and let me explain.

I love you. I love Brett. You two are the most important people in my life. We've been through a lot in the last three years. I tried Cole, I really did try to get myself together at Penn, but I'm still in pieces. I don't know if college is what I need or even want anymore.

I'm lost.

B has Ruby. You have Sam—don't try to tell me any differently! —and I have nothing. I don't mean love. I'm not pouting because I don't have a boyfriend.

I don't have me.

I can't find me at Penn.

I'm not sure if I can find me in Europe either. I've been here two months and I'm still not sure what I'm looking for.

I only know I must try. I have to do this on my own. You two can't keep picking me up and protecting me.

I love you, big brother.

Always, Amber

Sam touches my back as I lower the letter in shock. The phone appears in my face. I take it, bringing it to my ear.

"Two months?" I ask numbly. Brett's half-grunt, half-laugh

greets me. What does he find funny about this? "I spoke to her last week."

"I called Hope after I left you the message. Amber left right before school started. She's been lying to us when she calls."

"That's why she never answers when I call. Why the only time I talk to her it's because she called me. Why? What did Hope say?"

"Mostly what the letter said. I assume yours says pretty much what mine does. Hope said Amber wanted to get there and see if she liked it before she told us. Hope apologized, by the way."

"Apologized? Why didn't she call you and warn you?" Anger seeps in replacing the numbness.

"She thought it was another one of Amber's whims. Hope has always stood by Amber's side first and foremost. She wasn't going to rat her out. Which is why Amber trusted her with the information."

"And the only reason we're finding out now is because she knew there was no way she could have talked me out of seeing her for Thanksgiving." Unbelievable.

"She has plenty of money. She's staying at hostels, and according to Hope she's already worked on a few farms picking up extra cash. She seems to be doing well. She's always happy when we talk."

Is he trying to talk me into liking this idea? My twenty-year-old sister, alone, backpacking around Europe. Are you freaking kidding me? "We have to get her to come home."

"She won't do it."

"You want to bet? We'll call the bank and cut her funds. When she calls—"

"Cole," Brett cuts me off, his exhale heavy. "She won't do it. She needs this."

My eyes close. When I open them again, Sam is in front of me. Right, Sam. A car full of groceries, and work.

"Brett, I've got to go. I need to be at the hospital at five and I need to get Sam home and help her unload groceries."

"Okay. Ruby and I fly out in the morning. I'll page you with her dad's number later."

"Sounds good."

"Hey, man, she'll be alright. I'm sure she'll call in a few days, too. She's probably giving us time to process and cool down."

"Yeah, sure. Give Ruby my love and you guys have a safe trip. Love you, man."

I turn the phone off, and nearly throw it across the apartment.

"What happened? Is everything okay?"

I hold up the letter my fingers have crumpled between us. She hesitantly removes it from my hand. Drawing back, her spine hits the counter behind her as she reads. Shadows cover her expressive eyes. Her jaw drops slightly as her mouth forms a small 'O'.

"She mentioned going to Europe to me, but—"

"Wait. What?"

"At the Fourth of July party, Amber talked to me about it." Sam lowers the letter, meeting my gaze. "But she was supposed to tell you and Brett before she left."

"At the Fourth of July party? I'm sorry, please explain this to me. She told you she was going to Europe?"

She sets the letter on the counter with an unsteady hand. "Everyone had ditched us, and she wanted to talk to me privately. I was a little confused at first. I told her she should talk to you about it, but she was concerned about you and Brett and wanted to make sure I'd take care of you. I told her I would."

I step back. "I don't even know where to begin." I can't breathe. My fingers clasp on top of my head and I exhale. "Amber ... No, she told ... she asked ..." I drop my hands, cursing. My brain unable to form a coherent thought.

"I'm sorry. I should've said something, but it wasn't my place."

"Wasn't your place? Are you kidding me?"

"She was confiding in me," she tries. "She said she would tell you!"

"My then twenty-year-old sister tells you she's dropping out of college to go gallivanting around Europe like a freaking hippie, and you didn't think it was your place?"

"I see why you're upset. A college education is important, but c'mon, Cole. If I'd had the opportunity to go to Europe when I was her age, I would've gone in a heartbeat."

"Oh, sure. Since you think it'd be awesome, she should pack up and go."

"She'd already made the decision," Sam emphasizes. "I wasn't telling her to go."

"No, you just didn't bother to tell me about it."

"I should've. I know I should've. But it was before this." She gestures between us, her voice wavering. "I was trying to be a listening ear for Amber. I knew it was going to upset you. Of course I didn't want to be the one to break the news. It seemed like something to be discussed between family, not this outsider."

Amber gave me such a hard time about my feelings for Sam that day. She told me life was too short to pine after the girl I was meant to be with. Dang it. She spurred me into making the decision to go after Sam, then she went to Sam and confided in her? I can't believe her.

"Outsider?" Is that what she thought of our relationship at the time? "You were my best friend. You were not an outsider. Look, I know you didn't keep it from us to be hurtful, but you did keep it from me. This isn't something of little importance. This is her life."

"I know." Her lip quivers and she steps closer. "I'm sorry, but think of it from her perspective. She's still young. We all know firsthand how quickly life can be taken away. She's living with no regrets. Let her have this."

"Living with no regrets? You don't think she'll regret walking away from school? Throwing away her inheritance?" I flex and unflex my fingers, making fists to control the energy coursing through me. "Is your easy acceptance of this stemming from your own wishes, or do you truly think this is good for her?"

Sam takes a shaky breath, her mouth parting in reply, but I throw a hand up, stopping her.

"Because I've got to tell you from where I'm standing this has disaster written all over it. You don't know Amber like I do. She's not you. She's not Brett. She's a wreck. She's impulsive and uninhibited and ... all I can picture is her knocked up on a street corner or living in a French brothel."

The color drains from Sam's face and she sucks in a surprised breath. "I ... You're right. I don't know her. I don't know what else you want me to say."

"I'm supposed to take care of her, Sam. I would have thought, if nothing else, you would have understood that much."

I pull the ring with my car key from my keychain as I check the time once again. "I've got to go. You take the car and I'll grab the train from here instead of going to your place first." I toss her the key.

"Let me drive you to the station." Her hand reaches for my arm. I scoot away.

"Nah, it's fine. The walk will do me good. Do you want me to call you before I leave the hospital tonight? You know how it is. I'm off at one, but if it's busy—"

She heavily exhales, her eyes drooping with dejection. "Cole, I know. Just use your key. Whatever time you get there is fine."

"Okay." I throw my bag over my shoulder and open the door. Sam sniffles behind me. I can't do it. I can't walk out of the apartment without saying goodbye, no matter how angry I am. I drop my bag in the hall and turn.

She crashes into my chest. "You were just going to walk out?"

One hand presses her cheek to my chest as the other encircles her waist. "No. No, I was about to turn around." I kiss the top of her head. "Baby, it'll be fine. I'm sorry."

"No, I'm sorry. I could've prevented this. I didn't think."

"I'm angry and confused." And a bit hurt by the idea that she thought she was an outsider. That she didn't realize how important the information Amber told her was to me and Brett. "I need to go. We can talk later."

Sam backs away with her head down and rubs her finger under her nose as she sniffles.

I lift her chin with my fingers. "I love you." My lips brush hers.

"I love you, too."

33

WHEN YOU SAY NOTHING AT ALL
SAM & MONICA'S—NOVEMBER 22, 1995

TWO AM ROLLS AROUND and worry hits me. Is Cole not coming to my place? He's working late, it makes sense for him to go home. I'll understand.

I close my eyes and try to find sleep. The bed jostles and I sigh deeply when he crawls into bed beside me. I peek at the clock beside my bed. 3:00AM. He doesn't curl up behind me like he normally does. He remains on his side of the bed, and I remain as still as possible so he thinks I'm asleep, so he won't have to pretend. My heart sinks. I've slept alone for three years, but tonight I ache like never before.

COLE FINDS ME IN THE KITCHEN ALREADY PULLING OUT recipes and dishes for pre-baking, and he doesn't say a thing about Amber. I don't dare bring it up. We go right to baking.

It's nearly four o'clock in the afternoon and we've avoided our fight all day. What are the chances he's gotten over it? Slim to none.

The kitchen is covered with baking dishes and mixing bowls.

Empty soup cans and baking supplies fill the trash can. Dishes already pile high next to the sink.

"These leftovers are going to go bad before we can eat them all. I hope you and Jamie have a huge appetite tomorrow."

"I always have an appetite for Thanksgiving leftovers. Honestly, I like them better than the meal." Cole covers yet another casserole with tin foil.

"Well, that makes one of us. So you'll have to eat leftovers for two."

He props himself against the counter and surveys the mess. "Sounds like a good deal to me." He checks his watch. That stupid, stupid watch. "What time does Jamie get in?"

"I think he said 7:15. I'm gonna meet him at the airport to ride back here with him."

"I'm sorry I can't go with you. I hate when you ride the train alone."

"And you know I can take care of myself." I push the utensil draw closed with my hip and walk over to the sink to begin the dishes.

"Yes, Supergirl." He straightens and steps behind me, his lips skimming the skin directly behind my ear. The first touch since our fight. "And you know that I will worry no matter what you say."

Rolling up my sleeves, I flip on the water and wait for it to heat up, suppressing a shiver. Normally Cole can barely keep his hands off me. I've missed his touch all day. Now he's kissing my weak spot? Are we not going to address the giant-sized Amber in the room? I don't want to brush it under the rug.

"I should clean up and get going."

Of course. Another shift cutting into an important conversation.

"Oh, before I forget, I changed my machine's message for Amber, telling her to call here. If she calls, will you get a number for where she's staying and tell her to page me? Or you call me?"

There's uncertainty hiding in his eyes. It's as though he's not sure he trusts me to do what he asks. I hate him not feeling like he can trust me. It's unfair, and yet I understand, but I need him to forgive me. He knows my heart. I never meant to upset him.

"Trust me. I'll make sure she calls you."

I'm finishing up the dishes when Cole walks to front door. He stops, grabbing his coat off the hook. "Tell Jamie I'm sorry I had to work, and I can't wait to meet him in the morning. And please be careful."

He's going to walk out the door without kissing me goodbye? "I will." I dry off my hands, hesitating by the sink. "You be careful, too."

Cole doubles back and stands before me. His blue eyes hold mine as his lips form a sexy crooked grin. Gosh, he's so handsome it's painful. His thumb rubs the skin above my nose. "Stop worrying, everything will be fine." He leans down and presses a swift kiss to my lips.

He says that, but what is he referring to? The Thanksgiving dinner? Us? "Will it?" My eyes remain closed, my mouth hovering against his.

"It has to be," he whispers, our lips brushing with each word. I open my eyes to find him walking out the door.

34

I'M THE ONLY ONE

MONICA & SAM'S--NOVEMBER 23, 1995

"Do you remember the Thanksgiving when Mom burned the mashed potatoes and she felt so bad you pretended you liked them that way?"

I can't stop laughing. "Oh my gosh, I still regret that! The next time she made mashed potatoes she burned a portion just for me."

"And you ate it!"

"I had to!"

Jamie hops up onto the counter. "I wouldn't have. It was like eating cigarette smoke."

"The taste will be forever burned into my taste buds." I squeeze the stuffing in below the turkey in the oven. "Pray I don't burn anything, because whether you like it or not, you're eating it. I didn't spend all this time making it just for it to go to waste."

"Yeah, what were you thinking making food for an army."

"It was Cole! He made me do it."

"Who is this guy anyway? You barely tell me anything about him and now the three of us are eating Thanksgiving dinner together."

"Shhhh, he might hear you. He had a late shift last night. He needs the sleep."

"Late shift? What? Does he work the graveyard shift at a convenience store?"

"He's a doctor." Jamie straightens with a sly grin, ready to make some obnoxious comment. I. hold up my hand. "Before you say anything, I want you to know I've known him for a few years and he's a really great guy. I think you'll love him."

"That's what you said about Paul." Jamie's expression falls immediately after he says the words. "I'm sorry, Speedy. I shouldn't have said that. I wasn't thinking."

I brush him off, "It's fine. I know you never liked him."

"But I should've kept that to myself. I'm just looking out for you." He hops off the counter. "Let me help you with something. What can I do?"

"You're a little late on the offer." I make my way out of the kitchen, punching him in the shoulder as I leave. "Everything is prepped and ready to go. It just needs to finish cooking."

Jamie follows and kicks his leg up, throwing himself over the couch. He leans back with his head propped up against the armrest, his arms tucked under his neck. "Then I guess I should do what I do best on Thanksgiving and relax."

I whack him in the head with a pillow as I walk by him and sit in the recliner. "Yeah, some help you are, showing up after everything is taken care of."

The creak of my bedroom door pulls my gaze away from Jamie.

"It smells like someone will be having a turkey hangover in here soon." Cole walks into the living room dressed in dark jeans and a cream sweater. "I missed the parade, didn't I?"

Jamie swivels his head around at Cole's voice, his face sour as though he's expecting to meet the grim reaper. Scooting to the edge of my seat, I move to stand and introduce them.

"Roz?" Jamie shoots up, his feet planting on the floor. "You're the guy my sister's dating?"

What ... the ... heck?

"J.R.?" Cole's eyes bug out before he maneuvers around the couch to hug Cole. They hug each other like long lost friends! "You're Sam's brother? This is a joke, right?"

J.R.? Who the crap is J.R.?

"Speedy, why didn't you tell me Cole Rossner was the guy?"

"I—you two *know* each other?" My head spins. Is my apartment tilting? Maybe we're in the middle of an earthquake. I stand to test it, but my feet are on solid ground.

"Know each other? We were frat brothers at Penn," Cole laughs. "And who the heck is Speedy?" His brows arch.

Jamie steps back and throws his arm over my shoulder. "This one hasn't told you about the track star she was in high school? This girl won sprints at State her senior year."

"You don't say." Cole smirks, accusations forming. His eyes shift back to Jamie. "Man, it's been years."

Jamie's hands make like his head is exploding and steps away from me. "What's it been? Six? Seven years?"

"Yeah. I'm finally in my last year of residency. I was so busy with med school, I haven't gone to any alumni events or chapter parties."

"Yeah, I haven't bothered with those either. I've been too busy in Boston. Work, work, work. But you know all about that. Your hours must be insane."

"Boston, really? You said you were going to end up there. Good for you. It's still in the running for me."

Is my jaw on the floor? Even if I knew what to say, I wouldn't be able to get a word in edgewise. I guess I don't have to worry about them getting along.

"How did we not put two and two together?" I ask Cole.

Cole shakes his head, walking over to me. "Jamie Cooper wouldn't ring a bell. Cooper is common enough, and *Jamie* went by J.R. at Penn." He tugs on the hem of my shirt. "Good morning, by the way." He kisses my forehead. Stupid big brother in the room. "The fact that you ran track explains a lot. I should get a handicap next time we race." He winks.

"Yeah, I guess."

"Maybe if you'd mentioned his last name I could've told you," Jamie spouts.

That gets Cole's attention. "Huh? She doesn't talk about me much, I take it?"

"Speedy here is pretty close-lipped when it comes to her dating life." Jamie elbows me in the ribs. "I didn't even know she was dating someone until I called her last month and told her I was coming for sure."

"Interesting," Cole murmurs, his fingers tugging on my hair.

You're so not helping this situation, Jamie. "In my defense," I shift away from both of their reach, "Jamie isn't the warmest and most welcoming to the idea of me dating. I figured he'd need to meet you first, so he wouldn't pass too many judgments."

Would Amber tell you who she's dating? The question reaches the tip of my tongue and I swallow it down. It might reopen a wound we haven't healed yet.

"Like I could pass judgments on this guy." Jamie slaps Cole's shoulder.

Cole punches Jamie in the stomach and then they're hugging and laughing. What kind of alternate universe am I living in?

"It's so good to see you, man. So good," Cole says as they part.

As we're waiting for the food to finish up, the boys sit on the couch catching up while watching football. I let them be and set the table. Their laughter and cheers fill the apartment. As strange as it is, I'm grateful they know each other. It's really starting to feel like the holiday.

. . .

274

"So," Jamie finishes his bite of turkey, "How did you two meet?"

Cole explains how we bumped into each other at the memorial for Flight 397.

"Why were you there?" Jamie asks Cole, like it isn't obvious he lost someone. I kick his shin under the table.

Cole sets his fork on his plate. "Uh, my dad and his wife were on the plane."

"Oh, man." Jamie pauses mid-bite. "I'm sorry, Roz. That's rough. I hate that for you."

"Yeah, it's been hard." Cole turns his gaze to mine. "For all of us. I had to take guardianship of my half-siblings, if you can believe that."

"Ha, you couldn't stand them." Amusement dances across Jamie's eyes. "That change at all?"

"It did, over time. We're extremely close now. Losing our dad forced us all, especially me, to accept our relationship."

"Well, that's cool. I'm glad you had someone, that you could be there for each other. I know when Speedy lost Paul, she was a mess. I couldn't be there for her like I wanted to." Jamie spares me a glance before he looks back at Cole. "It's kind of hard to mourn a guy you never liked, but I mourned for her, for how it affected her, changed her."

"I'm right here, James," I bristle, glaring at him across the table.

Jamie ignores my stare. His brow rises, a thought dawning on him. "Roz, you remember that party years ago, when I told you my sister was coming for the weekend and I wanted you to meet her?" Everything comes to a screeching halt. My breathing. My heartbeats. "You left that weekend, I can't remember why." Jamie points his fork back and forth between Cole and me, chuckling to himself. "And yet, here you are."

Cole mutters a curse under his breath as his eyes go wide. "I completely forgot about that. That was the weekend I went home and finally met with my dad. He'd been bugging me about med school and wanting to help me." He looks at me, a dazed expression on his face, and I spare him a glance from the corner of my eyes.

The weekend I met Paul.

Don't cry, Samantha. Do. Not. Cry.

Nothing. I can't get my mouth to work to say anything.

"Do you know the crazy story behind our relationship?" Cole asks Jamie after a few moments.

"Can't say that I do since Speedy keeps me in the dark most of the time." Shut up, Jamie. Shut. Up. Now is not the time.

"A month after we met at the memorial, I ran into your sister two blocks from my hospital at a gyro cart. A few weeks after that, we ended up on the train ride home together. We bumped into each other at the market a few months later."

Jamie chuckles and leans back with his arms folded.

"And crazier still, my buddy Shawn lives two doors down from here and dragged me into Pure for a class several months after the market meeting. I've been pursuing this one," he throws me a smile, "for a long time."

"Well, isn't that something?" Jamie grins, but I'm on the verge of throwing up. "I guess you two were always meant to be."

"Had I not gone home—" Cole lets the statement linger in the air between us.

What if...

THE BOYS COVER EVERY TOPIC IMAGINABLE AS THEY HELP ME clear the table, but my lips won't form a coherent sentence, so I keep my mouth shut. When I turn on the water to do the dishes, Jamie nudges me out of the way. "Let me do this. You cooked a fantastic meal. Now it's my turn." He kisses my cheek. "Thank you for dinner, sis."

I nod, not saying anything as I escape to my bedroom. I just need a minute to process all of this by myself.

What if Cole had been there that night? Would I still have met Paul? Would I have chosen him over Cole? No. I can't go there because I think I know the answer. Pushing those thoughts away, I pick up some socks and toss them in the hamper. And another pair, and some jeans. My floor is covered in clothes. How did I let it get this dirty?

"I told you this was fate," Cole says, his voice light as he moves behind me and wraps his arms around my waist. How long have I been locked away? I wasn't ready for Cole to join me.

"You okay? You sort of disappeared suddenly." He nuzzles my neck, his lips trailing up and down.

I shift out of his arms, putting distance between us as I pick up more random clothes from my floor and put them in the hamper. "I'm fine. Just taking a minute to decompress."

"I can't believe J.R. is Jamie. I can't believe—"

I spin around, clutching crumpled pajama pants in my hands. "Cole, that was the night I met Paul."

He draws back at the bark in my words, sucking in a breath. "You met Paul that night?" He pushes his hand through his hair, a wry smile on his lips. "You were supposed to meet me."

I choke on a laugh, or maybe it's a cry, as I press my fingers to my temples. I can't believe he just said that. "But you weren't there! You weren't there and I met Paul and now he's dead."

"Exactly, he's gone. You've moved on. Why are you angry?"

"Why am I—why am I angry?" Who is this man and what has he done with my Cole? "I wasn't angry until you became so insensitive! *I was supposed to meet you*," I scoff. "Like Paul was some insignificant frat boy at that party, so easily disregarded. How can you talk to me like that? Who *are* you?"

"I'm the man you're with now. I'm the man I thought you loved."

"That's not even the point, Cole," I urge him to understand. I can't control the quiver in my voice. "You keep talking about fate. How we were fated to be together. Then tell me this, why did fate send you away that night and give me Paul? He shouldn't even have been at that party, either. He was visiting one of his friends for the weekend. Why did we pick that exact same weekend to visit if we weren't supposed to meet? Why make me fall in love with him and take him away from me? Was it some cruel joke?"

"He was taken away because you were meant to be with me." Cole shrugs. He *shrugs* like what he's saying is supposed to be obvious or romantic.

"Stop saying that!" I throw the pajamas on the floor. I will not let him spit on Paul's grave.

A bitter laugh springs from his chest. "Why? Why should I not tell you what I believe? You think I want to admit that fate took those lives that day? That people had to die for others to be happy. Look at Brett and Ruby. They would never have met if not for the crash.

"I've tried to be patient, I've tried to be your friend, but I can't because I've only ever loved you. I love you. I want to spend my life with you. Do you not feel the same? Are you still hung up on the guy who I can't believe made you all that happy to begin with?"

"Wow," I breathe, shaking my head. "You went there. You didn't even *know* Paul! You have no right—"

"Don't play all shocked with me. You didn't even tell your brother my name. *My name.* I took you on a trip for your birthday. My name didn't come up once? Is that how much I mean to you?"

"That's not what this is about. That's *totally* different. You don't know how my relationship with Jamie works. He's an overprotective, frustrating, hard-headed older brother who doesn't understand the first thing about my heart. It's no wonder Amber didn't want to tell you anything."

He lets out a humorless laugh. "Low blow, sweetheart."

"Hurts, doesn't it?" My nostrils flare as I try evening my breathing and angry tears stream down my face. "And what about Seattle?" I snap. "Were you ever going to tell me you were thinking about taking a job across the country? Talk about things that should come up in conversation. You say you love me, but if you truly loved me I feel like you would've included me in on that *minor* detail."

"It's not what you think it is, but I guess it's no different than the minor detail of not telling me my sister was running away."

"I knew you were still pissed about that! How many times do I have to say I'm sorry? She was supposed to tell you!"

"How many signs do you need to see to believe in fate?"

My hands fly up. "Who cares about stupid fate when we don't even know how to communicate?"

Cole's head shakes. "Nah, I think we just communicated perfectly. You're not over your dead fiancé and I am... I'm... I don't know what I am." The alarm on his watch goes off. "I'm going to be late for my shift."

"Perfect timing. Like always. Run off to the hospital when there are more important things at home. I know that's where you'd rather be anyway."

Cole shakes his head, his eyes filling with a pain I rarely see. "No." He steps forward, toe-to-toe. His hand presses to my chest, covering my heart. "This is where I'd rather be, but I'm not sure you have room for me there."

Then he turns on his heel, and I hardly make out his figure walking away through my tear-stained eyes.

I drop to my knees, exhausted. Mentally, emotionally, physically.

What just happened to us?

35

MISERY

ANGER FUELS my walk to the train stop. What was I supposed to say? We all make choices in life. Had I gone to that party and met Sam, maybe it would have spared her the pain of finding and losing Paul, but I never would have had those years with my father. Fate sucks.

Door number one gives me Sam.

Door number two gives me my dad.

We chose door number three. I got my dad, Sam got Paul, and now we have each other.

Once the train doors close and I'm sitting in the corner, heading into the city, my anger recedes and my chest aches. I drop my head into my hands and breathe deeply.

I practically told Sam I wanted to marry her, and she got pissed about Paul? I tell her it must have been fate that put us together, and she brings up Paul, again.

Paul.

The guy she fell in love with when she was nineteen. The guy she lived with and planned to marry. The guy she must have pictured her entire life with: babies, vacations, growing old. All the things I've pictured doing with Sam, she surely pictured doing with Paul once. Then he was gone. Two weeks before their wedding.

How could I be so selfish?

———

My head pounds relentlessly. A non-stop barrage of moments shared with Sam loop through my mind.

"Dr. Rossner?"

What was I thinking? How could I attack Paul like that? How dare I yell at Sam that way?

"Dr. Rossner?"

I blink at the paperwork before me, clearing my thoughts. My first-year shadow, Dr. Reynolds, stands at the counter. Her eyes narrow as she waits for my response. She's studied me all night. Pull yourself together, Cole.

"Yeah?" I rub the back of my neck.

"I've got the toxicology screen on our hit and run, and Murray has your x-rays."

Time to be a doctor. "Great," I clear my throat, forcing a smile and grabbing my coffee as I stand. "What are the tox results?"

"High as a kite." Her head shakes.

"Of course he is. Guy's lucky the victim lived." Reynolds hands over the chart and I scan the findings. "You want to let the officer know while I grab the x-rays from Murray?" I ask as I hand the results back.

"Really?"

I nod.

My head shakes at the eagerness in her eyes as she hurries away. Was I that bright-eyed two years ago? I was. I was that bright-eyed two days ago. I love my job, but tonight ... tonight is the first time I find myself hating it. Sam's complaint about my leaving her for work won't leave my mind. As though I would put my job over her. I wouldn't, but I can't not show up. This is what I do, I save lives. Maybe that's my problem—a hero complex? Maybe that's why the mere mention of Paul sends my blood boiling.

My pager goes off as a code goes out over the intercom system. I rush to triage, once again pushing my personal life into the background because that's what I'm trained to do.

THERE'S NOTHING LIKE AN ER WAITING ROOM ON Thanksgiving night to help the hours speed by. I push Sam and our fight out of my mind as I move from patient to patient. Grease burns, allergic reactions, indigestion, and turkey carving injuries. Is this what I went to school for eight years for? By the time midnight rolls around, my patient load has dwindled down to nothing and I've caught up on my paperwork.

"Why don't you head out early?" Rivera pops around the corner into the locker room while I'm switching shirts, thanks to some projectile vomiting by a turkey overindulging kid.

His suggestion is surprising. "I'm good, thanks though."

"You're good?" He rests against the locker next to mine. "You've been on a mission all night. Have you stopped for air once?"

"Just doing my job."

"We're overstaffed and you've signed off on all your patients. Don't get stuck. You know it'll happen, some crazy case is going to walk in here at 12:55 and you'll be roped into working it up for two hours." Rivera pushes off the locker and slaps my shoulder. "Get back to that girl of yours."

Get back to my girl? The chaos of the night kept me from thinking about it all, until now. If I show up, will Sam let me in? Her tear-streaked face as I walked out of her room hours earlier assails me. It's such a sharp contrast to the face I typically picture of hers. The one she made on her birthday, lying in bed with me. The smile she gave me knowing that that time, it was right.

I don't care if she wants to let me in or not, I need to see her. We need to have this out. One stupid fight isn't going to tear this relationship down. We're stronger than that. We've got to be, because imagining my life without her isn't an option.

36

LET HER CRY

"WELL, THAT DIDN'T SOUND GOOD." Jamie leans his shoulder against my door jam.

"I don't even know what happened," I rasp, glancing up at him from my place on the floor.

He grimaces as he walks into my room, crosses his legs, and sits down in front of me. "Sounds like you had a fight."

"Thanks, Captain O."

"I do my best." Jamie's lip twitches into a side-smirk before his eyes soften. "Cole left here pretty upset. You wanna talk about it?"

"I don't know how it got so out of hand." My jaw works from side to side. "I don't know how to make him see. He just doesn't understand. He doesn't respect Paul."

"Who does?" Jamie retorts.

My jaw clenches. "I mean the memory of Paul."

"I know," he commiserates. "But I'm serious. Does Cole know the real Paul or the Paul you created after he died? I know I shouldn't talk ill of the dead and you loved him, but don't you think you're remembering him a little differently?"

"I know he wasn't perfect, James," I snap.

"Wasn't perfect?" he snorts. "Coming from the woman who sat in a restaurant alone for hours on her twenty-first birthday because her fiancé got caught up at work and forgot all about their plans and didn't bother to call. Coming from the woman who made excuses for her fiancé every time he'd come home hours after he was supposed to be home from work, drunk and smelling of cigars, but it's okay because he just needed to unwind after work. Or how about all the times—"

"Enough," I exhale. I won't dwell on those things. I can't. "I know. You don't have to remind me of his downfalls. I remember them well."

"Do you? Because I think even when you were with him you did everything in your power to ignore them. You know what I think?"

I don't want to know. My head shakes.

"I know you don't want to hear it, but I'm going to tell you anyway. I think you settled for Paul. I think he was the first guy to make you feel special and he provided a solid sounding future. You were in love with the idea of security. He wasn't Dad." One of his shoulders shrugs. "I can't blame you for that."

He's right. I never wanted to believe Paul wasn't the one. I fell fast and I fell hard. And I was young. But it's wrong to not respect his memory now that he's gone. Just because he wasn't perfect doesn't mean I didn't love other things about him.

"Sam," Jamie clutches my hand resting on my thigh, "I know you loved him and he loved you in his own way, but you've got to take him off this pedestal you've created since he died. He wasn't good to you. He didn't deserve you, and I think you know that."

When Ruby told me about her story meeting Brett, it had fate written all over it. It's like fate said, *"Okay, this terrible thing has to happen, but here you go. Let me give you something good to get you through it."*

Is that what fate did to me? *"I'm sorry I have to take away*

Paul, but let me give you Cole. He'll be good to you. He'll understand you. He'll make you irrevocably happy." Or was I never supposed to get Paul?

I sniffle and wipe under my nose. "I just keep thinking, what if Cole had been there that night? Would I have picked him over Paul? Who was right for me that night? Was I supposed to lose Paul? Is that why Cole wasn't there? Or was I always supposed to be with Cole, so fate found another way for us to be?"

"Stop it." Jamie takes my shoulders, gently shaking me. "You shouldn't look at that night and imagine what if. You don't have to choose. You don't have to do anything. I never should've brought up that night. I forgot that's when you met Paul. Whatever happened doesn't matter now."

"I think Cole got a job offer in Seattle." My shoulders fall as I blink away tears, and Jamie removes his hands.

"Is he taking it?"

"I don't know, but that's not the point. He didn't even tell me about it."

"Maybe because he wasn't going to take it, so it didn't need to be shared."

That sounds like Cole.

"You're making issues out of nothing, Sam."

"I know. He was just so *insensitive*."

"Well, I might get a little impatient, too, if the woman I loved kept second-guessing her feelings for me."

"I don't. I know exactly how I feel about Cole."

"So, you love him?"

Exhaling my worry, I answer, "More than I thought possible. I think that's why everything kind of blew up tonight. It's like I'm self-sabotaging because he has the power to destroy my heart. Every road leads back to Cole." Looking down at my hands, I admit, "I can't bear the thought of losing him. Knowing what that kind of loss feels like. If Cole left me, I'd never recover."

"You need to tell him. From what I could hear, because you

two were *not* quiet, he needs to know Paul is in your past." Jamie leans forward, his elbows resting on his knees. "Cole is your future, Speedy. And he seems like a pretty dang good one."

37

I CAN LOVE YOU LIKE THAT, ALWAYS

N TRAIN—NOVEMBER 24, 1995

THE TRAIN RIDE to Astoria is agony. I replay our words the entire way and I come back to the same conclusion every time. I have no idea how our argument escalated so quickly.

How did one flippant comment from Jamie blow everything?

The train slows as it pulls into Sam's stop and I stand, throwing my bag over my body as I move toward the doors.

Dang Jamie. How crazy is life? How crazy is it that six years ago I could have met Sam? How crazy is it that we would both suffer losses in the same crash? That I would meet her a year after that loss? That I would I know within an instant of meeting her that I needed to know her better? That she would turn into my best friend? That I would fall in love with her six years after we missed our first opportunity? How crazy is it ... that as the doors slide open Sam stands in my path?

The site of her nearly knocks me to my knees.

"What are you doing here?" My hands immediately reach for her arms, shifting her back so I can move out of the train and onto the platform.

"I was coming to you," she says breathlessly. "You got off early?"

"You were coming for me?" I yank her into my chest and loop my arms around her. It's almost comical how perfectly in sync we are. "*I* was coming for *you*," I explain, pulling back just as quickly, steering her two steps away. I drop my hands and she immediately turns her head, angling her face away from me.

Oh, no you don't. My head dips and I catch her eyes. "We need to talk about everything that happened, but I need you to know one thing right now."

"What?" Her fingers fidget with the buttons on her coat nervously.

"I will never walk away from you. Ever."

Sam exhales, her shoulders dropping as she releases her tension and searches my face. Inside I'm smiling because I was right. I knew she was worried about more than Paul.

"I couldn't figure out why you were angry about my job, about my having to get to work. I know you understand my hours and the crazy stress being a doctor can put on us as a couple. We've talked about it so many times." Her head bobs enough for me to keep on. "Your father left your mom, he walked out on you and Jamie, but I won't do that. I will not walk out on you. On us." My hands grasp her cold ones, squeezing them between us. "I will always come back, Sam."

Her lips press together tightly the way they do when she's fighting tears, and her head shakes slowly from side to side, as though...

"Unless you don't want me to?"

"No. No, it's not that." Her head shakes adamantly. "I think you know me better than I know myself."

How wrong she is. "If that were true, tonight would never have gone down the way it did."

"I think that's exactly why it went down the way it did. Love makes us mad."

The wind picks up, whining as it slices up from the street into the elevated tracks. "We need to talk, but it's nearly 1 AM and freezing out here. Can we go back to my place since Jamie is at yours?"

"Yeah. I told him not to wait up for me."

We walk down to Broadway from the train platform and head south. "C'mere." I wrap my arm around Sam's shoulder, pulling her into my side so we look like one person walking. "We'll share body heat."

"Sound logic."

"So, where do we start?" The wind makes easy work of the thin scrubs I'm wearing. Why didn't I take the extra minute to throw on my jeans?

Her hand grabs my wrist hanging over her shoulder. "Let me go first."

I nod, then stop and look down at her. "Wait. No, let me go first."

She inhales through her nose. "Okay."

"About Amber," I exhale as we begin walking again. "I'm sorry for blaming you. Amber has a way with people. I can see how she must have confided in you, knowing it would put you in a tough position. Obviously, it's not your fault she left."

"If I could go back, I'd have told you. I'd have put you first."

My arm tightens around her neck and I lean down, pressing a kiss to her hair. "I know you would." And I believe it. There's no doubt in my mind that Sam knows how much I care about Amber; I merely allowed my anger to override rational thinking.

"She didn't call today," I admit painfully. "She didn't call me, or Brett, and she didn't call her Gram either. I'm worried about her, Sam, but it wasn't fair of me to take that out on you."

"Thank you," she says softly. "You know Amber is a tough girl. I'm sure she's fine, but she probably knows you guys got her letters. I doubt she's excited to call and deal with the consequences. Give her a few more days. She'll call."

I pray she's right.

"Okay, your turn." I'll try to keep my mouth shut.

"I think I need to be more straightforward with you about Paul." She curls deeper into my side, shying away from the cold. "Jamie helped remind me of a few things after you left, things I subconsciously avoided. Or maybe consciously. Paul wasn't some perfect fiancé, though I think you might have already caught the drift of that at dinner."

"Sam," I interrupt. I can't even let her get out three sentences before I have to make a point. "I don't want you to point out his faults," I explain, not wanting her to misunderstand where I stand. It's not fair of me to make her feel as though she has to pick apart the type of man he was.

"No, I need you to hear this."

I want to stop so we can talk face-to-face. This is too important to gloss over as we huddle together, but it's too dang cold. "Okay," I sigh. She has the right to say what she needs. I'll listen.

"I'm not going to list all of his flaws. I just ... I shouldn't have gotten upset with you for stating a fact about him not making me all that happy. There are a lot of things about Paul that didn't fit with me, but I chose to ignore them. There were probably a lot of things about me that he chose to ignore, too. If I'd gone through with the wedding, it wouldn't have been right. It would have been a mistake."

I suck in a long breath, the cold air burning my lungs.

"I—"

"Wait. Before you say anything else." I glance around. We're at the corner of Broadway and 36th Street. Turning, I study her face under the streetlamp. "We can't have this conversation like this. I need to look at you. It's half a mile, are you up for a run?"

She lifts a side smile. "I'll race you."

God, I love this girl! "You're on."

Sam's hand slips from mine as she takes off down 36th Street and I lay chase. The frigid air burns my lungs and numbs my face, but I don't stop. Her hood falls back from her speed, letting her dark strands fly in the wind. I run faster, but I let her win. Maybe she would have won regardless, but I wasn't giving up the view I had of her.

COLE'S PLACE

"I can hardly breathe," I gasp, pulling out my keys and letting us in the building. As usual, she's barely winded.

"Wimp," she quips. "You should probably workout more."

I grab her hand, bringing her frozen fingers to my lips and kissing them. "You should probably remember who had to pull who up that ridge a few weeks ago."

"Let's not forget who couldn't handle one kickboxing class, and who teaches three a day."

I chuckle. She's got a point.

It's so tempting to joke with her. We could step into my apartment and I could kiss her and we could let everything that happened earlier tonight fly by, like nothing. We could ... but, then it would linger. Like my anger over Amber. No, we're not doing that. Earlier today Sam insinuated we had no clue how to communicate? Well, we're about to communicate this issue into the ground.

"The only thing I have hot to drink is coffee. Do you want some?" I ask as I open my door and flip on the lights. I toss my jacket on a chair as Sam peels hers off.

"Here." I grab her favorite blanket from my trunk and hold it out to her.

She wraps it around her shoulders with gratitude. "Coffee sounds perfect."

I head into the kitchen as she situates herself into the corner of my couch. "Can I ask you how you feel about me knowing Jamie?" I ask as I put a pot of coffee on.

Silence.

"I know it freaked you out a bit. Does it bother you?"

"Yeah, it threw me off at first, but the fact that you two know each other and he likes you makes this all so much easier."

I move to the kitchen door so I can see her face. "He likes me? Even after I left you crying as I walked out of your apartment?"

"Truthfully?" She smirks. "The jerk took your side. Some brother."

A smile tugs my lips, then falls. "I'm the jerk here."

"You weren't great, but I didn't help."

Neither of us acted like the adults we are. She's right. Love makes us mad. The coffee sputters behind me and I throw her a look before turning and fixing two cups.

"You seemed mad that I didn't show up with Jamie at that party, but you also threw it in my face when I said it must be fate bringing us together." I walk to the couch with our coffees in hand.

"Cole, I was feeling a lot of different things." She takes her mug, wrapping her hands around it and holding it in front of her face, letting the steam curl up and warm her as I sit on the opposite end. "I think I was mad you weren't there and that I met Paul instead. For several reasons. Obviously, losing him, but also knowing if I were faced with the option, I would have chosen you." When Sam looks at me, I see her truth. Me. She would've chosen me over Paul. She shifts her eyes downward, shame covering her confession. "And that makes me feel guilty, but it shouldn't. I shouldn't have been with Paul for as long as I was in the first place. I just don't want to disrespect his memory."

"Why did you hang onto his memory for so long?" I immediately feel badly for phrasing it that way. "I don't mean that insensitively. I'm just ... I'm trying to understand your feelings."

She doesn't hesitate. "Guilt, mostly. I've never admitted this aloud. When I found out about 397, I felt a mixture of emotions.

Initially, grief, of course. I'd lost the only man I'd ever loved, the man I thought I was supposed to spend the rest of my life with. But, then when I thought about canceling the wedding, I felt relief, which in turn transformed to guilt."

She spares me a glance before focusing on the wall across from us and takes a sip of her coffee. "Paul had given me everything I wanted. Stability, security, loyalty … and here I was, following his death, feeling like a weight had been lifted. So, I punished myself. I wouldn't let myself move forward. And … we haven't talked about this yet, but I have a feeling it's something that will come up eventually."

Sam leans forward and sets her mug on the trunk in front of the couch. She twists her fingers into knots as she looks down at her lap, clasping her hands together. "Paul's parents gave me quite a bit of money after the crash. It's how Monica and I could afford the studio. I didn't want it. I didn't ask for it, but they wouldn't take no for an answer. They wanted me to be able to have a life after his death. It was money that was supposed to go to Paul."

Money. She lives off his money?

"I haven't used much of it, but in months when things get tight, I have it to fall back on." She swivels and peers at me, pulling her knees to her chest. "So, yeah. I think after time I pushed away all the bad and focused on the good in Paul. As a way of preserving what I did love about him. It wasn't his fault he wasn't the one."

"It's all more complicated than just losing someone, isn't it?" I ask, and she shrugs with a little nod. "I'm sorry, now that I hear of that—the money, the relief you felt—I guess I understand why you had such a hard time moving on."

A sheen of tears glazes her eyes. "I didn't think I deserved to be happy with someone else."

"Oh, baby." Her words rip my heart to shreds. "Of course you deserve to be happy. That's what this has all been about, isn't it? Every time I thought we were taking a step forward, you'd step back. Is that what you think he'd want?"

"It was never about what he'd want. I thought I needed to be punished. The day before he left, I called off the wedding." I drop my head, gripping my hair. "He told me to think about it while he was gone. Said I was just stressed and getting cold feet. He didn't want me to make any irrational decisions." A tear drips off her quivering bottom lip. "I told him I wasn't being irrational, but he wouldn't hear it. The business man in him always needed his way. Paul thought he could talk his way out of anything. He didn't want to believe it, but I think he left knowing it was over. I didn't even tell him I loved him."

"Aww, Sam." This is all such a mess.

"That's why I've been so complicated." Sam brushes the tears from her face. "I'm sorry. I had to come to terms with it all."

"Why didn't you tell me?"

"Because I didn't want to face it. I never even told Monica." She chews on her lips. "Meeting you was the last thing I expected to happen."

"Since we're being honest, I have to tell you that I cringe every time I hear his name. I think when Jamie reminded me that I should have met you at that party it gave me permission to not feel guilty for not liking Paul."

"Why do you have such an issue with him?"

That shouldn't be such an easy answer for me to give, but it is. "Because I want all of you. I'm selfish like that. I'm not good at sharing. I was an only child for years." I attempt to look guilty, but I most certainly fail. "I want to be the one who takes care of you and provides you with stability, security, and loyalty. I don't want to share your love with the memory of Paul. But I will because if those are my choices—you and Paul or no you—I'll choose you every time."

"You don't have to make a choice. You have me. Only me."

I slide over on the couch, twisting my body so we're face-to-face, my chest leaning against her blanket-covered legs. My hands rub over her thighs as I rest my chin on her knees. "I'm so incredibly sorry about tonight," I say as solemnly as I can. "I love you."

"Me, too." Her hand traces my jawline. "I love you, too. But I need to know," she holds my gaze as she proceeds, "what's going on with Seattle?"

"First, let me go back to the beginning of this whole conversation. To the part where I told you I'm never walking away.

"Seattle was unsolicited. Or somewhat unsolicited. Dr. Bannon and I had talked a while back about my doing a fellowship in peds. I've been considering doing research in pediatric cardiology after—" I pause, holding back Celia's name. Sam runs her fingers along the back of my neck, soothing me. "Bannon went to school with Dr. Rushdie out in Seattle. He's one of the premier pediatric cardiologists in the country, and I guess Bannon put a bug in his ear. He asked me to fill out an application for a fellowship position out there, and I figured why not. I didn't expect anything to come of it. Do you know how much competition there is for fellowships nationwide? I don't even know if I want to throw myself into a year of research.

"Sam, at this point anything I do with my career will include you. I'd banked on getting an attending spot somewhere locally. That's the benefit of living in New York City. There are plenty of hospitals to choose from."

"Cole, you need to do what's best for you. We've talked about a future, but we're just dating. I don't want to be a reason you feel held back."

"Baby, you are what's best for me." I cover her hand against my jaw and stretch up, grazing my lips against hers.

"And, you're what's best for me," she murmurs against my lips.

"That dating status you just threw at me, though. I'm not a

fan." I turn my face into her palm and kiss it. I'll happily kiss every inch of her tonight.

"Yeah?"

"We're more than two people dating. Certainly, the last year has taught us that. How important we are to each other."

Sam leans back, her teeth catching her bottom lip. "You're so sure of us that you're willing to make all of your decisions about your career and your future based on things I want?"

My hands cup her cheeks. How can she ask me that question? "You really don't believe me?" Her brows snap together, confusion marring her beautiful face. "I'm so sure of my love for you, of us being meant for each other. Yes. Yes, I would plan my life around you and your wants and needs."

Sam's eyes shines as they trace my face. "Let's get married," she breathes.

My stomach turns over.

"You're crazy." My lips touch the tip of her nose.

She swats me away, sighing. "Don't look at me like that."

"Like what?"

"Like I'm silly and … cute." She pushes at my shoulders, her face scrunching with irritation as she huffs, "I'm completely serious."

"I am, too," I chuckle. "And you *are* cute."

Her lips twitch. I slide to the edge of the couch and fall to my knees on the floor.

"What are you—"

Shuffling around, my hands grasp her knees and spread them as I wiggle my way between them, pulling her butt to the edge of the couch until she's pressed against my waist. I slide my hands up her thighs, squeezing once when they pass over her tickling hip joints, before wrapping them behind her back.

"Cole?" She breathes, desire and confusion mingling together as her eyes scour my face.

I tilt my head back. "I love you and I don't think you're silly."

Her breathing picks up before she playfully knocks me in the chest. "Then don't patronize me."

"I want to marry you."

Sam's mouth snaps shut, holding her words hostage for too long. "You do?" she finally whispers.

I massage her lower back, my hands loving the feel of her warmth, of the strength of the muscles in her back and the dip of her spine, the curve of her waist. Her eyes widen as my lips part, her face full of expectancy as I speak.

"Someday."

Sam's stuttered exhale tears a chunk of my heart away, her shoulders slouching.

I inhale deeply to clarify. "I want you to be my wife. My Mario Kart racing buddy. My trainer. My personal photographer. My off-key karaoke partner for life. One of these days I'm going to ask you to marry me, Samantha Cooper, and I'm going to ask you to let me love you for the next seventy years of our lives. Let me give you babies, and lake houses with front porches, and Rangers tickets."

She buries her face behind her hands. Her shoulders shake. Is she laughing? Is she crying?

"Sam, baby?" I tug on her wrists. I need to see her face. Her hands fall away and tears streak her cheeks. She's doing both. Laughing and crying, a smile spreading across her face.

"One of these days?" she whispers.

"Yes, one of these days. God, I love you. I am so in love with you it drives me mad, but not yet. We're not ready. You're still working through your grief—"

"No." Her head shakes. "No, I love you. This has nothing to do with Paul."

"Hey." I reach up and grab her face gently, holding her still. "I know you love me. I know."

Her head rolls forward, her lips parting with a light laugh. "I can't believe I proposed to you." She covers her face as my hands drop to her thighs. Her laughter growing louder as she falls against the back of the couch.

She erupts into a fit of giggles and I sit back on my haunches. All at the prospect of us getting married. Really?

"I'll try not to take offense," I say drily, biting back laughter at her antics.

Her feet run in place as she continues on and on. Her breathing heavy as she drops a hand and grabs her stomach. "I'm sorry," she wheezes, wiping a tear from her red face. "I just can't believe I did that."

I force my face to remain straight. "I told you women lose their heads over me. Evidently, you're the perfect case in point." I shrug.

Sam sits up and snorts. Her eyes swimming with tears of hilarity. "You're so full of yourself," she grumbles.

The bark of her tone is downplayed by the way her hands reach out and grab at my shirt, pulling me back to my knees. My arms wrap around her back, once again, and I press my face into her stomach as her hands weave into my hair. She kisses the top of my head.

"Are you going to stop loving me after those seventy years are over?"

"Baby, I'm never going to stop loving you."

Sam's fingertips press against my scalp, drawing circles. "And you'll get us amazing Rangers tickets any time I want?"

My lips stretch into a wide smile. "I knew you were using me for the tickets."

"Yes, it's true, the tickets are a perk." Her fingers tighten in my hair, tugging my head up. "But there are other things I'm using you for."

My hand twists the back of her shirt, my fingers searching for the heat of her skin. "Yeah, what's that?"

She smiles. It's the Heavens and Earth. The best sunrise and the most beautiful sunset. The finest wine and the most scrumptious morsel of food to ever pass my lips and touch my tongue. Her smile. *This* smile is life. Mine. Then she adds fuel to my fire. "Let me show you."

————

SAM STIRS. HER DARK HAIR TICKLING MY SKIN AS MY fingers continue their journey, stroking up and down the length of her arm. A sultry moan teases me as she stretches and fidgets against me. She peers over her shoulder, glancing up at me.

"I fell asleep," she murmurs as though it's news to me.

"I wore you out," I tease, pressing a kiss to her hairline.

She lifts my arm from her waist and rolls over, facing me. Her fingers glide up my chest as my hand snakes around her. My fingers splaying low on her back. I'll never get enough of her silky skin.

Her tongue peeks from her mouth, wetting her lips as they stretch into a smile. She grazes my jaw with her fingertips. "I love you."

She speaks the three words with such deference, such solemnity, my breath catches.

"I never thought I would find someone like you." I turn my face into her palm, kissing it. "Someone I could fall so completely and utterly in love with."

She moves forward. Our bodies skin to skin as she kisses me. "Me either," she admits.

And I know what she means. I know that I am her forever, just as she is mine.

My fingers push her hair out of our faces once I'm able to pry my lips from her mouth. "Are we crazy?"

"Of course we are, but why do you ask?"

"We've been dating for three weeks and we're already discussing marriage, and summer homes—"

"And Rangers tickets?" The corner of her mouth quirks up.

She bucks against me as my fingers tweak her side. "Fine, we're crazy. But who cares?" She kisses me once, twice, lingering. "I think I've belonged to you from day one."

I run my thumb along her bottom lip, the day I fell for her so clear in my mind. "My entire world changed at that subway stop."

The tip of her tongue darts out, wetting her lips and touching the pad of my thumb, sending passion soaring through my body. "The subway stop when I nearly punched you?" she asks with an arched brow. "Not the first time we met?"

Of course she finds a way to work the punch into this conversation. "No, Supergirl. It was the subway. I couldn't ignore our connection after that meeting. You know the saying, the third time's the charm."

"It *was* a little freaky by that point."

"Baby, what you call freaky, I call fate. I mean, how could we ignore the signs. You were everywhere."

"I'm sorry it took me so long to come around. To allow myself—"

My lips stop her apology. "I would have waited longer," I admit as we part.

"Just think, we never would have met if it weren't for Amber."

The irony. My crazy sister. Her flair for theatrics, and butting into other people's lives, and making crazy decisions. I ran into Sam on Long Island because Amber flipped out. I admitted my feelings—to myself—for Sam because of Amber. We nearly broke up, because of Amber.

Sam's fingers brush across my forehead, sweeping my hair to the side. "She'll be okay."

I believe her. Something deep within me tells me this trip will be what Amber needs to find herself, to find her peace. Just as I've found mine.

"You're right," I nod. "We never would have met if it weren't for Amber, but we never would have fallen in love if not for fate."

"And gyro carts, and subway trains, and..." she adds. I kiss her lips. "And ... the market ..." she continues against my mouth. My teeth catch her bottom lip between them, tugging lightly. She sighs, her hands trailing over my back.

"All the places we met," she gasps against my needy mouth.

"Yes, Sam." I growl, releasing her bottom lip. "We fell in love at subway stops and all those other places we met. Now stop talking and kiss me back."

Her leg tangles with mine. "You're so bossy," she chastises. "Is this what I have to look forward to when we get married someday?"

"This—" I laugh against her neck as she arches upward. My lips trail the graceful curve up and along her jaw. I lift up, propping up to my elbows. I hover over her face until her eyes open. Hazel orbs full of such craving they shoot burning sparks of desire throughout my body. Controlling myself is an effort as we lock eyes. "And so much more," I promise, finally finding my voice. "For the rest of your life."

"I think I can handle that."

ACKNOWLEDGMENTS

MICHELE

I'm always so very grateful to the people who support me through the book process and life:

My husband and kids deal with me forgetting laundry, dinner, carpool, emails—how they put up with me I'll never know!

My amazing crew of readers, bloggers, and friends on Facebook and 'in real life' keep me sane and make this solitary life a little less solitary and a lot more lifelike.

My PR agent, Rick Miles and the crew at Red Coat PR—You're the best pimps ever. Thank you for your advice and for making me look good.

My Literary Agent, Italia Gandolfo, and Gandolfo Helin Literary Management—Your fire is contagious. Here's to the future!

MINDY

To my husband, who puts up with my crazy and continues to encourage me to follow this dream.

To Jeremy Van Pinxteren, thanks for knowing some stuff about hockey. You're cool, I guess.

To my office family, I'm so grateful I had you to brighten my days and fill me with inspiration to pursue what I love most.

To my AWESOME readers and bloggers and friends and family, thank you for your support and shares and reviews. Because of you, new readers continue to find my books every day. I will be forever grateful for you.

The professionals who backed us up on Subway Stops:

Our editor, Samantha—Thank you for always telling us to go deeper! You help make all of our ideas shine brighter!

KEEP READING!

ABOUT THE AUTHORS

We're pretty awesome! We like singing in the car, eating white cheddar popcorn, and going on road trips together. You'll find us sharing a table at a few book signings each year. We have a love of romance, New York, anything sweet, and great books.

To find out more you can hunt us down on social media. We're all over the place!

Track down Mindy:
Email: mindy.hayes.writes@gmail.com
Website: www.mindyhayes.com
Facebook: www.facebook.com/hayes.mindy
Twitter: @haymindywrites
Instagram: @haymind

Connect with Michele:
Email: authormichelegmiller@gmail.com
Facebook: www.facebook.com/AuthorMicheleGMiller
Twitter: @chelemybelles
Instagram: @chelemybelles
Website: www.michelegmillerbooks.squarespace.com

 facebook.com/mindymichelebooks
twitter.com/MindyMicheleBks
 instagram.com/mindymichelebooks
bookbub.com/authors/mindy-michele

Made in the USA
Las Vegas, NV
28 February 2021

18784381R00184